THE HALLS OF HADES

D.V. WILLIAMS

Published by Claw Mark Publishing

www.dominic-williams.co.uk

This book is a work of fiction and any resemblance to actual persons, living or dead, is purely coincidental.

This book contains themes of a sexual nature. It also contains scenes of drug abuse, mental cruelty, and sexual assault which may be upsetting. It is not suitable for persons under the age of 18.

Typeset in Palatino Linotype

Photography by Brian J. Davies

ISBN: 978 0 9957715 8 1

This book is dedicated to everyone who struggles or has struggled with their inner demons. In the dark night of the soul, as with any other night, the darkest hour is always just before dawn.

To Yasmin,

Don W. xx

CONTENTS

ALSO BY THE SAME AUTHOR

INTO THE WILD
(A tigers Tale)

tigers Book One

EMBRACING THE WILD

tigers Book Two

THE GILDED TOWER

tigers Book Three

LIFE IN THE WILD

tigers Book Four

ACKNOWLEDGEMENTS

So here we are at the penultimate part of Rebecca's story where she faces her greatest challenge yet: her own, personal demons. I always knew these books would eventually come around to exploring the darker corners of Rebecca's head as the cumulative effect of betrayals, mistreatment by others, the pressures of fame, and the topsy turvy world of life on tour take their toll on her. Yes, they have their erotic side, but they are also so much more. Each of the books in this series has been, instead of repeating a formula, building on what came before it as Rebecca's life moves on. We are already a long way from where we started and there is still much to tell.

My thanks to all the usual team of people who have lent their time and their talents to bring this book into being, including MD for graphics and cover design, Brian Davies for his photography, and Kathy for proofreading.

My thanks also to Maria Lazarou at Obsessed By Books Designs for eBook formatting. Since it's not exactly my favourite job you saved me from much frustration.

Special mention should go to Tracy Wood for her PA services and going above and beyond the call of duty in order to promote these books and maintain my online presence. You are a lifesaver.

The world of independent publishing continues to be an adventure and I have met some wonderful people along the way, readers, bloggers, reviewers, other authors, and the providers of the many services we rely on to get our books out there. The one thing we all share is our love of books. There are far too many of you to mention by name, and I'm bound to miss somebody vital out if I try, but you know who are. 2020 may be a strange one for the book world, just like everybody else, but there are better times around the corner. We will meet again. I'll see you on my stand at future signings, when they eventually happen, and up at the bar. Cheers!

Dominic

'It is always darkest just before the day dawneth.'

Thomas Fuller, theologian and historian

CHAPTER ONE

'Come on! Up you get, Rebecca!' It wasn't the voice of my housekeeper Francesca, or Karina, my daughter's nanny. It was softly spoken with a hint of County Antrim. 'You can't stay there all day.'

I rolled over, burying my face in the pillow and groaning.

'I don't want to,' I huffed. 'Just close the door behind you on your way out.'

But Linda was having none of it. She swept the full-height curtains aside, allowing light to stream into the room through the glazed doors that opened onto the balcony, and made a tutting sound, presumably at the room's state of disarray.

'No can do! I didn't come all this way to take no for an answer and the morning's already half over.'

I squinted against the glare of a fine, bright, autumn day that now flooded into the room. Linda was right; it was a shit heap. I'd barely come out in days, not even returning my family's calls, just messaging them to say I was fine and needed some time to be alone.

Fine: it's funny how that word hardly ever means what it says.

'For starters, you need a shower,' she continued, 'and for fuck's sake open a window; this room's as stale as a North Sea trawler man's waders. Poppy needs you. She's alright, by the way; Karina's with her, but she wants and needs her mummy, perhaps more than ever now that...' Linda stalled, hesitating to utter the words that she knew would sting me. 'Your friends want you back too. I know what's happened sucks, but life goes on. You need to hold your head high and get back to being you.'

Nobody argued with Linda when she was on a mission; that much I'd learnt long ago. I heaved a sigh and sat up, rubbing my eyes, resigned to at least humouring her.

'Why aren't you in work? Surely all the goings-on at Pulverton Manor and Passion Flower are keeping you busy.'

'They are, but a friend in need is a friend indeed and besides, Ryan is quite capable of holding the fort for a while; he can deal with anything that needs seeing to for the next event. Tamzyn does most of the day to day running of the manor house and the Aphrodite Rooms. Ryan sends his love, by the way.' She gave a wry little smile. 'You've barely shown your face in three days by all accounts, so it's time to get your arse in gear whether you like it or not. Are you just going to curl up in the dark and let Guy win? That's not the Rebecca I know. She would come out of her corner fighting.'

Linda thrust a mug of tea under my nose and I took it automatically, not knowing whether I actually wanted it or not. It turned out I did.

'I just...' I sniffed and took a welcome gulp, trying not to let my emotions get the better of me. 'I just can't believe Guy would do that to us. I mean, I know we had our ups and downs like all couples do, but after everything that's happened, I really thought he was one person I could trust. That's why it's so hard to take. I mean, you know as well as I do that we had a semi-open relationship,' I said, raising one eyebrow at her; she knew why, 'but there were boundaries, there were rules. Not only did he not stick to them, but he'd been covering his tracks and lying through his teeth for months. It was always one rule for me and another for himself. I can see that so clearly now. Guy's the kind of person who takes whatever he wants because whatever he has is never enough. There's no room in my life for people like that anymore.'

'Why his co-star, Anna Gateshead? Why her? She struck me as a bit false when I met her at your Boxing Day party.'

I shrugged my shoulders.

'I think she's got him wrapped around her little finger and he's just too blind to see it. Guy's not always the most insightful of people. It's not even the sex that bothers me; it's the deception. He even squirrelled away a nest egg of almost two hundred thousand pounds of my money just in case I found out what he was up to.'

Linda's jaw dropped.

'You're fucking kidding!'

'I wish I was. The first thing I did was to withdraw all my funds and freeze the account. He won't get another red cent out of me beyond what he's already taken. Now he's made the break into films, he won't need my money anyway.'

Linda nodded.

'Very wise. You know, if you need any impartial advice, Ryan's very good with the financial side of things. I guess that's the advantage of being business partners with my brother; I trust him implicitly.'

'Thanks. I'll bear that in mind.'

In all honesty, I didn't know who to trust anymore. If I couldn't put my faith in the father of my own child then who could I rely on? I'd been let down, first by one of my manager's employees who'd sold details of my comings and goings to the press, then by a dodgy accountant, and now this. All the bad apples had to be removed from the barrel before they turned everything rotten. There could be no exceptions.

Linda, secretive and unconventional as she was, remained a constant in my life despite all the changes of the last few years. I knew I could rely on her. Even Sadie, the tiger who inhabited my imagination and shared all my highs and lows, but especially the highs, owed her name to Linda.

'So what's next for Rebecca Taylor?' Linda sat on the edge of the bed and gave me a searching look. 'It's important that you make plans to move forward from this. I know you; you'll just mope otherwise like you did when you broke up with Steve. I can't believe that was six and a half years ago now.'

Neither could I.

'Well, I'm supposed to be meeting with the band in Mitchell's office at the end of the week. We need to discuss the tour and I've got to find a way to let them down gently about my next album project.'

Linda knitted her eyebrows together and looked at me. 'What do you mean?'

I took a deep breath before explaining.

'Mitchell thinks that since I want to branch out musically into doing something different, it needs to be under a different banner, not just as Rebecca Taylor, and that includes collaborating with different musicians, not my usual band. I've got mixed feelings about it. I mean, I'm excited to be trying out new avenues but I don't want to sour things with the band; we've been through so much together.'

'It sounds like you feel a lot of loyalty to them.'

'I do.'

'Then the fact that you're all gearing up to tour again should put their minds at rest. Right now, you need to focus on the positive, and it sounds like getting back to work will be the best thing for you. You can't maintain a career on just being the face of your own perfume brand, lovely though that might be in the short term. You always wanted to make music, so it's time to get back to doing what you do best. That said: life can't be all work and no play. Guy had you right where he wanted you, didn't he? You brought other women into the bedroom but no other men. I think, in the interests of fairness, it's high time you redressed the balance. Sometimes the best revenge is living well.'

Oh, here we go!

I should have known it wouldn't be long before Linda was up to her old tricks.

'What have you got in mind?'

'Well, I think maybe some old friends of ours might be interested in getting together. What say we join forces with Janine and Alan and really make their night? I don't mean right now, but sometime soon. It'll do you good to get Guy out of your system.'

I had to admit, the thought of sharing Janine and Alan's bed had always intrigued me, and time spent in Janine's company was always…an education to say the least. But sex, to me, had always been a celebration of life. I hardly felt like celebrating. Facing the world in any capacity still felt like an uphill struggle.

'I'm just not ready for that yet.'

'Of course not, but you'll reach the stage where you want to break out of your shell again. You've always tended towards introspection; I suppose all artists do, but it's not particularly healthy.'

I nodded.

'I'll think about it. I just need some time to get my head together.'

Maybe Linda was right. I'd sworn to be more like her, to be strong and self-reliant, to listen to my head, not my heart.

'That's fine, sweetie,' she reassured. 'Just remember you've got friends, real friends. It just so happens that many of them come with benefits.'

She winked at me and I smiled thinly back in her direction, but behind the smile lay the tears I still couldn't find it within me to shed and the pain I daren't let show. My Guy was gone, and his betrayal was the worst kind I could imagine. First, he had stolen my heart, and now he had shattered it. I wasn't sure if it would ever be mended again.

Maybe, on reflection, I would be better off without it.

-0-

Since Linda left me with no choice but to face the world, I started with the remaining members of my own household. Once I had showered and dressed, I followed her downstairs. It was a warm enough day so we joined Poppy and Karina on the patio and Poppy toddled over with her arms outstretched. She was definitely steadier on her feet now and making something that at least sounded like the beginnings of words, even though they didn't make much sense. There was no denying her delight at seeing me. I scooped her up and hugged her, all my pent up emotion finally welling to the surface. I held her tight.

'It's alright, sweetheart. Mummy's not going anywhere now; she's just been feeling sad, that's all.'

Francesca appeared from the swimming pool area, through the partially retracted glass wall that looked out over the patio and the lawn.

'Ah, there you are! I thought I heard voices. Breakfast? I don't think you ate one proper meal yesterday.' She gave me a look that managed at the same time to be both warmly affectionate and gently chiding.

I checked my watch, with the sour realisation that it was the Cartier one Guy had given me for Christmas, bought predominantly with my own money, of course. He'd been quite good at spending the stuff, and mostly on the kind of status symbols I cared little for. It seemed a little late for breakfast, but now I thought about it my tummy was rumbling.

'Thank you, Francesca. Has everyone else eaten?' They all indicated that they had. 'Well, if it's not too much trouble.'

Francesca's expression invited me not to be so daft.

'It's no trouble at all. You've got to look after yourself,

young lady.' She'd snapped into mother hen mode. I could hardly complain. 'I'll let you know when it's ready.'

While she disappeared back inside to prepare what promised to be one of her typical feasts, we sat in the autumn sunshine and watched Poppy inspecting some of the first leaves that had fallen from the surrounding trees. She seemed fascinated. Poppy's first birthday would be coming up in less than a week and there were still preparations to be made. I needed to pull myself together. For the first time in days, I felt a ray of hope. Maybe there could be life beyond Guy after all, and it would be mine to make, for both our sakes.

CHAPTER TWO

I knew I had to face the day, there were important things to do in London, but still, I moped over my cereal without the energy to really get going. When Francesca bustled into the kitchen as she always did, she was quick to notice.

'Come on,' she encouraged, still removing her coat. 'Talk to me.'

I put my spoon down and pushed the bowl away. It appeared I didn't have many secrets from Francesca, so what was the harm in asking? She was, after all, practically family.

'Francesca, you've been together with George for years, so what's the secret?'

'Honestly?'

'Honestly.'

She paused for a moment, turning it over in her mind.

'Well, since we're speaking woman to woman here, in my humble opinion most men are very straightforward; keep their stomachs full and their balls empty and you won't go far wrong.'

I snorted, not quite believing my ears. This was a whole side to Francesca I had an inkling of but had never really seen. Perhaps it was a good thing I hadn't taken another mouthful of cereal; I'd have choked on it.

'I'd say you've got nothing to blame yourself for on either of those counts, even if you have enlisted some help with the latter.' She raised her eyebrows slightly at me, but her expression remained kind. 'Perhaps that way he's got even less excuse for going behind your back with things. I suppose there are some people who, no matter what they have in life, are never content; they always want more. To them, the grass will always be greener on the other side of the fence. It's not your fault that Guy Draper,' she spoke his name with far less deference than had previously been her custom, 'is one of those.'

When she'd first met him, Francesca had been as swayed by his looks and charm as anyone else; she'd treated him almost like royalty. In the light of recent events, that shine had certainly worn off. She sat down at the breakfast bar and took my hands in hers.

'Somewhere out there is the right man for you, someone who will see you for the giving soul that you are, who will stand by you through thick and thin, someone mature enough to think of more than just himself.'

'But what if I never find them?' I moaned. 'In my position, how can I be sure of anyone's motives? Everyone is out to feather their own nest, and I'm just an easy target. Then there's Poppy to think about. They don't just need to be a partner to me; they would have to want to be a father to her. I can't let just anyone get too close; it wouldn't be fair. She's better off just having me and a nanny than a succession of substitute fathers who turn out to be dead-ends.'

Francesca thought for a moment.

'What about Guy? He'll still see Poppy, won't he?'

I sighed.

'He may be a self-centred, faithless bastard, but I can hardly deny him access. He adores her in his own way. He's still her dad, and he'll be better to her than my father ever was to me. Until Jeff came into Mum's life, I grew up without mine. I couldn't do that to her; she deserves to have a relationship with him. I just don't think I can face him right now without wanting to tear his face off.'

'What about Poppy's birthday celebrations?'

Everything had been arranged well before I'd uncovered Guy's duplicity and I couldn't bring myself to cancel. Why should Poppy pay the price just because her father was a selfish, lying prick?

'Shit, I hadn't thought about that! I suppose I can hardly turn him away or rescind any invitations, although it's going to be pretty awkward. Mum's ready to kill him. As Linda used to say, she doesn't take prisoners. I suppose you get like that when you have to raise a family on your own.'

'You're not alone, though. Just remember that. Have faith. God has a plan for all of us.'

I shook my head.

'I'd love to be able to share your faith in divine providence, but I don't. Life isn't that kind to everyone, and perhaps I've already had my share of luck. No, I've just got to be prepared to stand on my own two feet, at least for the foreseeable future. Maybe I should take a leaf out of Linda's book. Perhaps she has the right idea after all.'

A thought struck me. I needed to get on with clearing

the decks but I just couldn't face doing the job myself, and anyway, I was due at Mitchell's offices in London in two hours time.

'While I'm thinking about it, could you go round gathering up all of Guy's things for me? We need to hire a van driver to take everything over to his apartment in Chelsea. I want his stuff out of my sight and out of my house, including that bloody great contraption over there.' I pointed to the fancy coffee machine that was taking up half the countertop. 'He'll want his stuff since possessions are so important to him. How he fits it all into a one-bedroom bachelor pad is his problem.'

-0-

By the time I reached the premises of Sacker Management, the rest of the band were already in Mitchell's office. I could hear their laughter and excited conversation from outside the door. Derek, my usual driver, hadn't been available to take me into London, and the other chauffeur, Colin, who occasionally filled in, hadn't been as punctual.

I knocked and entered the large but by now comfortingly familiar room. Mitchell's collection of tribal masks and gold disks crowded the walls, and a shiny, never-ridden, customised Harley Davidson motorbike stood to one side. He made sure it was always kept well polished.

'Ah, Rebecca!' Mitchell seemed quite upbeat, perhaps more so than necessary. 'We've only just started so you haven't missed anything. Take a seat. I think Penny's making a pot of coffee if you're interested.'

I was glad to see everybody. Daniel and Helena, our drummer and keyboard player, looked refreshed after their travels in North Africa and the Middle East, happy and contented now they were finally together after years of circling each other but never actually taking the plunge. Alex, our lead guitarist, livewire on stage but quiet off it, and Rafael, who many might have expected to have a fiery Latin temperament but instead displayed the laid-back nature typical of many bass players, looked relaxed too. It seemed the time off had helped everyone to recharge, except perhaps me; I still didn't feel at my best. In light of recent events, it was hardly surprising.

Mitchell's wife and PA, Penny, came in with the coffee just as we were all hugging and catching up. These days, with her shoulder-length auburn hair and smartly conservative dress sense, she looked very different from the young woman who sported spiky, brightly coloured locks the first time I'd met her. Since she must have been twenty years Mitchell's junior, news of their relationship had come as something of a shock to people at first.

'Thank you, darling.' Mitchell smiled at her. 'You'd better sit in on this one, too, since the things we'll be discussing will have an effect on all of us. First things first, though, I was sorry to hear your news, Rebecca.'

'News? What news?' There was a chorus of concern from the band members. I supposed they had been rather out of the loop.

I sighed, figuring I might as well tell them now. It seemed as good a time as any. Mitchell looked surprised I hadn't told any of the others but I hadn't really felt like making announcements.

'I guess you all ought to know, Guy and I have split

up.'

Helena looked startled.

'Oh no, honey! Why?'

'Well,' I drew my chin back and steadied myself, 'it seems he has someone else.'

There were a couple of audible gasps and collective murmurs of disbelief.

'Not only that, but he's been pulling the wool over my eyes in other ways too.' I didn't really want to go into the details. 'It's all still a bit raw at the moment but I thought you should know.'

'Jesus!' Rafael planted himself back down on a chair with his hands in his pockets, puffing out his cheeks. They all looked a bit shell-shocked.

'Anyway,' I waved my hand, 'that's not what we're here for. I'm keen to move on, so that's what we should do.'

'We'll have to make a formal announcement to the press at some point soon,' Penny interjected. 'I know it's probably not what you want to hear, Rebecca, but it's better that way than the tabloids finding out through other channels. Never mind any political turmoil that's going on; it'll be front-page news. At least we're in control of it that way.'

'I'll speak to Guy's agent if you'd rather I coordinated it,' Mitchell suggested. 'A joint statement will help diffuse things.'

'Whatever.' I still wanted nothing to do with him. 'Do what you have to.'

Not wishing to prolong any awkwardness, everybody turned to the business at hand, although Helena gave me a concerned glance.

‘So what’s next?’ Alex asked.

Mitchell took charge of the conversation again, much to my relief. Things would sound better coming from him rather than me. He spent the next quarter of an hour explaining the timescale for tour preparations before getting to the part I knew was coming.

‘In the meantime, Rebecca has been busy writing songs she is keen to record. We are, however, presented with a dilemma in that a lot of them don’t fit style-wise with other music you’ve made together, so the project won’t be marketed as Rebecca Taylor, but as a side project under the working title of Taylor Made. Ariva records are, as I suspected, keen to put a cushion between this and the main thread of Rebecca’s music so it will involve different musicians.’

Seeing the concerned looks on their faces, Mitchell held out a placatory hand.

‘But before any of you start to panic about your positions, don’t. By creating a side project we deflect risk and ensure that there is a separate identity for it. The tour and future Rebecca Taylor albums will continue as planned. Nobody, I repeat, nobody is being sidelined. I hope we’re all clear on that. Between you and me, Ariva records would rather avoid musical experimentation altogether. Like all record companies, they’re not interested in creativity, only profit, but they are, given Rebecca’s high profile, prepared to take a flyer on this. I’m sure you’d all like to offer her your full support because, who knows, it could open other doors musically for all of you.’

Alex nodded. I knew he had plenty of his own songs up his sleeve. He’d written or co-written at least a couple on each of the three albums so far. Helena and Daniel looked at each other, not quite sure what to make of it, while Rafael didn't seem fazed in the slightest.

'What prompted this?' Helena asked.

'I started writing some things that just didn't fit with what we've been doing but were too good to ignore,' I told her. 'I didn't want to tour until Poppy was at least two, and at least this way we keep our profile up for the future. Ultimately, Mitchell made the decision to play things that way because of the record company.'

'But what are the rest of us supposed to do?' Helena asked. 'Sit around waiting for the tour? Surely that should be happening off the back of a Rebecca Taylor album, not a side project. Wouldn't it be better to focus our energies on that?' Helena had a point but I didn't want to abandon the idea of doing something different.

'We could do both.' The words had escaped my mouth before my better judgement could stop them.

Mitchell looked like he was about to have a heart attack.

'Are you sure, Rebecca? That's a hell of a lot of work.'

'Right now that's what I need, and besides, it's no more work than recording a double album is it?'

'Maybe not for you it isn't!' Mitchell puffed out his cheeks. 'You lot will be the death of me.' Something told me he was only half-joking.

'Maybe…' Penny appeared to be thinking out loud. 'Maybe we need to consider bringing someone else on board to at least manage part of Rebecca's affairs.'

Mitchell remained unconvinced.

'I don't know. There's nobody within the organization with enough clout and in the light of recent experiences

I'd be wary of who we bring in.'

'Then delegate more of the legwork. You take on too much.'

'Well, that's it then.' Mitchell grinned. 'The boss has spoken. Seriously though, Ariva would be more than happy about another Rebecca Taylor album prior to the tour. Just make sure you don't spread yourself too thin, Rebecca. You can't afford to have a dip in quality. It will all depend on the strength of the songs. If I were you, I'd complete the recording of one project before committing too heavily to the next, but by all means, keep writing with both in mind. In the meantime, there should be plenty to keep everybody's hands full, as long as you're all happy with that.'

All heads nodded in agreement.

'Then you'd better get cracking. You've got just over a year before attention switches to the tour and rehearsals begin. It's a big ask. In the meantime, we've been lucky once again to secure the services of Clive Dunsmore as tour manager. You've all worked with him before so there'll be no surprises there. He'll be overseeing the bulk of the preparations and accompanying you day to day for at least the European leg and probably the US leg. His first task is going to be assembling a new road crew since many of them moved on to other projects after we had to cancel the last tour.'

I cringed.

'Sorry! There's no escaping biology. Poppy was as much a surprise to me as anyone else.'

Maybe focusing on getting my career back on track would be the best way to fill the emptiness that gnawed away inside me. I needed to do something, and music had always been my solace, my escape from the world, my reason for being. I knew such ambitious plans were going to demand a lot of me but even so, at that moment I had no idea what I had just let myself in for.

CHAPTER THREE

'Hey, beautiful birthday girl! Look at you! One today and you're already walking!'

Mum opened her arms to Poppy, who toddled across the Persian rug towards her, beaming. The spacious, high-ceilinged reception room seemed like the best place to welcome everybody since so many people were coming over at some point in the afternoon to share in Poppy's big day. Far from being put off by all the attention, Poppy seemed to be lapping it up. Nanna and Pappy looked on proudly. Even Jeff, in his own quiet way, doted on her too. She may not have been his granddaughter by blood, but that didn't seem to matter at all. She was surrounded by love.

'Hello, sweetie.' Linda's voice diverted my attention. 'How are you doing?'

'Keeping busy, I suppose.'

Linda shook her head.

'That's not what I asked.'

Not much ever got past her. I tried a more honest tack.

'Holding up,' I said.

This time she nodded.

'Good. You know Ryan and I are both there for you.'

Behind her, an equally tall figure with sandy blonde hair entered the room.

'Hi, Rebecca. I was sorry to hear about…' he looked suddenly less sure of himself when it came to actually uttering the words, 'about what happened.'

'Thanks, Ryan. We're okay. What about you? I've hardly seen you since…'

'Since I split up with Christine? It's alright; you can say it. What a pair we are!' He smiled, but his eyes betrayed his emotions: sadness along with something else I couldn't quite place.

I wished I knew why his relationships never lasted. Christine seemed such a good match for him, but a few months into their engagement he suddenly ended it. Now she wasn't even speaking to him. It wasn't as if he had any difficulty finding girlfriends; Linda often joked there must be a queueing system, but he seemed to have trouble making the leap to long-term commitment which was such a shame. He would be a real catch. Sickeningly clever at everything, just like his younger sister, he had an infectious, easygoing charm. And then there was that smile. I could have watched that smile all day, even if it had looked a little strained of late.

There had always been something unspoken going on, an attraction I couldn't quite shake, and there was even the one time we'd…but that didn't really count. It wasn't exactly just between the two of us. After that night, we hardly ever mentioned it. I touched the gold letter S that invariably hung around my neck and had done ever since he first placed it there shortly after my eighteenth birthday. Ryan was quick to notice.

'You've still got the bauble then, I see.' He nodded his

head toward it and I smiled shyly.

How does he do that? How does he always make me feel like a teenager again?

I put the thought from my mind. Whatever his issues around relationships were, I didn't need them in my life and neither did Poppy. Inside my head, I was still trying to pick over the wreckage Guy had left behind. As much as I always loved being around Ryan, leaping out of the frying pan and into the fire would be a huge mistake. I had no wish to add to my problems by becoming another casualty in his long list of failed relationships.

There was a knock at the front door so I excused myself and went to see who it was, but Francesca got there first. Guy's parents, Tony and Bernice Draper had arrived. I supposed Guy wouldn't be far behind and the thought set my teeth on edge.

'Hi! Come on in,' I encouraged, trying to remain cheery. They were, after all, Poppy's other grandparents. I could hardly deny them access to their only grandchild on a day like this.

'Thank you for inviting us.' Bernice wore her usual, plastered-on smile. 'I was so sorry to hear about the two of you...you know.'

I'll bet he hasn't given you the full story, though.

'It's so sad when work commitments take their toll.'

So that's what he told you. I thought as much.

'You know, I often say there's only room for one career in a relationship.'

And that would be his, then, would it?

For the sake of keeping the peace, I bit my lip and kept my sarcasm at bay. I wasn't sure if, beyond a bit of charity fundraising, Bernice Draper had ever worked a day in her life. Tony Draper made all the money; she simply made it her mission to find ways of spending it. On reflection, the origin of Guy's attitudes to a lot of things made perfect sense. There was no doubting he was his mother's son.

I waved them through, glad to set the awkward conversation aside rather than risk speaking my mind. Perhaps thinking I was no longer looking at them, Tony briefly glared at his wife as they crossed the marble-floored hallway.

'What?' Bernice protested. 'I was just saying.'

Always a man of few words, Tony Draper just rolled his eyes. I'd never quite been able to make up my mind about him. He always seemed to be wedded to his business, and I'd yet to meet a successful property developer without a ruthless streak. That said, if I was married to Bernice Draper I think I would have buried myself in my work too.

The next arrival was that of my brother Rob and his girlfriend, Chloe, and behind them, I could see Guy's silvery grey Aston Martin pulling up. At least he'd had the sense not to bring…her.

Man-stealing bitch!

That really would have been rubbing salt into the wound. I forced a smile for Rob who, sensing that something was wrong, glanced over his shoulder and caught my eye.

'You alright?'

I pinched my lips together and nodded, gratefully. Chloe just knitted her heavily pencilled brows at him, confused. She never was the sharpest tool in the box. Rob steered her out of the way so I could deal with Guy, one to one. Drawing myself up to the modest height I had available to me, I set my jaw, unsure whether to smile or scowl.

I had to admit, he looked uncomfortable as he came up the steps.

Good! I should fucking hope so.

'Hello, Guy. Just remember you're here for Poppy's sake. If it was just down to me, you wouldn't be coming back through this door. I hope you understand that.'

Guy maintained a mask of neutrality and stood, waiting to be invited over the threshold like the bloodsucker he was.

'I'm not here to cause any trouble. I just want to spend some time with my daughter, that's all. Don't forget I haven't seen her in over two weeks. We need to sort out arrangements.'

'You should be hearing from my solicitors this week. I'm trusting we can reach some kind of agreement without dragging this through the courts. Consider yourself lucky. If you'd helped yourself to money from anywhere other than a joint account, I'd be throwing the book at you. I'm sure you don't want that kind of publicity, and fortunately for you, neither do I.'

He moved forward to come past me, and as he did so I drew in close, lowering my voice to be sure no one else could overhear.

'I don't want trouble, but if you start any, I will personally end you. Got that?' I hissed.

Tightening his jaw, he nodded.

'Understood.'

I softened, just a little.

'Then go and see Poppy. She's in the reception room.'

As much as I hated to admit it, she'd missed him; I could tell.

Two old school friends, Jayne and Sophie, were making their way up the steps, so I left Guy to get on with it. I had no wish to spend any more time with him than was absolutely necessary.

These days Jayne had about her the healthy glow of a woman in love. I envied her. Sophie, too, seemed to be bouncing back after her disastrous relationship with Guy's friend Brett. He may have been out on bail in the wake of his arrest, but with a restraining order in place, unless he fancied being locked up again he wouldn't be going anywhere near her, thank God.

Steering them to one side of the hallway, I enquired about the upcoming court case and Sophie shook her head.

'It could be months away, but at least he keeps his distance now. I'll let you know when, so you can come and see justice done. I'd still be living in fear of him if it wasn't for you.'

'I just did what I could,' I told her. 'Three Rs Security certainly know what they're doing. Listen, I, um… I'm not sure it's a good idea I attend. Right now, the case hasn't attracted too much press attention, but if I showed up, it would turn the whole thing into a media circus. I'm speaking from experience here. Trust me; you don't need that sort of shit in your life. It's going to be hard enough reliving what he did to you without my presence stirring things up.'

'Oh!' Sophie looked like she'd just swallowed something unpleasant. 'I see.'

'It's not that I don't want to be there, but it's actually

better for you if I stay away.'

'Fine.'

That word again.

She made her excuses and stalked off on the pretext of going to the loo, leaving me with Jayne.

'You do understand why my being there wouldn't be helpful, don't you?' I asked.

She nodded.

'Yes, I do, but I don't think the reality of being the plaintiff in a trial for stalking and attempted rape has really sunk in. She just thinks it's all going to be a piece of cake, her moment in the limelight, but you and I both know Brett's defence barrister is going to put her on the stand and attempt to discredit her. They'll do anything they can to try and make out he's the model citizen and she's a needy attention seeker.'

'Just because they're right about Soph doesn't make him any less guilty, though.' Jayne's eyes widened. Perhaps I'd been a little too honest. 'Sorry, that was uncalled for,' I said, backing down, but she shook her head.

'No, you're right. She wants you there because it makes her feel like somebody, but if they do try to paint her in that light, I can understand why your presence might not help. The jury needs to understand that she's the victim in all of this and playing to the gallery won't help her any. The tough bit's going to be getting her to see it that way. She'll just feel abandoned.'

'What can I do, though? If I don't go, she's going to resent me for it, thinking I don't want to be associated with it all, but if I do go, it could make it harder for her and even damage her case by creating unwanted attention. I'm just trying to do the right thing, even though Sophie might not see it that way.'

Jayne assured me she'd work on winning Sophie round.

'Anyway, how's Simon?' I asked, hoping to change the subject.

'Oh, he's alright.' Her expression came alive again. 'He's working today, otherwise, he'd be here.'

At least something good had come out of the whole situation. Not all of Guy's friends turned out to be jealous, manipulative psychopaths.

Sophie reappeared, looking chirpier again.

'Right! Isn't it about time we said hello to the birthday girl?'

'I guess so.' I gestured them through to the reception room, glad to leave the topic of the trial behind.

When we entered, I could already sense the atmosphere as everyone tried their best to keep conversation convivial. The sound of all the unspoken words hanging in the air made my ears ring while oblivious to all the subtext of the goings-on around her, Poppy had tumbled into Guy's arms. How she loved her daddy! It warmed my heart and broke it at the same time.

I could see Mum chomping at the bit to say something, but Jeff held her back with a touch to the arm and a little shake of his head. Now was not the time for harsh words. It was, after all, Poppy's day.

By the time people began to leave, the mood had softened considerably. I wouldn't have called it relaxed, but at least it was less strained. Jeff accompanied Guy to his car to have a quiet word and came back looking thoughtful.

'What did he say?' I asked.

'Not much. It was probably more what I said.'

'And?'

'I just told him it would be best if he used me as a channel of communication. Things are obviously still raw between the two of you and your mother's ready to tear him a new one. I'm not trying to undermine how much he hurt you, far from it, but it's important for Poppy's sake to keep talking. Perhaps it's less painful if that's done through me for the moment.'

I guessed it was. I had no wish to deal with Guy but whether or not I spoke to him, the tangle of emotions the day had stirred up wasn't about to go away in any kind of hurry.

The day's ups and downs weren't done yet, either. Once the last of the visitors had left, I could tell by the way Karina stayed close by, fidgeting and trying to look occupied, that she was working up to something.

'What? What is it?' I asked as we took an exhausted Poppy upstairs. 'You've obviously got something you need to say. I can see it eating away at you.'

She looked relieved I'd broached the subject.

'Listen, I know you didn't want to hear it at the time when you split up, but seeing how Guy won people over today made me realise I need to tell you what I've heard. I hope you don't think I'm speaking out of turn but I can't keep it to myself any longer. You need to know the truth.'

We reached the top of the stairs and turned down the landing toward the nursery. I tried to hold on to Poppy but she was wriggling.

'I'm listening.'

'I know some people at the agency who are still in

touch with Emily.'

I stopped in my tracks.

Suddenly she had my full attention. Our previous nanny had left with no warning, no explanation, and no forwarding address, just a few words of apology to Francesca and a rather brief note before disappearing while I was out of the house. Even her phone number had changed. At the time I had thought she might have had something to do with the way the press seemed to know where I was going and when, how they were able to dog me at every turn. She turned out to be innocent of that so I was still none the wiser about her. The mystery surrounding Emily's disappearance continued to niggle at me.

'Go on.'

Karina took a deep breath.

'She left because of Guy.'

'Why?' It didn't make any sense.

'Well, from what I've heard she wasn't exactly worldly-wise.'

'Yeah, and?' I prompted, waiting for more. This wasn't news. My friend Janine and I had joked about her being a twenty-two-year-old virgin. She wasn't much younger than me but considerably less versed in the ways of the world. If the way we conducted our private lives had troubled Emily then maybe I could understand that, but she'd never said anything and we never shared the details with her. Besides, I still didn't see what that had specifically to do with Guy and not me.

'Apparently…' Now Karina seemed hesitant to take the final step and tell all. 'Apparently, he was hitting on her, making passes at her all the time. She didn't like being around him whenever you weren't there, and once he'd finished filming and was at home more, it got worse. She didn't want to let you down, but she also didn't feel it was her place to tell you. I don't even think she was sure if she'd be believed. Faced with the way he was behaving she decided she would rather leave than have to deal with it anymore.'

I reeled in shock. Surely we weren't talking about the same Guy.

'Maybe she just overreacted. His humour can be a bit childish sometimes.'

Karina shook her head.

'I don't think so. He didn't actually do anything to force himself on her, but the whole thing made her feel uncomfortable enough to just up and leave. I think it had been going on for a while.'

Even after everything else that had happened, it seemed so out of character. I had thought I knew him. It would seem not.

Rebecca, meet the real Guy Draper.

If this was true then underneath the surface he was almost as much of a selfish, entitled prick as his friend Brett. Linda's first impressions of Brett had turned out to be incredibly accurate despite his smokescreen of respectability, but Guy must have had everybody fooled, not just me: Linda, Mum, everyone. I needed more evidence, and I had a good idea where I could go to find out.

-0-

I stood up from the weights machine, still red-faced

and dripping with perspiration. Seeing as I must have looked like I had some irritation to burn off, Marie had been working me extra hard with more reps than usual. She handed me a towel.

'Better?' she asked in her slow, Australian drawl. Toned and tanned, she always looked to me like she'd just stepped off Bondi Beach or out of an advert for gym equipment.

'I don't know,' I told her. 'I'll tell you when the aching stops and my lungs no longer feel like they're about to explode.'

I flexed my back and placed the towel across my shoulders, dabbing the sweat away from my temples. No matter what she did, Marie never seemed to get flustered or even out of breath. I knew Guy had noticed her lean physique as soon as she began coming to the house to do my regular gym sessions. Neither of us had pretended not to find other people attractive, but outside of our dalliances together, I had thought his roving eye would stop there. How naive I had been!

'Marie, this might seem like a strange question but I'd appreciate your honesty here; you don't have to hide anything from me. In fact, I'd rather you didn't.'

'Okay,' she hesitated, looking up from packing her gym bag, obviously not quite sure where I was going with this.

'Did... Did Guy ever...?'

She stood up straight.

'Did he come on to me? Is that what you're asking?'

Her directness was refreshing, and the fact that she had pre-empted me already provided some clue as to her answer.

'In a nutshell, yes.'

Marie puffed out her cheeks and fixed me with a gaze like a firm handshake.

'Well, I didn't want to say anything before, but in the light of recent events, I might as well tell you. Yes. Yes, he did, and it wasn't just the occasional offhand comment either; it happened quite a bit. At first, it was kind of flattering coming from someone like Guy Draper. I wouldn't have done anything about it in case you're wondering; that would be totally unprofessional, but let's just say the novelty wore off after a while. I get that sort of thing all the time, though, so I'm quite good at brushing it off with a smile, but your ex-nanny, what was her name?'

'Emily.'

'Right, Emily, well she wasn't quite as adept. When he started to get a bit handy with it too, I get the impression that might have been the last straw for her. I think it was a bit of a power trip for him, you know? He probably thought it was just harmless fun, but I don't think Emily saw it the same way.' Marie could obviously see the look of horror on my face and glanced downwards. 'Sorry, have I spoken out of turn? You did ask.'

'I did, and thank you for your honesty. Did she say something to you, then?'

She nodded.

'Little things at first. After a while, she piped up a bit more and asked if he was the same around me. I told her straight. I'm sorry; none of this is probably what you want to hear.'

Whether I wanted to hear it or not, I needed to. All the time, while so jealously insecure and possessive of me around other men, he'd been coming on to other women, even a sheltered innocent like Emily, and despite our welcoming the likes of Linda, Janine, and the mysterious Svetlana into our bed.

The latter, having received her education at the finest private schools Britain had to offer, seemed to prefer being called Lana since it was a more Western European sounding version of her real name, although she had originally introduced herself as Anya. Either way, this sexual revelation and regular at Pulverton Manor, Linda's posh little country retreat and BDSM club I had the pleasure of part owning, intrigued me.

In a strange kind of way, Guy's possessiveness made sense; he thought everyone else must be as faithless as he was. There was only one real love in Guy Draper's egocentric world, and that was himself. Well, fuck him! I owed him no more of my pity, or my affection, or my tears. I was a free woman now. I belonged to no one, least of all him.

I'll show you, Guy Draper. Two can play at that game.

That evening after dinner, when I bathed, changed, and settled Poppy down to sleep, I sang her a little song and watched her breathing settle as she drifted off, before quietly closing the nursery door and reaching for my phone. It was time to put Guy behind me and redress the balance, and I finally knew just how to do it. Wheels were about to be set in motion.

Linda, you shall go to the ball.

Having my revenge on Guy was going to be so, so sweet.

CHAPTER FOUR

'I knew you'd come around to my way of thinking eventually,' Linda said with a hint of smugness as we made our way out to her car. 'Best thing for it!'

'Janine didn't seem too upset by the idea either,' I replied, 'and when she told Alan how in-demand his services were going to be, neither was he.'

Linda chuckled.

'I hope he knows what he's let himself in for. Just keeping up with Janine would be more than enough for most men, but then Alan isn't most men as I'm sure you're aware by now. I'm really looking forward to this. It's time to move on, sweetie, and I can think of no better way to do that than in the company of good friends.'

'Friends with extras,' I reminded her.

'Listen, honey, most of my friends are friends with extras, but they're still friends and that's what matters most. Just because I choose to live a life without unnecessary attachments, don't assume it's a life without affection.'

We slid into the front seats of Linda's new Audi and I placed the gift bag containing a bottle of wine in front of me in the footwell. It felt good to have taken a day off the songwriting in order to be pampered for a few hours. Having my hair done and dressing up for the evening had helped to restore at least some of my confidence and self-worth. There was now a renewed and much-needed spring in my step.

'So what happened to the Mini?'

'It was time for a change. I miss my Esmerelda, though, but I needed something more in keeping with the image of the business.'

Esmerelda? She had a name?

Of course she did; Linda had a track record in that regard. I just hadn't heard her use the name for the car very often. Given the growth of Linda's empire of naughtiness, an Audi TT was still hardly extravagant. It wouldn't look out of place next to all the expensive cars parked outside Pulverton Manor but it wouldn't outshine them either. Maybe that was her thinking all along.

'Besides,' Linda continued, 'she was getting a bit long in the tooth. None of our clients these days expects to see me driving round in anything older than about three years, and Esme was way older than that, so I got this one on a lease. It's just good business, keeping up appearances. You ready?'

I nodded, feeling excited and strangely nervous, like I was about to do something irresistibly naughty and against the rules. I hadn't been that way with another man since I met Guy, and that was well over two and a half years ago, but what's good enough for the gander is good enough for the goose. Now I had my independence back, I was free to serve Guy a dose of his own medicine. It gave me a certain satisfaction to know the thought of it would drive him up the wall.

Good! Cheating bastard!

'Ready as I'll ever be!' I admitted.

'Good, then let's go.'

Linda eased the Audi up the driveway toward the trees, on the other side of which stood the gates of Spensford Hall. Beyond them, the wider world beckoned, a world still full of experiences yet to be had. It occurred to me that perhaps I should make more use of Pulverton Manor and the Aphrodite Rooms now I was a single woman again. We turned right out of the gates, which closed smoothly behind us, and accelerated away down the country lane. While we drove to Sevenoaks I took the opportunity to ask Linda a little more about her clientele, though she seemed more dismissive about them than usual.

'The thing is it's not really about them. Yes, the business is focused on them, of course, but they're not the point of the business.'

I creased my brow.

'What do you mean? You're talking in riddles again.' She did that a lot.

Linda took a moment, gathering up a basket of words to scatter in front of me.

'It's a pretty selfish world we live in, and the higher up you go, the more selfish it becomes. I'm just doing my small bit to redress the balance. I give wealthy clients exactly what they want in return for some of their cash. It's a perfectly fair and equitable arrangement.'

None of this was exactly new information, and she'd somehow managed to sidestep the point of my question.

'But you don't spend much of it on yourself,' I pressed. 'Neither does Ryan.'

'True, but we have what we need. The rest gets put back to work.'

'But why do all this, though? I still don't understand what drives you. You've never really explained.'

Linda looked serious as she drove, keeping her eyes on the road.

'Like I said, it's a shitty world. We all do the best with it we can. I suppose you could think of Pulverton Manor as a microcosm of society, except on my terms. The richness of life's opportunities and experiences is reserved for the few, and no matter how successful either of us might be in our chosen fields, we're not part of the inner circle. That's a whole other club the likes of you and me are still excluded from, so imagine what it's like for most people. The doors to opportunity aren't open to them, nor will they ever be. Life's more fortunate individuals will try to tell you that as one door closes another always opens, but the reality for the majority of the population is that as one door closes, another one slams in their face. They're not invited to the party and never will be.'

I snorted.

'You may be many things, Linda Maloney, but I never had you pegged as a cynic.'

'I'm not. It's not cynicism if it's true; it's just good observation. I see things as they are, not as I would like them to be. Haven't you ever heard the story of The Emperor's New Clothes? Honest observers of the world are often labelled as negative, maligned and misunderstood. I could take the approach of the child in the story by speaking up and risking derision, or worse still, being ignored and ineffective while remaining on the outside of things, or I can quietly subvert the world around me from the inside in a way that does no harm to anyone. No one has to lose face. I chose the latter path. In the real world, it's a much more effective strategy.'

'But everything worked out in the story, though.'

'True, but that's what it is: a fairy story. In life, whistleblowers and dissenters rarely prosper, no matter how justified they are. I decided I could make more of an impact by being closer to that inner circle than most will ever be, while not sacrificing my independence.'

I leant back in the passenger seat, pondering her cryptic words. Linda might have known what she meant by all that. I was damned if I did.

-0-

'Darlings, do come in! I'm so excited,' beamed Janine, her flame-red hair catching the light spilling from the hallway and out into the darkening street. 'They're here, Alan!' She called over her shoulder, even though he wasn't far behind her.

Alan glowed quietly, smiling more with his eyes than his mouth. Slim and slight of build, he wasn't a particularly big man and yet possessed a gentle sense of command, a presence. Always the quiet one, I found it hard to imagine him as the sexual force of nature Linda seemed to think he was, but then I'd never have imagined he'd turn out to be a master of Japanese rope bondage techniques either. Fizzing with anticipation at the rest of the evening to come, I rather hoped his expertise would be put to good use at some point.

We followed them into the spacious and modern,

split-level lounge with its grand piano by the double doors that opened out to the rear of the house, taking in the ever-present faint whiff of incense. I handed my bottle of wine to Janine.

'Oh, good! We'll keep that for later on because I've just opened one. Fancy a glass of Sancerre?'

I did. It might help to loosen my jangling nerves a little.

Lucy, the Ashton's West Highland Terrier, fussed around my feet while Alan poured the wine.

'So how are you keeping?' Janine asked. 'I still can't believe how Guy went behind your back like that.'

'I can. The more I think about it, the more I realise I should have seen it coming, especially after your tarot reading. I think you did, though, didn't you?'

Janine shook her head.

'It isn't an exact science. Sometimes you don't want to believe what your own instincts are trying to tell you, and for your sake, on that occasion, neither did I. It's hard to separate emotion from intuition sometimes. If you wanted, I could do another reading to see where things are now.'

'Thanks, but I'll take a rain check on that one for the moment. I'm still getting over the dreams left behind from the last reading you did.' I didn't like to tell her how much they still haunted me, but every now and then I would wake up in the middle of the night, trying and failing to shake the image in my mind of a dark figure with eyes glowing like hot coals, who presided from his throne over a cavernous, underground kingdom with shadows and dangers lurking behind every one of its myriad columns.

'Here you are.' Alan handed each of us a glass of wine. 'This ought to be just what the doctor ordered.'

'Thank you, Alan. It'll be nice to let my hair down for the evening.'

'Until I plait it for you to keep it out of the way.' Janine gave me a look of wicked intent and winked. 'We don't want it catching in the ropes, do we?' For a moment she looked like she might have overstepped herself. 'Sorry, was that too far, too soon?'

I shook my head and assured her it wasn't. After all, it came as no surprise to any of us what the point of the evening's entertainment was.

'Just remember, there's no rush.' Janine reassured. 'Nobody's going to push things any further than you want to. Emotionally, you must still be a bit…'

'I'm fine. Really. I'm just claiming my life back.'

Janine nodded thoughtfully while Linda took a sip of her wine.

'Ooh, that's nice!' she said, changing the subject before the good mood of the evening dissipated. 'Why don't you play a bit of what you've been working on for Janine and Alan? See what they think. I know how excited you are to be doing something new and different.'

Alan extended his hand toward the piano.

'Be my guest,' he said. 'We'd love to hear it. You know how big a fan Janine is.'

I sat at the stool of the piano and lifted the lid, exposing the keys. Despite Alan only claiming to tinker at it, he and Janine had invested in a good one. It wasn't quite as nice as the Steinway that lived in my recording studio but seeing as Janine ran a television production company and they had no children, they hadn't cut corners.

'This is just something I'm working on for a solo project without the band. It's still a work in progress. We're going to be recording with a full orchestra to fill out the sound but you'll get the idea.'

My fingers found the comfortably weighted keys and sought out the opening chords. By the time I'd played the first few bars and relaxed into the music, I almost forgot where I was. The melody and the words just took over me, like they always seem to when it matters. When I had finished singing and the last chord died away, I opened my eyes to see Alan with his arm around Janine and Linda's waists. Linda looked on with pride. Janine was staring at me and welling up.

'Oh, wow! That's amazing and so different from any of your other stuff. It's so much more…'

'Grown-up?'

'That too but I was going to say soulful. You're digging deep for this album, aren't you?'

I nodded.

'I think we can safely say I've had to re-evaluate a lot recently. It was bound to come out in the music.'

'Well, whatever you're doing, it appears to be working,' Linda assured me. 'It's good to see you back on a creative roll, sweetie.'

From that point on, having played and sung for my friends, I felt much more relaxed. The conversation flowed and so did the wine. Things gradually became more tactile as we lounged on the cream leather sofa, laughing about the goings-on at Pulverton Manor and the idiosyncrasies of some of its clients. Some unexpectedly high profile people really did have the most unusual fetishes and preferences and Linda had her own inimitable way of sharing the stories. Her graphic tales of others' peccadillos might have come across as shocking had they been told by anyone else, but coming out of her mouth they sounded so matter-of-fact it was impossible to take offence.

Engrossed as I was in conversation, I barely noticed when a pair of gentle hands came to rest on each of my shoulders and I looked around to find Janine leaning over me. I melted into the upholstery and put down my wine glass as she began to massage the base of my neck with her thumbs. Looking across, Linda too had abandoned her wine and entered into a deep, open-mouthed kiss with Alan.

'Why don't we…?' said the dark-lined lips close to my ear.

'Take this upstairs?' I asked, finishing Janine's sentence for her.

Cradling my jawline with her hands, she leaned right over me and I tipped my head back to meet her, our lips meeting gently at first, then with more committed enthusiasm.

My God, that woman can kiss! I knew what a fearless adventurer she was, but I'd missed out on her more tender side.

In fact, I'd missed tenderness altogether. I'd forgotten, in all honesty, what real, passionate lovemaking could be like, how overwhelmingly emotional it could be. It was something I hadn't really experienced since my early, clandestine explorations with Steve. Even though his heart had always belonged to someone else, I knew he adored me and it showed in everything he did. They were wonderful, carefree times. Nevertheless, it hadn't prevented losing him from breaking my heart. It took a long time to eventually put it behind me, but the respect we had for each other had never waned. I would always be grateful to him for showing me what real tenderness could be. I missed that. Nowadays, though, he was just my producer, and along with his wife Valentina, a good friend.

Sex with Guy had been exciting, never dull, and he knew how to fuck alright, but that was just it; it was just fucking. When I thought about it, what intimacy there was had gone missing from our lovemaking for the last few months while he was busy directing his attentions elsewhere. I owed him nothing any more.

Hungry for Janine's touch, I intensified the kiss and drew her down towards me so she almost lost her balance over the back of the sofa. When we broke away from each other, Linda and Alan were both watching us, lips parted, with one hand in each other's laps, stroking firmly. Linda gave his hard-on a final squeeze through his trousers and stood up, stretching her long arms above her head and arching her lithe body.

'I think it's time, don't you? I don't know about you guys, but I'm feeling as horny as fuck. Lead on, Mr Ashton.'

He stood and took Linda by the hand, leading her out of the room. Janine and I followed, hand in hand while Lucy the westie, obviously accustomed to such cues, tottered off to her basket in the kitchen. I followed the generous sway of Janine's hips and the tattooed angel wings that led down to her slender waist up the stairs while behind me, four great orange and white paws padded along in our wake. Purring loudly and tail waving proudly in the air, Sadie was back in business.

Linda clearly knew where she was going. Walking backwards from the top of the stairs with Alan's hands in hers, eyes shining with excitement and biting her lip, she pulled him in through the bedroom door and they tumbled onto the oversized bed. Janine and I weren't far behind, kissing and feeling our way to begin removing each other's clothes.

Linda stood up to undo the buttons on Alan's shirt, working downwards until she had exposed his chest, and teased one of his nipples between her teeth, flicking its piercing with the tip of her tongue. Why it should have surprised me he had rings in his nipples and a Celtic knotwork tattoo across his left shoulder and down his left arm I don't know. After all, I already knew about his wife's tattoos, including those that only the most intimate of acquaintances would ever be aware of, and also the piercing in her clit, but the voluptuously fairytale Janine had always come across as larger than life anyway. It was just such an unexpected thing in so normally quiet and unassuming a man. Minus at least some of their clothing, they made such a perfect pair.

Janine slipped her backless dress over her shoulders and wriggled it down over her hips, letting it fall to the floor and stepping out of it before helping me out of mine. In the meantime, Linda had undone Alan's trousers and sunk to her knees with the fingers of one hand wrapped around his not exactly insubstantial erection. It was pretty obvious to me what was coming next and Linda didn't shy from it. Sweeping her long, dark hair over her shoulder she wrapped her lips around the head of his cock and holding him by the base, sank him into her mouth.

Janine shot me a look of collusion and tossed Alan's trousers towards the corner of the room before standing behind him and whispering something into his ear. She gestured me over to join Linda, who slipped Alan wetly from her mouth, wiping a trace of saliva from her bottom lip with the heel of her hand.

'Come on, sweetie, I think you should show Alan your party trick. Try as I might, you've always been better at that than me.'

I knew exactly what she was talking about and I think Janine did too. Shooting me a knowing look, she whispered into his ear again and I could have sworn his cock grew even harder at her words. Joining Linda on my knees I prepared myself while she gripped him by the base and held him in my direction.

'All yours, honey.'

Janine looked on encouragingly too with no hint of jealousy at what the two young women in front of her were doing to her husband.

It's now or never.

I was about to do something I hadn't expected to do to anyone else other than Guy for…well, forever.

Not anymore!

I teased the tip of Alan's cock with my tongue and drew him into my mouth, gradually working him deeper and deeper, listening to his groans of pleasure and Janine's little gasps of surprise and delight. I could feel him press against the back of my throat as Linda let go of him and I wrapped my lips around the base of his cock, cradling his balls in my hand. He throbbed in my mouth as I rocked my head back and forth and Janine clasped her hands together in excitement.

'Oh, well done you! Even I can't do that. What's that like, Alan?'

He stroked my hair and closed his eyes while Linda took over caressing his balls and I mouth-fucked him deeply.

'Oh, fucking hell!' he snarled, apparently having some trouble breathing. 'That's…that's really rather nice.'

'Rebecca, you are going to have to teach me the secret,' Janine insisted. 'I swear he's about to blow his top and Alan can go on for hours usually. Can't you, Alan?'

He just growled, trying not to think about coming in case it tipped him over the edge.

Eventually, I had to come up for air and Linda took over again while Janine kissed me, delving into my mouth with her tongue. I wondered if she could still taste her husband's cock. The thought of it turned me on even more.

'You realise you're going to have to show me the secret to how you do that,' she said, eventually breaking away from the kiss, 'even if I have to torture it out of you…in the nicest possible way, of course.'

'It's just a knack,' I told her. 'I learnt with bananas at first. It's all Linda's fault; she kind of dared me.'

'Guilty as charged, I'm afraid.' Linda looked over at the pair of us. She didn't exactly come across as penitent for her misdemeanour.

'What do you think, Alan? Should I try and add that one to my repertoire?'

Alan just grinned. I got the feeling he wouldn't complain.

'Come on then, Rebecca, let's get those cute little knickers off you,' Janine insisted. 'I think you deserve the royal treatment tonight. Doesn't she, Alan? You are going to get properly fucked like the naughty young lady you are.'

'Please,' I gasped as she slipped her hand inside my lacy knickers and her fingertips found my sensitive spot. I wrapped my arms around her neck because my knees were giving way underneath me. By this point, getting 'properly fucked' sounded like music to my ears.

Several eagerly reverend pairs of hands helped me out of my underwear and I stood, naked except for my heels.

Janine bit her lip.

'Stunning! You're beautiful enough fully dressed but you are breathtaking without your clothes, my lovely. Aren't we lucky, Alan? Come here, my darling.'

She drew me towards her and lay back on the bed, taking me with her. I leant over Janine, locked in her embrace while Linda stroked down my back with her hands until they found the smooth cheeks of my arse and gave them a playful slap before parting my thighs with the flats of her hands. I soon realised why.

Two strong hands grasped my hips and Alan positioned himself behind me. Before I knew it, he was sliding effortlessly into the welcoming depths of my pussy and I melted into Janine's arms, resting against the fabulous pillows of her breasts while he fucked me with smooth, even strokes.

'There now!' she soothed into my ear, cradling my head while my body undulated on top of hers. 'Isn't that nice?'

I had to admit it was. What made it all the sweeter was

the thought of the revenge I was exacting on Guy.

Every time Alan pushed forwards a little gasp escaped from my mouth, mingling with Janine's breaths which mirrored mine. She wrapped her legs around my waist, pulling me up her body a little. At first, I wasn't sure why until Alan withdrew from me and Janine let out a long sigh when he entered her instead. I glanced across at Linda who was kneeling up on the bed with one hand pressed between her thighs, watching.

'I'm sure you'll get yours too,' I assured her.

'Oh, don't mind me; I'm just enjoying the view. We've got all night. It's Alan I'm worried about. You'll be a stone lighter by morning, won't you, Alan?'

I could feel him shaking with laughter behind me.

'Don't worry; I'll live. If not, I'll die a happy man,' he said before shifting position and plunging into me again, taking me completely by surprise. I rested my head on Janine's shoulder as he began to fuck me, this time more vigorously than before, rocking my lips against Janine's pale skin.

'Yes... Oh, fuck yes!' I gasped, gritting my teeth as he slammed into me. 'Like that...harder...harder!' He really was going for it now. 'Oh my God, I'm going to come! I'm...'

Janine crushed her lips to mine and held me close as I began to convulse, sobbing as I came. But there was no let-up; Alan powered right through it, only slowing down as I came out the other side, twitching and gasping for breath with my hair cascading over Janine's face. She brushed a damp strand of it away from my flushed cheek while a bead of perspiration ran from my brow and down the bridge of my nose.

'There now! Isn't that better?'

I nodded, still rocking to and fro in time with him and unable to speak. Since my mouth had fallen open and remained that way, it felt rather dry. Although Alan had settled into a much more leisurely rhythm, he showed no signs of letting up.

'Good girl,' Janine said, stroking my face.

'What about Linda?' I asked. 'I think she deserves her share. She's been very patient.'

Alan slowly withdrew, teasing the head of his cock against my clit, and I shuddered at the sensation, still very sensitive after my orgasm.

'Come on, Lindylou,' I said, holding out my hand to stroke her thigh. 'Your turn.'

'Oh, alright then!' she said with an air of mock resignation. 'If I must.'

She lay on her back with her legs in the air, gripping behind her knees and exposing herself to full view. I brushed my fingertips up and down the lips of her pussy, gauging her readiness.

Fuck me, Linda; you are so wet!

I needn't have worried on that score.

'Come on, Mr Ashton; do your duty!' Linda ordered. 'I need fucking too.'

'Alright, Miss Maloney. You asked for it.'

He moved across and sank smoothly into her while Janine and I held onto one leg each, kissing Linda's feet and sucking her toes into our mouths. As was her way, Linda went into silent paroxysms of delight, throwing her head back and gasping for breath every time he pushed forward, going at her with deep, purposeful strokes.

'That's it, Alan,' Janine encouraged. 'You give that

young lady a good seeing-to. I want to see Linda come. Let's make it one she won't forget.'

Faced with three insatiable women in full flow, how the hell he hadn't blown his stack already I had no idea. His self-control must have been off the charts.

An idea crossed Janine's gothically beautiful features.

'While Alan fucks that lovely young pussy of yours, Linda, I think mine might be in need of a little attention. Quid pro quo, as they say.'

She knelt astride Linda's face and lowered herself against my helpless best friend's outstretched tongue, parting her labia in readiness and tugging on her piercing.

'Oh yes, get that tongue in there,' she snarled. 'Make me come all over your pretty young face.'

Linda needed no further encouragement, holding her open and lapping at Janine's flower like a butterfly eagerly gaining its fill of nectar while Alan ploughed into Linda's pussy, building up the pace again.

Where does that man get his stamina from?

Not wanting to be left out, and enticed by Janine's ample breasts, I cupped one in my hand, feeling its weight, and lowered my head to take her nipple in my mouth. She stroked my head while I teased at the sensitive bud, her mouth opening and closing silently.

Now Linda began to twitch, arching her back. I recognised her cues well enough by now to know she was close and reached out with my other hand, running my fingers through the neat triangle of dark hair and caressing up and down her labia, stretched tightly around his cock, while Alan fucked her with zeal, slamming against the backs of her thighs with every stroke.

Your turn now, honey.

A stifled moan came from between Janine's thighs and Linda bucked her hips, rising them off the bed as she came, gripping the bedclothes between whitening fingers before completely dissolving again.

'Good girl. Don't stop. I was just getting into that,' Janine insisted.

She wiggled her hips by way of a reminder, and Linda gradually recovered herself enough to put her tongue back to work while I sucked hard on Janine's nipple, pinching the other between thumb and forefinger.

'Oh yes, that's it,' Janine breathed, her body tensing. She began to quiver and shake, issuing a string of obscenities as her own orgasm took hold, visibly relaxing as it subsided.

'Ooh, that was nice! Linda, you've been practising.'

'You know me, sweetie,' came the slightly muffled reply.

We all flopped back on the covers while Alan leant over Linda. She languidly stroked his face and gave him a deep, wet kiss, her face still smeared with his wife's wetness. I knew from previous experience Janine had a tendency to squirt when she came, although to say the least it had been a bit of a surprise the first time I'd encountered it.

'I think…' Janine mused, 'I think Alan deserves a treat for all his hard work, don't you, ladies? It seems only fair.'

It did.

She gave her husband an adoring look.

'And I think I know just how.' Sitting up on the bed, she encouraged Alan to lie back on the bed while she cradled his head and kissed him lovingly. 'I think you know what to do, ladies.'

Linda and I looked at each other. I think we did.

'I'm bagging first go,' I said. 'Let's see who wins the prize.'

'You're on! Winner has to share though.'

'Deal.'

I dived on Alan's cock, enthusiastically sucking him like a lollipop and stroking up and down on his shaft, applying what I hoped was just the right amount of pressure. Every man seems to have a slightly different threshold but with any luck, I'd found his. He still tasted of Linda; I knew that sweet, hot flavour well.

Linda appeared to be counting to herself, her lips moving almost silently as she breathed out the numbers.

'My turn!'

Reluctantly, I passed the baton and she took over, alternating between sweet and nasty, trying every trick she knew. I would need to come up with something truly original if I was going to be the one to take Alan across the finish line. When it came to my turn again I raked my teeth over his sensitive tip before sucking hard and engulfing him to the hilt. It was the one thing I knew Linda would struggle to do. I could see Alan's orgasm building while Janine looked on in fascination, holding his hand. He wasn't there yet, though. When my time was up, Linda took charge again.

Damn, I almost had him!

Alan started to twitch, breathing heavily. It was all going to be a matter of timing. Sporting to the last, Linda relinquished him at the appropriate moment and I knew I had to go all out. I alternated between a twisting motion with two hands and taking him as deep into my mouth as I could. I could feel him tensing.

'Oh, good girl!' Janine encouraged as I felt him begin to throb. 'I think you might have him.'

Maybe I can make sure.

Taking a leaf out of Janine's book, I found his anus with one hand and slipped my index finger carefully inside, pressing my advantage. Janine had to have developed that technique somewhere and she had used it to remarkable effect on Guy. Maybe that was what it took to push Alan over the edge. Not being an expert at it, I hoped I'd found the right spot.

'Oh fuck!' They were the first words Alan had uttered in some time and they arrived just as I released him from my mouth, rubbing the tip of my thumb against the underside of his glans.

Got you!

With a loud groan, a fountain of come erupted from Alan's cock, raining onto his belly and running down over my fingers.

'Oh my God!' It took a moment before I even registered the words were mine. 'How long have you been saving that one up for?'

Alan exhaled slowly and sank back against the covers, regaining his breathing and trying not to laugh. Janine chuckled to herself and Linda clapped her hands in delight.

'Well done you, Rebecca! Whatever you did, I think you just found the secret to unlocking Alan's code.'

'So!' announced Janine. 'Come on then, girls,' she encouraged, leaning in. 'Let's finish this job properly.'

For a moment, and only a moment, Linda and I looked

at each other. As one, the three of us descended like ravenous succubi to the feast.

-0-

I awoke with a need to use the bathroom and gently disentangled myself from Linda's endless legs. The others were still breathing quietly as they slept. It may have been a deliberately large bed, but the four of us still didn't leave much by way of empty space. When I returned, Linda had stirred and was propped up on her elbows, looking at me enquiringly.

'Morning,' she whispered. 'How are your wrists?'

I checked them over, rubbing the place where a few hours before there had been a series of red lines extending to a network covering all the areas where I'd been so deliciously bound. Not only did Alan possess Olympic level endurance, but he was also an absolute artist with his shibari ropework; a true kinbaku master. I had already seen him give a demonstration at Pulverton Manor, but now I fully understood why Linda held him in such high regard. He had a seemingly endless repertoire.

'Not too bad now the marks have faded. You?'

She checked her ankles and wiggled her toes.

'I'll recover. Fun, though, wasn't it?'

'Oh yeah!'

Janine stirred and sat up, stretching. Alan was still out for the count, bless him.

'Up already, you two? What time is it?' She answered her own question by glancing across at the clock. 'I'd better go and put the dog outside. Help yourselves to robes; there are fresh ones on the shelf in the bathroom. I'll start some breakfast going in about half an hour.'

By the time Linda dropped me home, Francesca had already started work. Karina was wrapping Poppy up warm to take her outside, presumably to play in the fallen leaves. She seemed to love that. I decided to join them for a while before heading into the studio. I had some fresh ideas swimming round in my head and I wanted to try them out before they left me.

'Morning all!' I breezed.

Francesca gave me a momentarily enquiring look but her face remained otherwise impassive. It still made me wonder whether she could read my thoughts. Hopefully not, although what I got up to and with whom was nobody else's business anyway.

For the first time in a long time, despite the obvious physical tiredness resulting from only about four hours sleep I felt refreshed, energised, and empowered. I'd had my first taste of being truly free again and I liked it.

I wanted more.

CHAPTER FIVE

Having listened through the tracks we'd already recorded for the song one final time, the arranger put down his tablet and looked thoughtfully through the triple glazed window into the performance area of the studio, tapping his finger against his top lip before turning his attention back to Steve and me.

'It might be best to hold off on the French horns and the bassoons until the third verse, keep it mainly strings on the suspended chords through the first half of the song. That should help it to build going into the last chorus. You'll have it all as a sequenced file to approve the arrangement before we do it for real anyway. Then I can get parts out to all the musicians involved.'

'Thanks, Trevor.'

Steve sat back in his swivel chair while I leaned one elbow on the mixing desk, half-listening to the conversation and half playing the orchestral parts through in my head. He seemed pleased with the morning's progress.

'We've already got the orchestra and the main soundstage at Oxygen Studios booked for two weeks time. There'll be a full rehearsal the day prior to recording so we can iron out any wrinkles, but basically, we need to work quickly. It looks like we're going to be recording two separate albums back to back, and all before Rebecca has to prepare for the tour that follows.'

Trevor raised one eyebrow in surprise and looked across in my direction.

'And when does all that kick off?'

'We've got about fourteen months before the first gigs, so the clock is ticking.'

'Jesus H. Christ! You don't do things by halves, do you? I wish you good luck on that one. You'll have your work cut out alright.'

I shrugged my shoulders.

'It's all about getting things back on track. If what Mitchell says is anything to go by, and I have no reason to doubt him, the general public has a short memory span and fickle allegiances. There are too many vested interests to consider if I want to continue making the kind of music I can be proud of, especially after taking my foot off the gas to have a baby. At this stage in my career, I'm lucky to be coming back from that one.'

Mitchell remained kind about it, but I knew cancelling the previous tour had hit the business side of things harder than he was prepared to admit. I owed him. I owed the rest of the band. As much as I would have been happy to spend my life hidden away in the studio making my own kind of music, it wasn't just about me. Truth be told, it never had been.

'Good, well I'll get right on it then,' he assured us.

Trevor packed up his things and I saw him to the front door of the studio annexe before returning to the control room. I had some more ideas to run past Steve. It felt rather like the excitement and the experimentation of the old days in Jeff's converted barn studio at The Gables, only without the romantic entanglement. I'd never have tried to take Steve away from his family, and at heart, he was a one-woman man anyway. If he hadn't been separated from Valentina at the time, nothing would have happened between us.

I picked up my favourite electric guitar, the Les Paul my family had given me for my seventeenth birthday, and was just about to start playing when the heavy, glazed doors from the entrance vestibule swung open and in burst Jeff with an expression like thunder.

'I thought I'd find the two of you in here. How very cosy!' He came right up to a startled Steve while I stood with my guitar slung over my shoulders, hands still poised ready to play. 'You've got your feet nicely under the table here, haven't you? Just like you did with me, I suppose.'

Steve's mouth opened but no sound came out. Somehow it was my voice that replied.

'Jeff, what the hell is going on?'

'Save it!' He rounded on me, pointing, his face red with anger. 'You're not innocent in this either, but I'll deal with you in a minute.' For now, he turned his attention back to Steve. 'I trusted you. I trusted you with my family, with Rebecca's future, and this is how you repay me. For fuck's sake, she was only sixteen!'

Almost seventeen, actually, and by the way, hello, she's standing right here!

So that was what all this was about, but how come he knew? We'd managed to keep Jeff out of the equation all this time. Someone must have let something slip.

Guy! It has to be Guy. I was going to fucking kill him.

Steve stood and said nothing, simply waiting for the punch he obviously thought was coming. Perhaps he'd resigned himself to the fact that eventually, Jeff might find out. He made no attempt to defend himself or to fight back. It was probably the only thing that made Jeff stay his hand.

'It's not his fault,' I heard myself saying. 'If anything, blame me; I started it.'

Jeff didn't even look at me.

'That's not the point. Steve should have known better. You should have kept your dick to yourself, Steve. Instead, you took advantage of an impressionable teenager.'

A young woman who was already quite capable of making her own decisions, thank you very much!

'It wasn't like that,' I protested. 'Steve never treated me with anything less than the utmost respect. Would you rather I lost my virginity to some snot-nosed, full-of-himself teenager who treated me like a possession or a conquest he could brag to his mates about? For your information, Steve turned me down at first. Nobody used anybody like your first wife used you. I'm not like Ginette and neither is Steve.'

It was Jeff's turn to look stung, but only for a moment.

'Oh, you know about that, do you?' he replied with an air of sarcasm. 'And I suppose you told her, didn't you, Steve? That's yet another confidence you've betrayed.'

Still Steve made no attempt to defend himself, verbally or physically. He just stood and faced Jeff square on, meeting his gaze passively, preparing himself for the worst.

'Just stop it, Jeff! Stop it!' I yelled. 'It happened while Steve and Valentina were apart and she knows about it. We've made our peace about the whole thing. It's all in the past.'

Jeff briefly glared at me then turned his attention back towards Steve.

'Valentina might have put it behind her, but don't go expecting me to. Steve, you might well have a cushy little number here and that's beyond my control, but you stay the fuck away from me and you stay the fuck away from my house. You got that? I don't want to see your face again. You wouldn't even have become the producer you are without all those years of my guidance. And as for you, Rebecca, I'm bitterly disappointed. While I spent a long time putting my own career on the back burner and using my energy and my contacts to gain you a foothold in the business, you were busy screwing around while you were supposed to be working on your own future. Who do you think paid for the guitar you're holding in your hands, huh? The fairies? If it wasn't for the opportunities I've put in front of you, you'd be scraping a minimum wage day job while hawking yourself round playing covers on the club circuit like your mother had to, and this is the thanks I get? I don't think you have any idea of the damage you've done, either of you.'

I put the guitar on its stand as gently as I could although my hands were shaking and rounded on him.

'I've always been grateful for what you and Mum have done for me and Rob. Don't think I don't recognise how much you've given and sacrificed to forge a family where there wasn't one and to build our futures, but there's more to my life than just a career. I was at an age where I was discovering who I am, and Steve was there for me when I needed him. We did nothing wrong. We committed no crime.'

'But you still felt the need to hide it from me, though, didn't you?' Jeff snorted. 'Both of you did. Rebecca may have her own way of rationalizing this, but you, Steve,' in his fury, he was practically poking Steve in the chest with one hand while gripping his shirt with the other, 'you should have known what you were doing. You crossed the line, with Rebecca, with me, and with my family, and there's no taking that back. You stay out of my way from now on.'

Jeff turned on his heels and stormed out of the door, leaving us standing open-mouthed in the control room.

'Shit!' Steve was the first to speak. 'I'd always thought this day might come. How do you think he found out?'

'Oh, I think I know,' I said, clenching my teeth. 'I'm beginning to realise it's just the sort of low blow Guy would stoop to.'

-0-

'I can't believe you did that! What on earth possessed you to tell him?' I paced up and down the library floor with my phone in my hand.

'It just sort of came out in conversation. I didn't realise he didn't know,' Guy pleaded. He sounded sincere enough, but then he always did; he was an actor after all. It wasn't washing with me, though.

'Don't give me that shit. You knew exactly what you were doing. You've known I was keeping that particular information away from Jeff ever since the night you blew up in a jealous rage at Mitchell's wedding. If you want to stir up trouble at my end because of some childish fit of pique, you can think again. I can always file for sole custody, you know, and then where would you be?'

'You can't do that without good reason,' he protested. 'I'm still Poppy's dad.'

'And you don't think your meddling in my business and wrecking my family's peace isn't reason enough? Just watch me!' Sadie snarled at him down the phone. 'I don't think you have any idea how much damage you've caused. I've already had Mum on the phone in tears because Jeff went off on one. Since she knew about it and hadn't told him, he's not even speaking to her at the moment.'

Guy, however, was ready with the counteroffensive.

'That's their business. Don't blame me! I wasn't the one who had an affair with my stepdad's studio engineer. I think you need to look a little closer to home for the root cause of that little mess.'

'Why do you think nobody ever said anything? No good would have come from Jeff knowing, and guess what? It hasn't.' I was more than livid now, but still just about avoiding the temptation to explode. 'Whatever the rights and wrongs, it wasn't your place to tell him. I've cut you more than enough slack up to this point, but if you want to get petty with me I can make your life pretty fucking awkward if I want to. Don't go thinking you're so perfect and untouchable, because I know exactly how much of my money you helped yourself to.'

'Look, I'm sorry. I wasn't thinking and it just came out, okay?' He'd backed off even quicker than I expected now I brought the money issue into it. 'I'm not trying to make waves, honestly; I've already done enough damage.'

This was a first: at least a partial admission of guilt. Maybe he had some semblance of a conscience after all. But then there was the other thing.

'It's not the only damage you've done, though, is it? You managed to drive Emily away. She ran off because she got fed up of you coming on to her.' I could almost hear his jaw drop on the other end of the phone. 'Did you really think I wouldn't find out the truth eventually? And don't even bother denying it either; I've got my sources.'

There was a moment of silence.

'I was only teasing. I didn't mean anything by it.'

'Even if I believed you, it would still make you an insensitive prick who lied to cover his tracks. You were always the one who went on about maintaining boundaries with people who work for me. What kind of boundaries were you maintaining there? It's yet another example of how you think the rules don't apply to you. I'm just glad I finally see you for what you are.'

Point made, I decided to change tack and at least ask him how things were going.

'So how's Anna?' I asked, still rather abruptly.

He went quiet again for a moment.

'She's alright. She's just... Well, she's not you.'

'Don't forget, you made your bed...'

'And I can lie in it. Yes, I know.' He'd actually begun to sound genuinely penitent, or maybe things weren't as rosy between them now everyday reality had kicked in. 'You don't need to remind me. I deserve what I get, right?'

With that shrew for company, I guessed he did.

CHAPTER SIX

Somehow it felt odd driving through the gates of Pulverton Manor in my little Honda. Sporty as it was, it still felt out of place among all the prestige cars lined up outside the entrance to the seventeenth-century manor house. I could see why Linda felt the need to change her Mini. Maybe it was time for me to ring the changes too. I still had my Volvo XC90, but I left that at home in case Karina needed to take Poppy out. The days spent in the studio working on new material had been long ones and the following week would see us recording in London with the orchestra, so what better way to take a break and unwind than an overnight stay at the club? Every girl deserves a treat now and again.

Tamzyn was at the front desk when I stepped through the stone-lined archway, pushing open the dark oak front door that led into the reception area. She smiled broadly when she saw me.

'Hello, Miss Taylor. We haven't seen you in a while. It's nice to have you back.' She handed me a key. 'Your usual room has been prepared for you. If you'd like to make yourself comfortable, I'll have your bags brought up for you.'

'Thank you. Actually, I was hoping to catch Linda if she's here.'

'I think she's in the upstairs office, along with Mr Maloney. Would you like me to ring up first?'

It took me a moment to realise she meant Ryan. To me, Mr Maloney had always been Brian, their father. I thanked Tamzyn and told her that wouldn't be necessary; I could make my own way up. Leaving my car keys with her, I ascended the wide, wooden staircase, doubling back on myself at the first-floor landing and passing through a door marked 'Private – Staff Only'. I found myself in the corridor outside the office which acted as the command centre for Linda and Ryan's growing little empire of high-class amusement. There were voices coming from inside, and I could have sworn I heard my name being mentioned a couple of times. When I knocked, the voices stopped.

Ryan opened the door.

'Oh, hi Rebecca! Come on in. We were just wondering what time you were coming.'

'I haven't come at an awkward time, have I? I just thought I'd get here early enough to catch up before things kick off in the Aphrodite Rooms.'

Linda came over and gave me a hug.

'Not at all, sweetie. Besides, the Aphrodite Rooms are open most of the time anyway. Some of our members prefer more leisurely and private daytime entertainment. Things do become a bit of a spectator sport in the evenings; there's more of a party atmosphere, particularly at weekends, so if that's what you're after you've timed it right. It can be a bit of a free-for-all but some people prefer it that way. It depends on how you like it. I think you might know a few of the faces here today, but you can never be too sure who will be around. Unless they're staying here or using the restaurant, club members don't need to book.'

'What about Svetlana?'

She gave me an amused look.

'I wondered how long it would be before you asked about her.' Linda went over to the window and glanced at the cars outside. 'Yep, she's here somewhere. That's her Ferrari outside: the burgundy red 488 with the custom plates. She's become something of a regular when she's in the country. Keeps asking about you, too. You and Guy must have left quite an impression on opening night.'

'I think we must have.'

In the form of angry red marks across her behind!

We didn't exactly hold back, and her very public punishment had been one of the evening's many highlights. Now it was just me, I wasn't sure if she'd be as interested. I guessed I'd find out in due course.

'Just…' Linda glanced across at Ryan who wore an unusually serious expression. 'Just remember to be a bit careful around her. Simply because she enjoys playing the submissive, don't be fooled into thinking she isn't getting things her way. Daddy's little princess always gets what she wants. I don't think she's ever had to face a day of responsibility in her whole life.'

It sounded a little like sour grapes to me. Linda's workload was the consequence of her own choices, as was mine, and despite welcoming her moneyed clientele with open arms and sometimes open thighs, she clearly didn't consider herself one of them.

'I'll bear that in mind,' I told her.

'Well now you're here, do you fancy some tea or coffee?' Ryan asked, gesturing toward the facilities to one side of the office.

I told him since this was my well-earned time off, I'd rather ease into things with a proper drink for a change.

'In that case, we'd better head downstairs to the bar. Are you coming, Linda?' he asked, but she shook her head and glanced at her watch.

'You two go on and have a catch-up. I've got some things to see to before dealing with one of our more specialist clients. I might be a while with this one.'

On our way back down the staircase, I took the opportunity to ask Ryan how he was doing since his rather awkward split with Christine.

'I'm... I'm alright.' His reply wasn't exactly unequivocal.

'Is there anybody new on the horizon?'

He shook his head.

'Nah. I'm kind of taking a break from relationships: holding out for the right one, I suppose. What about you?'

'Oh, I'm in no hurry to get involved again. The last thing I want is to get into another Guy situation, and the immediate future is all about getting the music career back on the rails. It's the single life for me, at least for the foreseeable future. There's always the Aphrodite Rooms for when I want to let my hair down.'

Ryan nodded thoughtfully as if there were some words on the tip of his tongue that never quite made it out of his mouth.

'Yeah, I guess there is,' he said eventually with what sounded like a hint of resignation.

We sat down at a table in the bar and I told him all about the recording plans and the tour to come while we sipped our gin and tonics. I recognised Preeti, the girl who brought our drinks over. Her dusky charms had caught my eye on previous visits, but I knew full well what the house rules were: staff would be firmly off-limits. That said, I'd been left with the impression on more than one occasion that Linda and Tamzyn had come to their own, more flexible arrangements. I supposed that was the privilege of being the one who makes the rules, or perhaps their terms predated Tamzyn's appointment as general manager of Pulverton Manor.

Shame, really.

I'd have to find my evening's amusement elsewhere, not that that was likely to be a problem around here. The advantage of a place like this was there were no ties or complications; even names could be optional. Famous faces and public figures were in and out of the club all the time, as well as the anonymously rich and powerful, but nothing was ever mentioned about it. In these circles, it just wasn't done. I could, quite literally, come and go as I pleased, and that felt…refreshing.

Ryan finished his G and T, rattling the remaining ice around his glass just as a familiar figure with a shock of strawberry blonde curls flounced through the door to the bar.

'Ah, there you are!' She flung her arms open. 'I heard you were here. It's so good to see you again. And Ryan!' Svetlana made big eyes at him. 'I didn't realise you knew each other that well.'

'We're old friends,' Ryan told her. He looked at me and smiled. 'We go back a long way.'

We certainly did.

'Well, I'm afraid I have some things to finish off in the office,' he continued. 'I'll leave you two ladies to it. Enjoy your evening, won't you.'

'Oh, we'll try,' I assured him.

'Rebecca. Miss Markova.' He nodded in each of our directions, stopping just short of actually clicking his heels together.

Lana watched him leave. Her eyes didn't stray from his behind until he'd disappeared out of the door.

'Now that's all man, don't you think? So polite, so reserved, so very...English!'

Even if he is actually Irish, I thought to myself. What remained of his accent had softened to the merest hint of a seductive lilt, even less pronounced than his sister's.

Preeti came over with a cocktail for Svetlana and asked me whether I'd like another G and T. I replied that I would.

Fuck it! Why not?

'So is this a flying visit or are you staying for a while?' I realised Lana was looking straight at me now, toying with the maraschino cherry on a stick propped up in her glass and parting her lips.

'I'm here till tomorrow so I can relax and enjoy myself a bit.'

'Oh good! There are so many appetites to satisfy once we allow ourselves the opportunity.' It appeared Guy's absence had done nothing to lessen hers. 'Which reminds me, I haven't eaten yet. Have you? The current visiting chef, Marco, is very good. I often pop into his restaurant in Naples when I'm passing by. Would you care to join me for dinner before making the most of the club later?' It sounded good. 'Now you're a free agent again, us girls can indulge whatever tastes take our fancy,' she said with a pout.

'I didn't realise you knew.'

'Darling, of course I know; it's all over the papers and the magazines. Is it really just career pressures that broke the two of you up?'

'That and a few other things,' I admitted. I really didn't feel like telling her the full story.

'Well, be that as it may, there's nothing to hold either of us back any more. It's been quite clear that Guy was a little uncomfortable getting too…involved when there were other men around. I think it's high time we remedy that situation, don't you think? We ought to party like the single girls that we are.'

I wasn't about to argue. Perhaps letting my hair down was just what I needed, and wherever Lana happened to be, the party was sure to follow.

We ate in the restaurant just through from the bar, which doubled on occasion as a function room, and I had to admit the food was exquisite. Pulverton Manor's opening night menu had not been a one-off. Francesca's cooking was always good but homely and uncomplicated. This went way beyond what I expected of Italian food, and the panna cotta with grappa caramel sauce was just to die for.

Lana dabbed the corners of her mouth with her napkin and fixed me with a smouldering look.

'Seeing as we have a couple of hours before things get interesting downstairs, I suggest we both go and freshen up in readiness. You don't fancy joining me, do you?'

I had to admit, I couldn't say no to a little appetizer

before the main course. I met her gaze with mine, slowly sucking the last of the caramel sauce from my bottom lip.

'Sounds good to me.'

CHAPTER SEVEN

Lana and I descended the main staircase together, holding hands and treading carefully on the way down in case we toppled in heels. To be honest, my knees still felt a little bit wobbly after the things we'd been doing to each other upstairs. Time, and a little fine dining, had done nothing to lessen either Lana's appetite or her creativity.

'You don't think I look too slutty, do you?' I asked. The dress I was wearing didn't leave all that much to the imagination, and I didn't generally go for such heavy make-up unless I happened to be on stage.

'I take it you do know where we are. What's wrong with slutty? It leaves no room for misunderstanding. After all, we're here to get laid, aren't we?' If I wasn't already fully aware of her capabilities behind closed doors, the words might have sounded coarse coming from her impeccably spoken mouth but instead, they just sounded direct. 'Which of the rooms takes your fancy tonight? What are you in the mood for?'

We reached the bottom of the stairs and I cupped my hand, whispering my thoughts into her ear. Lana's eyes sparkled with mischief.

'I like your style. You really are determined to break

free of old ties, aren't you? Well, I'm in if you are; the challenge is on.'

'Are you sure?' I asked.

'Darling, do you honestly think I'm breaking new ground here? Of course I'm sure. Call it a hunch, but I don't think there will be any shortage of willing volunteers.'

I guess that's that settled, then.

We turned toward the largest part of the manor, the east wing, and descended another set of steps, passing through the double doors that led to the Aphrodite Rooms. Beyond the fountains at the other end of the column-lined entrance, music could be heard coming from the club itself.

Suddenly my confidence waned. I was about to step into the club as a single woman: no man by my side, no partner, no safety net. At least I had Lana for company. Sensing my nervousness, she gently steered me to one side.

'Look, I know you're newly single again, but what are you afraid of? People's attitudes? You won't be judged by anybody I know, and I do this sort of thing all the time. The only barriers are in your head, my darling. Don't forget, two minutes ago you were challenging me.'

She was right, of course. I took a deep breath.

'Fuck it, let's go!'

'Good girl.'

We pushed open the doors to the main club room and it was like entering another world. Two performers, a man and a woman, dressed in nothing but thongs that could have doubled as dental floss, gyrated together on the low stage to an incessant beat, occasionally peeling away from each other to dance on poles. Their lithe, muscular bodies beaded with perspiration as they defied gravity in perfect synchronisation before coming together again.

In the main area, people in various forms of dress and undress sat or stood around in groups, sipping their drinks and occasionally applauding the performers. One man was speaking to another while a slim woman with waist-length, wavy, brown hair knelt in front of him, still with a glass of champagne in one hand, sucking enthusiastically on his cock. Occasionally he would look down, stroking her incredible, leonine mane and speaking encouragingly to her before returning to his conversation. One couple couldn't even wait to get to a side room and were fucking vigorously across one of the tables.

'Drink?' Lana asked. 'I think some champagne might be called for, don't you? After all, we are celebrating your independence.'

We were indeed.

She signalled to the young man behind the bar who seemed to know exactly what she wanted and reached for a bottle of her favourite Krug from the chiller. Once we each had a glass in our hand, she wasted no time making introductions. There seemed to be nobody there she didn't know. Occasionally she would share a quiet word with one or other of them, although it was largely drowned out by the music. They would nod appreciatively and glance in my direction with a smile before she moved on.

'I think we should be all set,' she said eventually. 'Not surprisingly, there seems to be quite a bit of interest.'

My nerves began to tingle with anticipation. It felt so wrong and yet…

Why shouldn't I? Guy could go and fuck himself.

Lana downed the last of her drink and took me by the hand.

'I think it's time we got more comfortable. I believe the Roquelaure Room should be free. It might be better suited to what you have in mind, rather than one of the more specialist areas.'

I agreed. She seemed to be quite happy to take charge on this occasion and, feeling almost like a beginner again, I was quite content to be led. I wasn't ready to go back to The Principal's Study anyway; it would remind me too much of the last time I was in there, and one or two of the other rooms weren't really to my taste, certainly not for tonight.

I put down my glass and followed Lana through the doors on the far side of the club to the place where the real action happened. I could feel eyes trained on us as we went, boring into my back and making my skin prickle. To either side of the wide corridor, a series of doors led off into the different themed areas. The sound of what was already going on inside some of them could be heard as we passed by; laughter and conversation, but also groans and gasps, and the occasional slap of something against bare skin, all in relative privacy but hardly in secret. Just thinking about everything going on behind those doors set my imagination whirling and I could already feel myself becoming wet with anticipation. On our right and about halfway down we found the room we were looking for. Lana knocked then opened the door, peering around to check inside.

'All clear: no unexpected guests. I think we should get this party started, don't you?'

Around the walls, there were beautifully photographed, black and white prints of men and women in various forms of bondage, a series of soft drapes which made the room more welcoming, and a number of gold-leaf, cushioned chairs, but the centre of the room was dominated by a huge divan bed. I could only call it a bed, although it was clearly not intended for sleeping. There were no pillows, but it was scattered with a number of plush cushions. Eight to ten people could have comfortably got up to no good on it without ever running out of space or even getting in each other's way that much.

Svetlana ran her hands across my shoulders and feathered the skin at the nape of my neck with her lips.

'Do you remember how on the night I met you at Miss Maloney's first event, you and Guy so deliciously ravaged me?'

I did.

'Well tonight it's your turn to get ravaged too,' she slipped the straps of my dress down my arms and began kissing across my shoulder blade, 'and I'll be right with you every step of the way, just as long as you don't mind sharing.'

I didn't.

'Good, then let's get this dress off you. I want to see you in all your naked glory first, and so will everyone else,' now her lips hovered so close to my ear I could feel her breath against my skin, 'right before they fuck you: every...last...one of them.'

I melted against her, my knees going weak at the

thought. It wasn't like I didn't know what was coming; I did. That was *why* my legs had turned to jelly. It had been a long time since I'd done anything so brazen, but I knew exactly what I'd let myself in for. With a wiggle and a bit of encouragement, I worked my dress down over my hips until it dropped to the floor and stepped out of it, placing it over one of the chairs while Lana did the same. Our underwear, what there was of it, soon followed, and we fell giggling onto the bed, hands exploring and tongues locked.

It wasn't long before there was a knock at the door.

'Come!' Lana entreated.

Appropriate.

Two well-toned men in their thirties entered, already unbuttoning their shirts. We had been introduced but I couldn't remember their names. It didn't matter much.

'Well, well! What do we have here?' said the more broadly built and probably slightly older of the two in a soft but clearly spoken Scottish accent, grinning. 'It looks like you've started the party without us.'

Nice eyes.

'Just getting things warmed up,' I assured. I wouldn't have said no to either of them, which perhaps was just as well; I ended up saying yes to both, and plenty more besides.

Behind them, a queue was already forming at the open door and several couples exchanging furtive glances entered hand-in-hand and sat down to watch. The two men quickly divested themselves of their clothing, rolled on condoms, and sidled onto the enormous bed to join us. I opened my arms to the one with the lovely, Scottish accent and he slid up my body, showering me with kisses before meeting my mouth eagerly with his own. I could feel his erection pressing against me. He wasn't especially big, but he was hot and hard and definitely ready, and when he started to move down my body again I began to gain an inkling of just how good he might be with his mouth and tongue. I couldn't wait for him to get all the way down.

I looked across at Svetlana who was receiving much the same treatment and reached out my hand to squeeze hers just as my new found lover reached his target. Sucking air in through my teeth I hooked my legs over his shoulders and arched my back as he went to work.

'Oh, fucking yes!' I snarled, grabbing the back of his head with my other hand and pulling his face into me, feeling his tongue swirling and pressing. 'That hits the spot.' Sadie agreed.

He looked up briefly and grinned again before returning to his task. I'd have been quite happy for him to keep doing that all night but he was eager to have his fill of me, and I wasn't about to complain.

By now, Lana had presented herself on all fours, rocking to and fro as her companion got into his stride. I could hear her little gasps coming from close by, mingling with his. My lover knelt up, grasping my upper thighs, and lifting my hips he eased himself into me.

Game on!

He didn't even do it particularly hard, but his timing was impeccable, catching me just right every time, and I was lost in the rocking motion of his hips, almost oblivious to the audience when Lana eventually tapped me on the shoulder.

'Time to swap over,' she panted.

Quickly, the two men moved around and picked up where the other had left off while Lana and I locked eyes, each aware of the sensations the other was experiencing. It wasn't long, though, before the man between my thighs altered his rhythm, his strokes becoming shorter and sharper and his breath beginning to catch. I wrapped my legs around his hips and pulled him into me as he lost control and slumped forwards, groaning as he came.

'Nice?' I asked.

'Oh, Jesus!' He rolled over next to me, still breathing heavily. 'I never thought when I got up this morning I'd…'

'You're welcome. Don't mention it.' I'd have been crazy to imagine people didn't know exactly who I was. 'No, seriously, don't mention it. What happens at the manor stays at the manor. Just remember that and we're all good.'

Next to me, Lana's eyes were starting to roll as both she and 'Highland Fling' behind her drew closer to their respective orgasms. She dropped forward onto her elbows pushing her delicate behind into the air and closed her eyes as she came while he followed suit with a slow exhale. Lana lifted her pretty head, brushing a mass of tight curls back from her face.

'Well, that's one, or is it two? How are we doing this?'

I felt slightly taken by surprise.

'Firstly, I didn't realise we were counting, and secondly, who decided it was a competition?'

'It might make it more interesting, don't you think?' she said with a sparkle in her eyes.

'In which case, we'll call it one each. It only counts if they come.' I pointed to another man who'd caught my eye earlier on and beckoned him over. 'You're next.'

The well-presented woman next to him defiantly shifted her weight onto one leg and placed a possessive hand on his shoulder. She had short, dark hair, clipped features, and an air of efficiency that said she was used to getting her own way with things.

'Only if I get to play too.'

I gave her a playful, tight-lipped smile, raising one eyebrow. She may have been a little older than either of us young whippersnappers already on the bed, but she kept her figure in fantastic shape and she looked like she meant business. I wasn't about to turn her down.

'You're on.'

'That's not fair,' Lana pouted. 'You didn't say girls were allowed.'

'No one said they weren't.' I was ready for her with that one.

Not really having an answer, she just nodded her head and pointed to the next two men in the line.

'You and you…yes, both of you. You're up.'

They acknowledged each other for a moment and began hastily removing the last of their clothing.

'What?' Lana shrugged her shoulders and gave me an unapologetic look. 'You think I'm ready to be left behind?'

'Not for a minute.'

If this was going to be all about who could go the distance, so be it! I had previous form. I knew I could last out, even if I was going to feel it in the morning. The man I beckoned to earlier came over and eased into me with a satisfied sigh, but instead of joining in with us, his companion lay down next to me, spreading her legs and stroking her neatly trimmed but unshaven pussy, hoping to entice some of the waiting men her way.

'I thought you meant...'

'Oh, don't get me wrong,' she said. 'You're very lovely, so please don't take it personally, but I don't do girls; I just wanted to join in. After all, if Niall gets to have you, I want my share of the fun. It's only right.'

I couldn't argue with that, seeing as I had my legs wrapped around her man's waist and his balls slapping against the cheeks of my arse, but now I was on my way to becoming one down in the competition. I reached my hand across to her.

'Rebecca.'

'Oh believe me; I know who you are. Who doesn't?' She accepted my hand and shook it. 'Sharon.'

Lana was already being enthusiastically seen to from both ends, making satisfied little noises while her pair of lovers went at her in stereo. I could tell she wasn't a long way off coming. Perhaps her friends wouldn't be far behind.

'Looks like we've...got some...catching up to do,' I told Sharon as her man thrust forwards, energetically pushing me into the bed.

Sharon gave me an enigmatic little smile.

'Slow and steady wins the race, my dear.' Another man sidled onto the giant mattress and positioned himself, making the most of the opportunity her open thighs afforded him. 'See, I'm catching up already,' she soothed, turning her attention to him as he eased into her embrace.

If this was now a serious competition, I needed to up the ante. Assuming Lana's two current admirers carried on the way they were going they wouldn't last particularly long, and then where would I be? I looked up at Niall.

'How about we flip over? I've got an idea.'

Curious to see where I was going with this, he eased off the pace and I flipped him onto his back in order to take charge, kneeling astride him and riding up and down, teasing the head of his cock against my opening then sinking my full weight down onto him.

'You like that?'

He nodded, looking up at me and growling with each downstroke.

In the meantime, the man in Lana's mouth couldn't contain himself any longer and let go with a shudder. Once he'd finished unloading, she swallowed his come down with a lick of her lips and waved him away.

'Next!' she announced.

Fuck! I'm going to have to get creative here. I needed to use every available weapon in my armoury.

I looked over my shoulder at the waiting queue and gave my backside a tempting little wiggle.

'Okay boys, who wants to fuck my arse?' Immediately, half a dozen or more eager volunteers stepped forward.

You lot are so fucking predictable.

'Well, form an orderly line. I can't handle more than one at a time in that department, but you'll all get your turn.' Actually, two at the same time in that regard was about the one combination I'd never quite had the courage to try. Perhaps even that would be a step too far for tonight. My tactics would have to be all about endurance and turnover, so maybe that was an experience best saved for another time.

As if to make a point about my state of readiness, I dribbled saliva onto two of my fingers, leant forward, and reached around to insert them while a suave, lean looking man of about forty took up position behind me. He captured my wrists firmly behind my back, dribbling lube into the crack of my arse, and slid smoothly home while I looked into Niall's eyes, panting. It took the two men a minute or two to find a rhythm that worked, but once they did there was no stopping them. I rolled my hips in time with their movements, revelling in the deliciously filthy sensation.

You're a dirty girl, you little slut.

That I may have been, but neither of the men offered any complaint, and the extra feeling of pressure would probably bring them off faster too, so it was a win-win situation.

It wasn't long before all three of us ladies had taken on new lovers, and the queue kept moving forwards. Several of the women also joined in. Lana and I devoured them with equal skill and eagerness, while Sharon focused solely on the string of men that came her way. In the spirit of friendly rivalry, we each took on two, sometimes three people at a time and some of the men lined up again, keen to go another round with one or other of us, but eventually, the queue subsided. Sated as I was, and having come several times myself, I was almost relieved when it did. Every joint ached, and despite the liberal use of lube and the fact that none of the men had been particularly rough, I still had the feeling it was going to catch up with me. Even my jaw was killing me. I could still taste the come of the last man I'd had in my mouth and some of it was in my hair too. Insatiable as always, and ever the showoff, Lana had licked the rest of it from my face while still being fucked from behind.

One of the couples sitting at the side of the room had decided to keep score for us, which I was grateful for because I lost count on my own behalf, never mind keeping track of what Lana and Sharon were up to. It had to be close, though. Each of us had used every wile at our disposal, every trick we knew, until eventually, only the three of us remained on the bed, waiting for the final pronouncement. It was the woman who spoke. She looked kind of familiar even though I felt sure I'd never met her before.

'I think I'm speaking for everybody when I say we'll all be talking about tonight for a long time to come. No matter who comes out victorious, I have to say all three of our valiant contestants deserve a round of applause and a visit to the spa for a massage to ease those aching muscles.' A general, appreciative cheer went around the room, followed by a smatter of polite clapping. 'By tomorrow morning, I think you're going to need it, ladies.'

The woman conferred briefly with her partner while the three of us sat, somewhat gingerly, on the edge of the bed with our arms around each other's waists in an act of moral support. Should that have been immoral support? Who cared?

'So in third place with a score of twenty-seven, we have...Sharon.'

Her late entry might have cost her. She can't have been all that far behind us, but I had no idea what the final tally would be.

'The other two scores were so close we had to double-check, but in second place is…'

She was enjoying keeping everybody on tenterhooks for the result, like the presenter of a reality TV competition. Come to think of it, now I knew where I'd seen her before. That's exactly what she was.

'…Rebecca, with a score of thirty-two!'

Were we really that far ahead?

Now there was louder applause and a series of wolf-whistles. I guessed there was no shame in coming a close second. On Linda's instigation, I'd probably taken on more at my eighteenth birthday, but she had imposed a time limit on the majority of them so it had been more of a sprint than a marathon for the most part. This had been an altogether different experience.

'Which means,' the announcer waited a moment for the noise to die down, 'that this evenings champion at, quite literally, taking on all comers, with a final score of thirty-three, is Svetlana!'

The room erupted. I had to hand it to her; she'd been relentless. I'd been one step behind her most of the way so it wasn't a total surprise. For someone so slightly built, she could certainly dish it out.

Sharon leaned across and held out her hand, patting Lana on the knee.

'Congratulations, my dear. That's some staying power.'

'Thank you. It's one lesson they never taught us at finishing school but perhaps they should have. We had to learn it for ourselves, and believe me when I say most of us did. One doesn't maintain one's place in the world by simply remaining on one's feet, you know.'

Not quite sure if she was putting on airs and graces in

jest, or if she was actually serious, I gave her a quizzical look.

'Skills have to be acquired if you intend to bag and keep a wealthy husband,' she told me nonchalantly, 'and it doesn't pay to lag behind the competition. You have to become good at getting horizontal if you want to stay on top, if that isn't a positional oxymoron.'

'I didn't have you down as the marrying kind,' I chuckled.

'Oh, I'm not! Not yet, anyway.' The humour of it seemed to have passed her by. 'I was never interested in the debutante scene; it's such a meat market, but it doesn't do to marry beneath one's station in life, does it? If anything, one ought to trade up, not down, and any advantage is still an advantage. It's alright to screw the help if you fancy a bit of rough but no one with any self-respect marries them.'

'But what about love?' I asked.

Lana raised one eyebrow and gave me a pitying look.

'What's love got to do with it? I'm talking about self-preservation.'

-0-

At breakfast, I felt like we should be wearing sunglasses. It wasn't so much a hangover as a fuckover; I could barely move. Even sitting down had to be done with great care: come to think of it, especially sitting down. Apparently, although I may have lost the overall contest I'd beaten the other two hands down in that particular department. I was paying for it now. Unfazed by the whole experience, Sadie sat by the side of the table, quietly licking her paws.

Sharon and Niall sat across the restaurant from Lana and me, looking remarkably fresh, but both Lana and I were in a similarly delicate state to each other. I picked up my gold-rimmed, bone china cup with the Pulverton Manor logo on it and took a sip of English Breakfast tea while waiting for my food to arrive.

'I can't believe we actually did that. The last time anything like that happened, I was eighteen. I should be old enough to know better.'

Lana shrugged her shoulders.

'You only live once. As vices go, it's probably one of the least damaging. After all, we've both had a pretty good workout. Shame is for the repressed, and is that how you'd really want to describe yourself?'

'No,'

'No, I didn't think so. What are you worried about, then? Besides,' Lana said, nodding in Niall and Sharon's direction, 'our friends over there seem to thrive on the lifestyle.' She tidied the cutlery on her plate, preparing to leave the table, 'I need to go and freshen up. I promised an old friend I'd be somewhere today and it wouldn't do to disappoint them.' She reached across to rest her hand on mine. 'Call me, though. I'm certain there's plenty more fun to be had.'

I felt sure there was.

Lana hadn't been gone long, and I was still tucking into my individually prepared breakfast when Linda came in, stopping to greet a couple of the club members before sitting down opposite me for a quiet chat.

'Well, well!' she cooed. 'And how are we this morning? I hear you had quite a night last night.'

'You could say that. How do you know, anyway? You weren't in the club, were you?'

'No, not last night; I had other things to do. I have my sources, though. News travels fast around here. I hear you almost kept up with our own resident Eskimo Nell.' I choked, almost spitting out my mouthful of food. 'That was either brave or foolish, I can't decide which,' Linda continued. 'That's like trying to drink rounds with Oliver Reed and not expecting to wind up under the table, God rest his sozzled soul. Never mind blood from a stone, I think she could milk other things out of it if she had half a mind to.' Her expression turned more serious. 'I just... I just hope you know what you're doing.'

'Of course,' I assured her, still recovering myself from trying not to choke at her previous comments. 'I'm having some fun, that's all. Don't forget, you introduced me to all this. Don't start getting all moral on me now, and certainly not in your line of work.'

Linda shook her head.

'Oh, there's no preaching involved and no judgement. You know that wouldn't be my style. It's not the what or even the who; it's the why that concerns me. Motivation is everything.'

'I'm fine. Stop worrying, will you! I'm a big girl now. I know what I'm doing and I don't need chaperoning.'

'Alright, alright!' she placated, holding her hands up. 'Just being a friend and looking out for you.'

'Like I said, I'm fine.'

Linda gave me one of her coolly analytical looks.

'Okay, sweetie. Well, I guess that's fair enough then.'

CHAPTER EIGHT

Trevor nodded to the orchestra and placed his baton on the rostrum in front of him before removing his headphones. A few moments later, Steve's voice appeared over the foldback monitors.

'Okay, everybody, I think we may have everything we need but we're going to run it through carefully for a few minutes to make sure. If anybody wants to grab a coffee or a nature break, now might be a good time to do it just in case we need to patch in with any overdubs afterwards.'

Finally able to relax a bit, eighty or so people set down their instruments, the murmur of conversation gradually increasing as they all stood up to stretch their legs. The previous four hours had consisted of fairly intensive final rehearsal followed by an extended series of takes so they all seemed glad of the break, and Steve had sounded fairly confident we were almost there. From where I had been sitting at the back of the soundstage it sounded pretty much exactly how I'd imagined it, all bar a few little additions courtesy of Trevor Mountford's experienced arranger's ear. We couldn't have recreated a sound quite like this, even with the technology available to us in the studio at Spensford Hall. It might have sounded okay using orchestral samples and piecing the whole thing together on keyboards, but the flow and the phrasing would not have been the same. Real instruments breathe in a different way, and it was such an important part of the song I'd insisted on using a full orchestra. Luckily, Steve had agreed with me, and at least we had the production budget to go the extra mile these days. By the time we'd paid the orchestra, the day's recording had probably cost almost as much as the studio time for my whole first album.

I made my way through two sets of heavy doors to the control room where Steve and chief engineer Rhodri were running through the track and adjusting levels.

'What do you think?' Steve asked.

'If the recording sounds anything like it did in there, it'll be amazing.'

'It should do. The in-house engineers have got the microphone placement down to a fine art. They know the acoustics of that soundstage like the backs of their hands and I've worked here before with Jeff.'

'How are things with Jeff?' I asked. 'Is he still not talking to you?'

Steve's expression tightened and he shook his head.

'No. What about you?'

'He's hardly said a word to me since that day. At least he's talking to Mum again but it's like there's a cloud hanging over the family. I'm sorry you got caught up in all that. It's not your fault.'

'I guess I have to shoulder my share of the blame. I shouldn't have…'

This time it was my turn to shake my head.

'You don't have to apologise, to me or to anybody. I started it, not you.'

'But I didn't have to act on it. I chose to.'

Although I wanted to reach out and touch Steve's hand in a gesture of comfort, I refrained. Rhodri pretended to ignore the conversation by finding something absorbing to do on the screen in front of him.

'Steve, it's history,' I told him. 'We've both moved on. Jeff needs to do the same.'

'Perhaps for Jeff, that's easier said than done,' said Steve contorting his face and twisting the corners of his mouth. 'Anyway, can't change that now. What's done is done. Are we ready with the playback?' he asked Rhodri, getting back to business.

'Almost ready,' he replied in his broad, singing, Welsh lilt. 'I'll have it for you now in a minute. It's sounding tidy, though.'

Steve and I looked at each other and grinned. Rhodri's turn of phrase had become a source of much humour, something he rather enjoyed playing up to. As part of his ongoing ribbing of Rhodri, Daniel had exhausted just about every sheep joke going.

When Rhodri hit the play button, I was blown away by the sound. The song now built from its quiet, intimate beginnings into something huge and sweeping. I wouldn't have called it operatic, it was more intimate than that, but it had an epic quality that made it so different from anything I'd done before. It afforded me the opportunity to let loose my full vocal range from soft and delicate through to full chest voice. Now I could hear everything in context, I wanted to re-record the vocals again. I knew I could do it even better justice.

For the moment at least, Steve was more concerned with the orchestra.

'I think there are still a couple of little bits with the strings I want to tidy up. Rhodri, if we can record the oboe melody again on a separate track, I want to double track it to thicken the sound and bring them out a bit more. We could just put an eleven-millisecond delay on it instead, panned hard left and right, but to my ears, it wouldn't sound as natural. At least we recorded each mic feed to a separate track; it gives us more options at mixdown, but it'll be cleaner still if we record additional parts in isolation. Apart from that, I think we're done.'

Rhodri nodded.

'Right we are, then. Mint!'

The conversation might have sounded like double Dutch to the uninitiated, even without Rhodri's turn of phrase, but having grown up around the studio with Jeff and Steve, it made perfect sense to me. I had no doubt Rhodri knew what he was doing too. He'd worked in a couple of the major studios in Cardiff before joining Steve as his right-hand man.

'So do you need me for anything?' I asked.

'No, it's just mopping up the details,' Steve assured me. 'If you want to stretch your legs or even go home, you're free to. You didn't even have to be here today.'

'I know, but I wanted to. It's my record. It's personal.'

Steve nodded.

'I know it is. All these new songs are. Anyway, we should be finished in another hour or so, once everybody gets back off their break.'

Which reminded me, I could use a cuppa myself. Leaving studio one behind, I made my way down the main corridor of the complex to where the drinks machines were located. Studio two was silent, but as I passed studio three I could just about decipher the sound of drums and grinding, dissonant guitar, a seven-string going by the extra low notes, bleeding through into the corridor. I could tell the studio door had been opened behind me by the sudden increase in sound level as I disappeared in the direction of the drinks machine.

On my way back with a plastic cup of disgustingly bitter-tasting tea in my hand, a figure I knew was standing outside studio three with another musician I didn't recognise. Normally, he would have been dark and brooding, all black eyeliner, tight leather, and attitude. Today, he was dressed for comfort in a faded pair of jeans and an old tour t-shirt. His eyes lit up when he saw me.

'Rebecca! I thought that was you disappearing into the distance. I'd recognise that cute little arse anywhere. I didn't know you were here today.'

I rolled my eyes and grinned at him.

'Likewise. I mean the not knowing you were here bit, not the butt recognition bit.' I pointed down the corridor. 'We're in studio one at the end, recording orchestral parts. What brings you here, Zakk?'

He grimaced.

'Nigel, please, or you can just call me Nige; the rest of the band do. We're not on show to the public today. I'm not Zakk Kaos to my friends and never have been.' He'd have freely admitted, though, that Nigel Smith didn't exactly make him sound like the internationally famous rock god he undoubtedly was. He gestured towards the man he'd been standing with. 'Rebecca, this is Pete, our new bass player. Pete, this is Rebecca. I'm pleased to say we go back quite a way.'

Pete shook my hand. He looked a little overawed. It was a far cry from when I was the overawed one, a still shy sixteen-year-old sitting at the back of Jeff's studio while Whispered Scream recorded demos for their second album.

'So what brings you guys here?' I asked.

'Same thing as you. We tend to do a lot of creating on the spot, so we're here playing around with a new song for our next album. It's missing something, though, and none of us can quite put our finger on what. You don't fancy giving it a listen, do you?'

'If you think it will help.' I wasn't so sure. As much as I enjoyed what they did, dark, angst-ridden metal wasn't exactly my area of expertise. Nigel seemed to think a fresh pair of ears were just what they needed, though, so what harm could it do?

I followed them into the studio where the rest of the band seemed pleasantly surprised to see me and sat down on one of the seats in the control room while they played the song back. Musically, it came as no great surprise: angular chord changes; dense, driven guitars; gruff vocals; and unusual structure and timings, but the lyrics fascinated me. They reminded me of the dreams I'd been having on and off ever since Janine's last tarot reading, but I still didn't understand what they meant, so naturally enough I asked Nigel.

'I often draw on aspects of mythology for the lyrics to our songs, seeing as it's kind of my background,' he explained once we'd heard the track through. 'I was studying for a Classics degree when we first started to make it big. Of course, I had to drop my studies to go on our first major tour, but maybe one day I'll go back and finish it. Our fans expect something grand and dramatic but not too prog-rocky, so we darken everything up a bit and give them exactly what they want: metal with a twist. We're still trying to do something a bit different again with it, though. Originally, when we did a rough demo, it was called Pennies For My Eyes and it was a much graunchier, more aggressive thing that focused on crossing over into the underworld, but it's kind of evolved. I'm thinking of renaming it The Halls of Hades. Are you familiar with the myths of Hades?'

I replied that I wasn't.

'Souls are carried across the rivers Styx and Acheron to reach the underworld, ferried by Charon,' he continued. 'It gave rise to the ancient practice of putting coins in the mouth, and later, over the eyes of the dead so they could pay the ferryman to carry them across into the afterlife. There's a lot of the story of Persephone the daughter of the goddess Demeter's descent into the underworld in the newer lyrics. She had to face the darkness in herself and come to terms with it by learning to love the lord of the underworld, Hades himself, despite his frightening appearance, before she could return to the world of the living. We kind of play on the dark aspects of it, particularly in the music, otherwise it gets a bit fluffy.' He shrugged his shoulders. 'We are a metal band, after all.'

A jumble of images raced through my mind: Janine's look of benevolent concern as my hand turned a tarot card over which a shadowy figure presided; the dark, cavernous halls that appeared in my recurring dreams; and the ever-changing face of a man, seated on his ebony throne, at times horned and others antlered, his eyes glowing with a fearful fire.

'Cross the water and enter my domain, but know this: the seed of light is often found in the deepest shadow. To return to the sun you must find your way through the darkness of these pillared halls. There is no turning back.'

'Are you alright?' Nigel must have registered my look of blank preoccupation.

'I'm fine. It just reminded me of something. You said you think the song needs a twist, something extra to make it stand out. Where's the voice of Persephone in this?'

'Go on; we're listening.' Now it appeared my ideas had the producer's attention too.

'It sounds to me like it needs a female vocal in places to give the song light and shade: perhaps not harmonies, that might soften it too much, but some interplay between male and female vocals to show both sides of the story, afford it some give and take.'

The producer was nodding. So was Nigel.

'Yeah, I can see that, although I've got nothing against adding harmonies. We are looking to try something a bit different to usual, after all, and I don't mind going a bit more conventional with my vocal style for a change, at least in places. It's all about the storytelling. Fancy having a go so we can try the idea out?'

'Why not?'

It wasn't like I was needed in the other studio so what did I have to lose? I wanted to experiment musically and this seemed like the ideal opportunity to try something totally out of the box. Its complex structure didn't even have simple verses and choruses and nothing seemed to quite follow the same pattern twice. I was completely out of my comfort zone but perhaps that air of uncertainty was what the song needed.

'I don't know if my voice will suit the style so if you don't like what I've done you can always scrap it or get someone with the right kind of voice to rerecord it. It's got to be worth a try, though.'

After singing it through and brainstorming a few changes and additions to the lyrics with Nigel's help, I took to the vocal booth. Nigel occupied the booth next to mine since he would also have to redo his parts. It was all just for the hell of it anyway, so I didn't feel under too much pressure. I slipped the headphones on and took up position while one of the engineers lowered the microphone and pop shield to adjust for my height.

'You ready?' asked the producer, his voice coming through loud and clear over the cans. I made sure I could see the amended lyric sheet properly and cleared my throat.

'Yep! All good!'

'Okay, rolling!'

An atmospheric intro layered with heavily reverbed guitar harmonies led into the body of the song and I settled myself while Zakk's voice came through the headphones. I could see the look of focussed concentration on his face through the connecting window as he growled his way through the opening words. I hope they didn't expect the same from me because that kind of vocal fry technique wasn't something I'd ever even tried to do. I'd be too worried about what it would do to my vocal cords.

Leave the sun behind
Cross the river
Set foot on the other side
Two coins to pay the ferryman placed across your eyes
Carried away to the land where dark presides
A sunless kingdom where all must face their fears
Daughter of grain
Welcome to the otherworld

Then it came to my turn. In my mind's eye, I could already see myself standing at the bottom of the steps leading up to Hades' throne as he towered threateningly over me. Flickering torches cast a pool of light onto nearby stone pillars that disappeared into the darkness of the vast cavern overhead. My voice echoed in the darkness.

Why have you brought me here?
Stolen from the meadow where I sought the flowers of summer
Why won't you let me go?

Zakk's voice came back at me, more melodic but with preening malevolence.

I would keep you to myself
And have you by my side
To be my queen, fair Persephone

Now it was back to me, this time with a hint of

desperation but opening up to the power of it, roaring from somewhere deep down.

I do not love you
I fear you
Your dark countenance repels me
I beg you
Release my soul

The music changed its mood, becoming less fierce but somehow maintaining its intensity. This time when Zakk's vocals came in again, there was an air of tender patience in his voice.

Alas my love I cannot
There is no way but through
Shadows haunt your every step
But they belong to you in the Halls of Hades

An instrumental section led into the inevitable guitar solo. This wasn't your typical fare, though. Soaring and melodic yet built on unusual scale patterns and sweeping, lightning-fast arpeggios, it made the hairs on the back of my neck stand on end.

And then it was my turn to sing again, the music transitioning to a kind of accepting calm.

Now I see your true face
And yet I have no fear
Only love
But let me return to my own kind
For half of every year in the realms above

This time Zakk's voice also became a little softer and kinder still than it had before, building up again towards the end.

Eat of the fruit I give to you
And I will let you go
Bound to me you'll be my wife
Queen of all the afterlife
I know you will return
(I will return)
You will return to the Halls of Hades

Both our voices combined, fierce and resolved, in a moment of impassioned drama at the end of the song. I really let myself go, ripping into the last note.

'Well? What do you think?' I asked once the sound in the headphones had faded.

Through the glass, I could see looks of surprise and various heads nodding in the control room. The producer reached for the button on the talkback microphone.

'I like it. How about we try it with a bit more of a raw edge in your voice at the beginning, though? Let's not forget she's a goddess in her own right, no shrinking violet. It sounds a bit too polite at the moment but the contrast with the two vocals is good and I love the powerful twin vocal at the end. Can you do that, shift it up a gear?'

I assured him I could.

We ran it through again, and this time I had a better idea of what I was aiming for; it came out with a lot more conviction on my part. At the end of the take, I could see the glances between the people in the control room. Nigel broke out into a broad grin.

'Now that's what I'm talking about,' said the producer's voice through the headphones. 'The storytelling's perfect. No disrespect, but you're wasted on pop music. There's a rock chick in you that's dying to get out. That sounds amazing in here. There are a couple of lines I'd like to tighten up on if you're alright to stick around for a few minutes, but it's pretty much there. You can't fake that kind of freshness and immediacy. Is there anything you can't do?'

I pinched my lips together.

'Let's just say I'm keeping my options open at the moment. It's fun to try new things. I grew up singing all kinds of styles in my stepdad's studio, so I've always been fairly adaptable. As long as you think it's alright, that's the main thing.'

'Oh, trust me; it's more than alright.'

Another fifteen minutes and they had what they wanted. That was it! The whole process from start to finish had taken less than an hour and a half. I don't think I'd ever worked as fast, but at least it gave them something to work with until they got a specialist rock singer in to do it properly.

I wandered back into the control room of studio one still clutching my, by now, stone-cold cup of revolting tea, just as Steve and Rhodri were clearing up, ready to go.

'Oh, you're still here!' Steve looked surprised. 'I thought you must have gone home ages ago.'

I shook my head.

'Naah! I've been down the corridor in one of the other studios. You'll never guess who I bumped into.'

-0-

The following morning I was getting ready to go into my own studio again when Mitchell called.

'Rebecca, what the hell do you think you're playing at?' he snapped without any preamble.

'And a good morning to you too, Mitchell. What do you mean, playing at?' I was immediately irritated by his tone of voice. He wasn't normally like that.

'Since when has recording with Whispered Scream been part of any plan? I've just had a request through from Keith Emmett, their current producer, to use vocals you recorded yesterday. I thought you were with the orchestra.'

'I was, at least initially.' I proceeded to tell him the story of how it happened. In my mind's eye, I could imagine Mitchell scratching his head in bemusement. 'Besides, I thought we were just trying out ideas,' I added.

'Well, it seems they like the ideas so much they want to run with them, including your vocal recording. You must have realised you were handing them an absolute gift. It's a massive coup for Whispered Scream, and they hardly appeal to your demographic so they'll be gaining a lot more from it than you will.'

'I wasn't thinking tactics. It was just a spur of the moment thing, something creatively different. After all, Elton John recorded piano with a rock band once, just because he happened to be in the same studio complex at the time, and Lady Gaga performed on stage at an awards ceremony with Metallica.'

Mitchell heaved a sigh.

‘I just wish you’d told me, that’s all. I’m not a big fan of surprises.’

‘Sorry, Mitchell, it was just one of those things. I didn’t even think about the wider implications at the time. We were just in the studio, getting creative, that was all.’

I could hear a slapping sound as he planted the heel of his hand against his forehead and let out a sigh, but I could tell by now he wasn’t being entirely serious. At least he seemed in slightly better humour now.

‘Well, at least they’re also giving you credit for your contributions to the lyrics as well as sharing the lead vocals. Artists! I think you lot will be the death of me.’

CHAPTER NINE

Passing me a large mug of tea, Mum sat down at the country style kitchen table that had replaced the old breakfast bar and poured some extra milk into hers, giving it a stir. Even though I'd moved out nearly three years before, and the house had continued to evolve, every time I returned to The Gables it still felt strangely like coming home, a return to solid and dependable reality, as if all the madness of life beyond the end of its gravelled driveway had been just an illusion: fantasy and nightmare rolled into one.

'How are things?' she asked.

'Oh, you know, I'm keeping busy. The recording's going well. Poppy's into everything, so it's a good job Karina's on the ball.'

'And with Guy?'

I shrugged my shoulders.

'He seems to be doing alright for himself. He always does, doesn't he?' If Mum registered the edge of bitterness in my voice, she didn't acknowledge it. 'He's got Poppy with him this weekend, so I don't suppose he'll be seeing much of Anna. Call it a hunch but I don't think she's really the maternal type. I get the feeling she keeps her distance when he's playing dad. What about Jeff?'

'Oh, he's... He's alright. In fact, that's part of what I wanted to talk to you about.' She paused, gathering up her words. 'I want... I need you to try and patch things up with him. Try holding out the olive branch to him again. It's important. We all need to pull together.'

Before I could ask her why particularly, I could hear the front door opening and closing. A few seconds later, Rob came through the kitchen door, looking a little surprised to see me sitting there. My old friend and adversary, Fluffy, the family cat, slinked through from the utility room to see what was going on. She'd probably been sitting on top of the boiler, keeping warm as usual.

'Hi, sis, this is a nice surprise. Was it a planned visit?'

'Mum asked me to come over. What about you?'

'Same.'

We both looked at her.

'What's going on, Mum?' I asked.

'Sit down, Rob,' she said with overt cheerfulness. 'There's some fresh tea in the pot if you want it.'

He poured himself a cup and sat down next to me.

'Come on then, spill the beans. There must be a reason you asked us both over at the same time.' He nudged me with his shoulder. 'Not that I'm avoiding you or anything, Beccs.'

I poked my tongue out at him. Some things never changed.

'Well, yes.' Mum's mask of levity was beginning to slip. She looked suddenly uncomfortable. 'Actually, there is. I don't really know how to break this gently, so I'm just going to come out with it.'

'Mum?' Surely Jeff couldn't be threatening to divorce her for not telling him about what happened between me and Steve.

'If anything happens to me, I don't want there to be any bad blood remaining between any of you. You all need to be a family…together.'

If it wasn't about divorce then what? What did she mean 'happens to me'?

'Mum!' we chorused.

She steadied herself and levelled us both with a steadfast expression.

'I've been to see the oncologist this week and she gave me some news I was frankly hoping not to hear. It seems I have breast cancer.'

'Oh, Mum!' Eyes wide, I put my hand over my mouth, desperately searching her face for more information, but she remained calm.

'Now before we all go off the deep end, they think they've caught it quite early so hopefully, it hasn't spread. My chances are quite good. I'm starting radiotherapy straight away and they're considering chemotherapy too, so things might get a bit rough. I just needed you to know what was going on before it all kicks off. I want us all to be strong for each other, whatever happens. Right now, Jeff's more of a mess than I am.'

Rob and I both got up from the table and put our arms around her. If she could keep it together under the circumstances, then we owed it to her to do the same. Nevertheless, what lay ahead filled me a cold dread, the likes of which I hadn't felt since I heard about the motorway crash Guy had been involved in on his way to the hospital when Poppy was being born.

'We're here for you, Mum,' I assured her, 'whatever you need.'

She gave us both a thin smile.

'I know, sweetheart. I know.'

'Where is Jeff, anyway?' I asked.

'He'd already made plans to play golf before we found out. He said he'd cancel to stay here with me but I told him to go anyway. I thought it would be best if we all keep on with normal things as much as possible. Life goes on.'

But it wasn't normal. Whatever the prognosis, the whole situation was a million fucking miles from normal, and somehow I instinctively knew we were going to be tested as a family like never before.

-0-

Mum waved me off from the front door. Although Rob didn't want to go so soon, he had to leave before me because of a match. It was a Saturday, after all. At least it was a home game or he'd already have been on the team coach to God knows where. This time he only had to drive into South London but he still couldn't afford to be late.

For Mum's sake, I couldn't let her see how worried and upset I was. Giving her a wave as I pulled off, I drove out of the open gate and for some reason turned left down the main road toward the centre of Westerbridge, the opposite direction to home, pulling over at the lay-by outside the park where I used to walk our dog Rolo. By now my emotions had overtaken me and I was trying to drive through a fog of tears that had suddenly begun to well up. I lay my head against my hands on the steering wheel. I couldn't breathe.

How could I face going home to an empty house? With Poppy away, Karina had taken some time off to see her boyfriend from the village and wouldn't be back until sometime on Sunday. Francesca never normally worked weekends. What was there to go home for? I needed some company, a distraction, and I knew just the place to go.

Pulling myself together, I set the satnav for my one remaining refuge, Pulverton Manor. I didn't even bother to go home and pack. In anticipation of future visits, I had left some changes of clothes at the manor since Linda assured me the room would be mine for whenever I stayed.

'Sweetie,' she looked at me as if it had been a foregone conclusion, 'you own twenty per cent of the place. The least I can do is make sure you have a bolthole for when you want to get away from it all. You could stay at my cottage but it's a bit of a trek across the grounds, which is the last thing you want when you come out of the club at the end of whatever play you've been indulging in, so the room's yours. I know we call each other quite often but the way both our lives are, it's the only chance I get to see you.'

I told her there was no need and surely the room could be used for other guests, not just me, but she held out her hand.

'We've got enough rooms. It's done. End of.'

Wiping the tears off my cheeks, I checked the coast was clear and pulled away again, still turning everything over in my mind. Despite the long drive, before I knew it I was driving through the imposing gates of Pulverton

Manor, flanked by two substantial, brick-built pillars, each topped with a large stone ball. I must have been preoccupied the whole way, driving on autopilot. I didn't even have any music on, and that wasn't like me. Normally, it would have been a case of no jive, no drive. Nevertheless, I somehow found myself pulling up outside reception and making my way inside.

'Good afternoon, Miss Taylor.' Preeti greeted me with a smile. 'It's nice to see you again.'

Seeing as we were now in early December, the first of the Christmas decorations were already up behind her. I wondered why she was on the front desk today; it wasn't her usual post.

'Thank you, Preeti. Is Miss Maloney here?'

She gave me a slightly puzzled look.

'No, Miss Taylor. Both she and Mr Maloney are away on business.'

Tamzyn appeared from the back office with some paperwork in her hand.

'Oh, hello! I thought I heard your voice. I'm afraid Linda is away for a Passion Flower event but it's business as usual for the Aphrodite Rooms, although they may be a little quieter than average for a weekend since some of the club members will be at the event.'

Linda had probably told me, but with everything else going on it had slipped my mind. I'd been hoping to talk to her, or more truthfully, vent my feelings. In fact, it was probably my main reason for wanting to come to the manor; I just needed company.

'Are you staying?' Tamzyn asked.

I told her I was and she motioned Preeti to collect my luggage from the car, but I saved her the trouble.

'I'm travelling light: no bags. This wasn't a planned visit.'

'In which case, if you need anything we can have it delivered from any of the major London stores in two hours. We have professional shoppers on standby.'

I thanked Tamzyn and told her that wouldn't be necessary. I would rather just settle in.

'Of course, Miss Taylor,' she said, handing me my key. 'If there is anything we can do, please let us know.'

Since neither Linda nor Ryan was around to talk to, I decided to go into the bar rather than up to my room. The last thing I wanted was to be alone. A handful of people were sitting around, relaxing. Most of them were dressed for the day rather than the evening, so I didn't feel too out of place. Given the way the day had gone so far, I needed a drink: a stiff one.

'Whisky, please. Better make it a double,' I said to the young, waistcoated man behind the bar. Why I asked for that, I had no idea. I hardly ever drank spirits on their own, never really having got the taste for them. Wine would normally be my poison of choice.

'Certainly, Miss Taylor. Which one?' he asked gesturing towards the long row of bottles behind him, one shelf up from all the boutique gins.

'Oh, I don't know. What do you recommend?'

A voice at the end of the bar with a soft Scottish accent piped up.

'Try the thirty-five-year-old Speyside single malt on the end. You won't regret it.'

I turned towards the voice and sure enough, I recognised the face that went with it. We'd met. In fact, it was safe to say we'd slightly more than met. I couldn't remember his name, though, but at least he was dressed this time. He did look quite different in jeans, casual shoes, and a cream-coloured shirt, and it had to be said he filled out his clothes rather nicely.

'Is that the voice of experience talking?' I asked.

He looked vaguely amused.

'Trust me; I have lots of experience, Miss Taylor.' I felt sure he did.

As if sensing the fact that his name still escaped me, he held out his hand.

'Gordon. I hope you don't mind if I call you Rebecca.'

'You may,' I replied, still slightly overawed by his politely commanding presence but applying a thin veneer of confidence.

I placed my hand in his and he kissed it before turning to the barman.

'Put it on my tab, please.'

'Really, there's no n…' I was quite capable of paying for my own drinks, even at Pulverton Manor prices.

'Please, I insist,' he said. 'It was my recommendation after all. It's the principle of the thing.'

I took the cut crystal tumbler that was offered to me and took a sip, coughing as the fiery liquid touched the back of my throat. I'm sure it was a very good whisky to those in the know but I wasn't exactly accustomed to it.

'What do you think?' His enquiring eyes didn't leave me.

'It's… It's very nice.' My eyes were watering slightly. 'I must confess I don't normally drink the stuff.'

He gave me that refined look of superior amusement again.

'You don't say. So what brings you to the manor on

this fine but chilly afternoon? It's probably somewhat quieter here than on your last visit. Many of the club regulars have followed the party up to Manchester.'

Come to think of it, I felt sure Linda had told me about the event up north. There were rich pickings to be had from the Cheshire set and Linda's events had gained quite a fashionable reputation among the bored and wealthy.

'I just needed to get away, that's all, clear my head a bit.'

'Well, if you want to escape, I can think of worse places to come. What's your pleasure this time?'

'I don't know. I hadn't really thought about it. What do you like to do?'

Gordon nursed his own tumbler of whisky between his fingers, rolling the amber liquid around inside, and fixed me with a firm but unthreatening gaze.

'I like to take charge, Rebecca. I like people to do what I tell them, in the bedroom and elsewhere. Do you do as you're told?'

'Sometimes,' I admitted. 'Sometimes not.'

'Oh, a challenge!' He set his jaw at me. 'We'll have to see about that then, won't we? You are here to play, I take it.'

'I guess I am.'

Fuck it, why not!

If I was looking for a distraction from all the things in my head I'd rather not be thinking about, then it looked like I'd found it.

He glanced at his watch and finished the remainder of his whisky.

'Good, then meet me in the Bondage Room in one

hour. Don't be late.'

With that, he got up from his stool by the bar and walked away without a backward glance or another word. The mind games had already started.

That was quick! Time for some Dutch courage.

I stared at my whisky for a moment and downed it in one, feeling the hot tingle as it slid down my throat and pulling a face. Replacing my glass on the counter, I thanked the barman and headed for my room. I needed to prepare myself in every sense.

A hasty shower, some all over personal grooming, and fifty minutes later, I handed my key in at reception for safekeeping and emboldened by the shot of whisky in my system, headed toward the Aphrodite Rooms. Rather than go through the club room, which wasn't open until later anyway, I followed the ground floor to the end of the building and descended the spiral staircase which led down to the play areas. Once at the bottom, I could hear sounds coming from one or two of them, including the occasional sobbing cry from the Electroshock Room. I thought it perhaps wise to give that one a wide berth.

Following the line of doors to the right-hand side of the corridor, I came to the Bondage Room and knocked, putting my ear to the door. Everything remained silent so I opened up and stepped in. Seeing as no one else was there, it gave me the time to take a closer look around than I had done previously. Various pieces of equipment had been moved around but essentially the room was much the same ultra-modern, brightly lit space as the last time I'd seen it. Movable suspension points hung from aluminium gantries overhead and there were two cages, one large, one small, a tilt-and-turn table with a number of straps attached, and a medical chair with restraints at the far end. Floggers, gags and other paraphernalia hung in organised rows on the wall. I was leaning in to take a closer look at some of them when I heard the door open and close behind me.

'You like the look of that one, do you?' asked the voice I was hoping to hear, still with an air of gentle humour. 'We'll have to wait and see, won't we? Come here, Miss Taylor.'

I walked slowly towards him, trying my best to be both nonchalant and seductive. I wasn't sure if I succeeded but by the way his eyes followed me across the room, I think he liked what he saw. The tight, yellow dress I'd changed into seemed to meet with his approval. I noticed he was now wearing more formal attire, a rather businesslike dark suit with a shirt and tie as if he'd just come back from a meeting.

'Kneel. Keep your back straight, please, and rest your hands flat on your thighs.' I did as I was told and he lifted my chin to ensure I was looking up at him. 'Before we go any further, we need to establish what your safe word is and what your hard limits are, otherwise, I'm going to assume everything you see around you is fair game. If anything specific is off-limits, now is the time to speak up.'

He held my gaze, waiting to see if I had anything to say. I didn't.

'Very well, then! From what we've established so far, I don't think you're likely to have a problem.' I didn't think I was, either. 'If things look like they're going too far for you, I want you to say 'yellow', and if we hit a definite no go area the word is 'red'. Do you understand?'

'Yes, I understand.' I knew well enough by now that tacit acceptance would not be enough.

'Good. Now remove your dress and shoes.'

I complied, unzipping and peeling myself out of the clingy garment I'd only changed into about ten minutes before, and stood on display, wearing only the flimsiest of lacy black briefs and stockings while he circled closely, inspecting every inch without actually touching me at first, inhaling my perfume. He smelt good too: clean and fresh with hints of citrus and sandalwood. His fingers skimmed over the recent tattoo at the base of my back which spread tendrils of ivy and little sprays of wildflowers out toward my hips, with a touch so light it made me tingle. Surprisingly, his presence calmed me, as if somehow allowing him to take charge provided the perfect escape from the whirlwind of thoughts and emotions I was so desperate to shut out. While I had him to distract me I could relinquish all responsibility and just be.

Gordon removed his tie and loosened his collar.

'Hands, please.'

I offered up my hands and he bound them deftly with the tie before leading me, rather appropriately, toward the St Andrew's cross positioned against the far wall, stopping first to position me below one of the suspension points hanging from the gantry.

'Well, young lady, I've got plans for you. I hope you're up for a little adventure. Are you ready to submit?'

Looking into those cool, grey eyes I offered up no resistance. My lips parted expectantly.

'Yes. Yes please, sir.'

'Good,' he said, nodding calmly. 'Then let's begin.'

CHAPTER TEN

After a cold, clear Saturday, Sunday began grey and wet. I'd woken up in a good enough mood after what turned out to be been quite an exhausting evening's entertainment, but as if the weather felt it somehow its duty to remind me of the situation, reality soon hit home.

Gordon wasn't at breakfast. I don't think he stayed the night and he certainly didn't stay with me; I wouldn't have asked him to. So, I breakfasted at a table by myself and left for home, nursing an even more confusing mixture of feelings than before. Now, in amongst the helplessness and the isolation and the anger on Mum's behalf over how cruel fate could be, there was a curious thrill, the fact that I had willingly given myself over to a relative stranger, mysterious and aloof as he was, to do as he pleased with me. And he had. Oh God, he had!

My wrists and ankles were still sore, along with quite a few other places, but the rougher he got, the more I could let go, the more I could pretend to be someone else like I wasn't even there. My body was, of course, but I was somewhere else, drifting on a tide of sensation. Whether it was pleasure or pain I wasn't entirely sure and didn't really care. He did what he wanted with me and I let him do it. I was in no mind to stop him. Whatever my body was feeling, it blocked out everything else for a few short hours and left me too exhausted to think or feel anything else.

He was a kinky fucker, though; that much could be said with some certainty. The soft brogue with which he spoke had probably lulled quite a few women into a false sense of security. A dominant to the core, he'd been just as determined to test my boundaries as I had been to allow him free rein, even if he did seem to rather enjoy choking me while he fucked me with unnecessary ferocity. My safewords went unused, perhaps even to his surprise. I guess we both got what we wanted. At least I believed within myself that if I had used them, he would have respected my wishes and stopped. As it was, I never found out.

Droplets of rain beat down on the windscreen for most of the way home, the insistent action of the wipers hypnotically brushing away the drops that ran like tears down the glass, purging them from my field of view. I knew I had to call in at The Gables before returning to Spensford Hall, so I could clear the air with Jeff. It was my stepdad who answered the door.

'Oh, Rebecca, your mother's through there.' He gestured with his head toward the lounge, still holding the door open.

'Actually, Jeff, it was you I wanted to talk to first. Have you got a minute?'

He nodded, looking grim.

'Yeah. Yeah, I suppose so.'

He closed the door and led the way through to the snug. I didn't know quite where to start.

'Look, I, um… I know you're still upset about what happened between me and Steve, and I guess you've got a right to be, but right now, it's Mum that matters most. She's going to need us to be strong for her. We can't afford to waste our energy on being divided.'

'I agree.'

Well, that was easy.

'Just don't expect me to welcome Steve back with open arms,' he continued. 'I put him in a position of trust and he let me down. You were young, impressionable and vulnerable. I'd given my word, to you and to your mum, to protect you from the pitfalls of the music industry while you were trying to make your mark, and I kept to that. I never thought for one minute that I'd be let down by someone closer to home, especially considering the fact that Steve knew full well what happened with my first marriage.

Maybe not quite so easy.

'And yes,' I'd been about to open my mouth but Jeff put out a finger to cut me short, 'Steve played a role in helping you become the artist you are, but he's also done very well out of it too.'

'Jeff, he never asked for anything from me. The only reason he's now my producer is because I asked him to be.' Jeff looked like he was about to say something but this time I put out my hand to stop him. 'He's bloody good at his job, and so he should be; he learnt his craft from you. The rapport, the friendship we have, has lasted well beyond anything else that happened between us. But what's happened between the two of you is your business. I won't interfere. All I'm saying is don't hold being human against him; we're all guilty of that.'

'Be that as it may.' He seemed keen to sweep the issue of Steve aside and return to more pressing matters. 'As you say, what really matters is your mum. What's she told you?' I recounted the conversation of the day before, but Jeff slowly shook his head. 'I'm pretty sure she's going to be having chemo. If they've talked about it, it means they've got concerns about it spreading and they don't want to take chances. I think if she's totally honest with herself, Avril knows that, but she doesn't want to alarm anybody. Things are going to get tough for her and her chances are much better if she knows the people she loves are pulling together around her. That's the most important thing right now.'

I put my arms around him and held him tight. He gradually placed his arms around me too and I felt the tension between us drop away.

'I don't want to lose you,' I confessed, 'and I know how much you love Mum. You're the only real dad I've got.'

-0-

Arriving back at Spensford Hall, I felt in better spirits. Even if Jeff wasn't ready to open the door to Steve again, at least the two of us had reached some kind of truce, which was a start. The rest might come in time.

Karina was the next to arrive back, followed by Guy with a grizzly Poppy in tow. He stepped around the car to get Poppy out of her seat.

'She didn't take a nap this morning so she's probably feeling it a bit. I thought she'd sleep in the car but she's been fighting it all the way here. To be honest, you look like you could use a rest too. Didn't you sleep very well last night? I thought you'd be making the most of the break with Poppy away.'

'Not that it's any business of yours, no I didn't. Things have just been a bit busy, that's all.' I wasn't ready to share any of the news about Mum. In fact, I was only still speaking to him for Poppy's sake. I certainly wasn't prepared to divulge any details of the last twenty-four hours.

Accepting Poppy from him, I turned to go back into the house.

'Aren't you going to invite me in?'

I stopped in my tracks and looked over my shoulder.

'No. Just because I'm not going to come between you and your daughter, it doesn't mean I'm prepared to let you back into my life in any way. If there's anything you're missing about the home we once shared, then you've only got yourself to blame.'

'I know that. I just...'

I turned around to face him fully again.

'Just because your charmed existence isn't working out quite the way you'd hoped, don't go thinking you can worm your way back into favour with me, especially after the way you treated Emily, amongst others, so you can drop the boy scout act. Alright?'

Leaving Guy open-mouthed on the doorstep, I went back inside and closed the door with a certain smug satisfaction. He'd been right about one thing, though. Perhaps both Poppy and I both needed the opportunity to rest up. I certainly needed to rehumanise. I'd enjoyed rubbing Guy's nose in the dirt just a little too much.

'Come on, darling,' I said hauling Poppy up against

my waist and pulling her close. 'I think it's time for both of us to have an afternoon nap.'

-0-

I awoke with Poppy beside me in the bed, pressing her hands against my face and trying to kiss me. I must have been sleeping with my mouth open; it felt like the sands of the Sahara had moved in. Daytime naps are never pretty.

'What's up, sweetheart?' I asked, trying to gather myself. 'Are you thirsty? I know I am. How about we go and get something to drink?'

'Mummum,' she said, holding out her hands and clenching them in a gesture of 'I want'.

Downstairs in the kitchen, I prepared Poppy a sippy cup of juice and poured myself a glass of water. Karina wandered in with a half-empty mug in her hand.

'Ah, there you are. Are you feeling any better? I was going to look at what to do for dinner. Are you hungry?'

'Not really. Not at the moment. If you sort yourself and Poppy out, I might have something later. It's been a bit of a weekend.'

'Anything you want to talk about?'

'No, I'm fine,' I lied.

'Oh, by the way, before I forget, I've paused the TV.' Perhaps sensing my mood, she'd changed the subject. 'There's something you might want to see.'

Curiosity getting the better of me, I followed Karina into the little TV lounge and put Poppy down in her playpen.

'Go on, then. I'm intrigued.'

She hit play on the remote. It wasn't even paused on a programme; she'd stopped it on the ad break.

'It's this next one. I don't think it's been on before; I certainly haven't seen it, although something tells me you might recognise it.'

Up popped a series of scenes with me relaxing in a gondola, wandering along the narrow, stone-paved streets of old Venice, standing in the Piazza San Marco, looking up at the elaborate facades of buildings, and dipping my toes in fountains with my shoes in my hand. Then, in a long, flowing, white dress I was looking over my shoulder, laughing and running barefoot through high-ceilinged, rococo styled hallways before becoming enveloped in billowing swathes of fabric. I reappeared, artistically draped over an elaborately carved, gilded bed and covered in just enough of the carefully placed material to make it suitable for family viewing, before an image of my perfume bottle with its distinctive, apple-shaped cap filled the screen.

'Rebecca Taylor's Seduction, the new fragrance by Lafontaine,' announced an alluring female voice. 'Come, fill up your senses. Temptation awaits.' It took a few seconds before I even recognized the voice as my own, even though we must have done a hundred takes of it when making the advert back in the summer, and in about fifteen different languages, most of which I didn't speak a word of.

'Well, what do you think?' I asked.

'It's very good. I'd buy it.'

I chuckled.

'But not for your gran.'

'No, but maybe for my naughty best friend.'

'Ah!' I said. 'Everybody should have one of those. I've certainly got mine. She's been responsible for quite a lot, I can tell you, although, in hindsight, nothing I didn't deserve and couldn't handle. Still, it's going to be competing with all of the other perfume ads that flood the telly every Christmas, so I won't hold my breath about it outselling the classics.'

I couldn't complain about the proceeds so far, though. Since its launch, I'd seen a steady trickle of money rolling in, and we were now heading into peak season. More perfume would be sold in one month of the year than the eleven that came before it.

'What do you think?' I asked Poppy, who looked at me, then at the TV screen and pointed. 'That's right, Mummy's on the telly. Daddy's on there a lot too. One day you might be if you wanted to.'

CHAPTER ELEVEN

Christmas was a much more low-key affair than the previous one had been. I didn't throw any grand parties. Although I'd been invited to a few rather showbiz ones, I didn't feel much like attending. With a little help, well actually quite a lot, Poppy was able to begin opening some of her presents herself, although she did look a bit confused at the sight of Jeff in a Santa suit and tried to pull his false beard off. I think the lights and the colour of it all fascinated her, even if she was still too young to understand what was going on. Mum tried to remain cheerful but she looked tired. We all kept our spirits up for her sake.

I was almost relieved to get back to writing and recording, both for my solo project and occasionally with the band. I could immerse myself in that and block everything out in the hope that work would fill the void. I didn't know what else to do for Mum apart from being there when she needed a comforting presence now her chemotherapy had started. I'd known she was going to lose her hair, of course, but there's a big difference between knowing it and experiencing it. It was the shock of seeing her with clumps missing that really brought it home to me what she must be going through. I'd heard her throwing up in the bathroom but she put on a smile and proudly announced she was going to get her head shaved that week. She asked me to go with her to help buy a wig.

Maybe pouring my heart and soul into music was the best therapy, and failing that I had my other life, my secret thrill. I could be Rebecca Taylor, recording artist, caring daughter and dutiful mother by day, before stealing away whenever I got the chance for a night away at the club.

I got to cross a few more firsts off my list along the way. I hadn't thought there were many left. I was wrong. On one occasion, it was only when we reached the playrooms that I realised why the two men who caught my eye in the club had come across as such a double act; they were already much more than friends. The ensuing triangle had three pretty equal sides, and it was fun every now and then to take a rest from the action to sit back and watch before launching myself back into the thick of things. Actually, when I say sit back and watch, that wasn't the entire truth. It was so hot watching the two of them together, my fingers kind of carried on the party, much to their delight.

Lana, of course, became a regular playmate. Since she brought out my competitive side, we tended to spur each other on to greater and greater excess. Wherever she happened to be, the party followed. A few times, in trying to keep up with her unquenchable thirst for champagne and kink, I'd regretted my overindulgence and had to wait until the following afternoon before driving home. Even if my head hadn't been pounding like my brain was trying to hammer its way out, my stomach was turning somersaults, and my legs still felt like jelly, I'd still have been over the limit to drive until sometime later in the day. At least that gave me some recovery time and the opportunity to use the spa. The masseuse knew exactly how to ease my aching muscles and her all-over massages were certainly very thorough and more than a little intimate. I guessed it was all part of the service.

My extended stays also gave me at least some chance to catch up with Linda. She never seemed to spend time in the club anymore unless it was in an official capacity, so tea and sympathy over at her cottage seemed to be the order of the day. To be honest, she was becoming the one thing I never thought she would: overly sensible. With all the demands the businesses placed on her, everything always seemed to be work, work, work. Even when she took time to herself, she preferred to read rather than indulge in more physical pleasures. It would have been true to say that outside of her dealings with a few select clients, she had begun to lead an almost monastic existence.

'Busman's holiday,' she'd say with a shrug of her shoulders when I broached the subject of why she never played in her own club, which while it might have been the truth, almost certainly wasn't the whole truth. While I was desperate to let my hair down whenever I had some time off, Linda seemed to have forgotten how to have a good time.

At least Ryan had learned the value of not working seven days a week; he wasn't generally around on Sundays. He didn't play in the club either, but then, to my knowledge, he never had. It did rather limit any opportunity to see him, and that was something I missed. It even felt at times like he was avoiding me, although as far as I was concerned I'd given him no reason to.

It was on one of my Sunday morning recuperative sessions that Linda came to seek me out. She found me in the sauna room after my massage. I'd just ladled more water onto the hot stones, the only other person in the cabin having left with an uncomfortable bulge in the towel around his waist. If he'd wanted assistance with that, he should have sought me out the night before. I was nursing the remnants of a hangover and no longer in the mood.

'Ah, there you are! I hope we've been taking good care of you,' Linda said from the doorway, peering through the steam.

'Of course! As always,' I replied.

'Why don't you come on over to the cottage when you're ready? I'll put the kettle on. I'll even make tea, although you won't catch me drinking the stuff.'

'If you'd rather just make coffee, I'll settle for that.'

'Listen, sweetie, it's no skin off my nose, but it would be nice to have a chat.'

'Sure. Give me fifteen minutes and I'll meet you in the bar.'

'Done!' Linda said before closing the door again.

I quickly rinsed off under a cool shower, towelled myself dry, and dressed. Linda was having a quiet word with the barman when I came in.

'There you are,' she said, looking my way. 'Shall we?'

It was spitting with a cold, February rain as we crossed the grounds in the electric golf buggy Linda used to get backwards and forwards from her cottage, so I was grateful for the overhead cover it provided and even more grateful to be back in the warm once we got inside. It wasn't the biggest place in the world but comfortably appointed and traditional. It had charm.

Linda filled the kettle at the kitchen sink and glanced out at a wooden bird table in the middle of the small, paved area outside.

'One of the nice things about being here is I get to watch the wildlife come and go. There are a couple of squirrels that visit the table and quite a few different birds. I keep a pair of binoculars handy.' She grinned at me. 'Back over in the direction of the manor, I've managed to spot some great tits, the occasional wild beaver, and even a few purple-headed custard chuckers from here.'

Normally her jokes would have had me roaring with laughter, but somehow this time the humour seemed forced. Seeing as I wasn't laughing, Linda cleared her throat and tried a different tack.

'How's your mum?' Linda asked awkwardly as the kettle came to the boil.

'She's putting on a brave face.' I didn't really know what else to say.

'Must run in the family.' She glanced my way and reached for the cups. 'Look, I know you probably don't feel much like sharing, but I'm worried about you. I can see the path you're on and it's not a very healthy one.'

'And what path is that?' I could feel my hackles rising.

'Believe me; I get that the breakup with Guy was painful for you, and I know you think you left all that behind, but you're still dealing with it, and now there's all this stuff going on with your mum too. I'm just not sure going off the deep end in the club is the answer to any of your problems; it's more like running away from them. '

That's rich!

'Now hold on just a minute,' I protested. 'Let's not forget who introduced me to the lifestyle.'

She handed me a steaming mug.

'Yes, but...'

I could feel my annoyance growing.

'No. No buts. Would I or would I not have got myself into all this stuff if it wasn't for you?' She had to admit defeat on that one. 'And what qualifies you to dish out relationship advice?' I put my untouched mug back on the counter. 'You've kept people at arm's length for as long as I've known you, always quoting the same pat answer about avoiding complications, so I hardly think you're in a position to give advice on how to deal with a breakup. You've never even had a proper relationship. Just because you've got a degree in psychology you think you've got the answer to everyone else's issues but this is real life, something you've got very good at avoiding on your own behalf.'

Realising I had already significantly raised my voice; I did my best to rein myself in, but the words were already out there, the damage done.

'I'm sorry you feel that way. You don't understand,' she said quietly, looking down at the floor, strangely subdued.

'No, you're right. I don't understand. I don't understand because you never share anything; you never have. You think that by putting on some public bravado that no one will ever get close enough to hurt you. Well, guess what? I took a leaf out of your book, Linda, and decided it was best to keep my distance, so if that means having my fun with strangers then so be it!'

'This isn't you talking, Rebecca. You weren't always the most outgoing person growing up but cutting yourself off emotionally has never been your style. That's one of the things I've always admired about you. You have a good heart.'

'A good heart?' I scoffed. I couldn't believe what I was hearing. 'That's about the least valuable asset to have when it comes to getting by in life. In fact, it's probably more of a handicap. It just makes you more vulnerable.' I gestured in the direction of the kitchen window that looked out over the grounds, raising my voice in barely controlled anger. 'The world out there doesn't care about good intentions; it only cares about results. What the fuck use is a good heart when the only people who seem to prosper in life are the selfish and the ruthless? You said so yourself years ago when you gave me all that spiel about shark tanks.'

Linda shook her head slowly.

'That wasn't what I meant. I was talking about removing yourself from the drama, maintaining a healthy detachment from all the shit that goes on. I wasn't encouraging you to become one of the sharks; you're better than that.' She stopped for a moment, studying me. 'Svetlana's really beginning to rub off on you, isn't she? I must admit I had my concerns about her.'

'You know what's really going on here?' I pointed my finger at Linda, all my pent up anger and frustration bubbling up to the surface and boiling over. 'You're jealous. You're jealous because she and I are out there having the good time you've forgotten how to. Now you think she's stealing me away from you and you can't stand that, can you?' I shook my head. 'Don't you lecture me on having a good heart! I don't think you know where yours is.'

A few times down the years, Linda had shown me a look as if she'd been mortally wounded. This was one of them. In the past, it had come about by accident rather than design, but this time I wanted my words to sting her; I wanted to break through her defences and make her feel some of my own anguish. At least that way I'd get a meaningful response out of her. Normally her injured expression would have won me round but this time I wasn't about to cave. I pushed my mug away and turned to leave.

'You know what? Keep your tea; I'm not in the mood anymore. I'm going back to my room.'

'Rebecca!' she called after me, searching for something else to say. 'At least let me drive you back.'

'Thanks, I'll walk.'

As soon as I stepped out of the front door I began to regret my words on several counts but I was in no mood to give in. An icy, penetrating rain had set in and I didn't have a coat with me. Whatever the truth was, I knew I had been rather hard on Linda, but I couldn't bring myself to turn around; my anger wouldn't let me. Closing the door behind me and choking back tears, I hunched my shoulders and set off on the path that led back to the manor house. I just wanted to get away from having to face any more of Linda's nonsense.

-0-

I was on my way home, somewhere on the M25, when the phone rang in the car. As if I didn't already know who it was, the screen on the dash confirmed it. I let it ring in the hope that she would give up. Two minutes later, it rang again. This time I picked up, resigned to making at least some sort of apology. It wasn't fair of me to take everything out on Linda, exasperating as she was.

'Hello.' I tried to keep my voice at least neutral.

'Rebecca, don't hang up, okay. I just... I wanted to make sure you're alright.'

'I'm fine.' Who was I trying to convince, Linda or myself? Perhaps I needed to give at least a little ground. 'Listen, I'm sorry I said those things. I was out of order and I know you're concerned for me.'

Linda softened too.

'To be honest, I probably deserved some of it. It's complicated.' Everything always was with Linda. 'Maybe one day I'll be able to explain everything. In the meantime, don't lose faith in me...or yourself. I don't think you understand how much I care. I'm your best friend; I'm allowed to worry about you.'

I sighed, keeping my hands on the wheel and my eyes on the road.

'I know you mean well, but I can make my own choices. You intended Pulverton Manor to be an escape from everyday reality, a place for people to unwind and live out their fantasies. That's what I'm doing so don't deny me my release valve. Right now I need this.'

I could almost hear Linda nodding grudgingly on the other end of the line.

'I know. I know. Just promise me you'll be careful

what you get into and with whom. Don't forget, I know more about some of the people who visit the club than it would be professional of me to say. I'm beginning to understand just what a powertrip some of them are on. You've a lot to lose, not least your self-respect.'

CHAPTER TWELVE

By the end of February, with only the mixing left to do on the solo album and Mum on a break from chemo before the next round of treatment, I needed to blow off some steam. Despite at least partly making my peace with Linda, I tended to keep my distance from her whenever I visited the club. The last thing I needed was more lectures.

I'd agreed to meet Gordon at the manor. He said he had something special lined up for me. Quite what that meant was anybody's guess, but I knew one thing for certain; the thought of the unknown pleasures that lay ahead turned me on, no matter how hard he decided to push me. The mystery surrounding his intentions only intensified my anticipation. Freed from responsibility and control after all the long hours in the studio, motherhood, and worrying about Mum, I could submit to him and just let go.

'Meet me in the bar at ten-fifteen on Saturday morning,' he'd said, 'and wear the yellow dress.'

Okay, bossy boots! Be specific, why don't you!

I think he just got off on the control, not that I minded too much. His domineering excited me. It gave me the tingles before he'd even done anything else.

Meeting him at the appointed time would have meant leaving rather early in the morning. If I didn't know better, I'd have thought he'd engineered things to make it as inconvenient for me as possible. In the end, I made an excuse about work commitments and travelled up on Friday night, leaving Karina in charge at home. Avoiding any awkward questions from Linda, I kept to my room, ordered up a bottle of wine as well as helping myself to the minibar, and lounged around in a luxuriously thick Pulverton Manor robe, watching any old crap that caught my eye on TV until I fell asleep.

I awoke, still in my underwear and wrapped up in my robe, in time to have a light breakfast before taking extra care over my preparations and donning the dress that had apparently made such an impression on its previous outing.

When I got downstairs again, a number of people were scattered around the bar, mostly sitting at tables, but there was no sign of Gordon. Having left my watch and my phone upstairs, I checked the clock on the wall. I was right on time, so where was he? Self-consciously, I looked down at myself. Seeing as I was rather overdressed for the middle of the morning, even at Pulverton Manor, I could feel curious eyes watching me closely, peeling the clingy material away from my form. In the club itself, I could throw modesty aside, strip naked and no one would care, least of all me. Here, although I was clothed I felt out of place, a curiosity to be dissected, mentally undressed and objectified. It didn't make any sense why I should feel this way, but then again less and less about my life did.

Rather awkwardly, I took a seat at a table in the corner from where I could keep an eye on the entrance and waited. I wasn't sure if it was my mind playing tricks on me but nobody seemed to be making eye contact, with each other or with me. In fact, I could have sworn blind they were avoiding it.

I endured another ten minutes of shuffling uncomfortably on my chair and telling myself not to be so stupid before Gordon finally appeared, breezing into the bar as if he had been early instead of late.

'Good morning, Rebecca. I see you remembered.'

I wanted to wipe that smug little smile off his face for keeping me dangling. Instead, I smiled politely.

'Well, you did say.'

'Indeed I did. Have you eaten and drunk this morning?'

Peculiar.

'Yes, of course.'

'And do you need to use the bathroom before we begin?'

I looked around, wondering whether anybody was listening to the bizarrely personal conversation. To be honest, everyone seemed to be studiously ignoring us.

'Why on earth…?'

He held out his hand.

'Please, just answer the question.' He remained impassive.

'No, I'm fine. I've just been,' I said, finding it hard to keep my irritation in check.

'Good, then follow me.'

With one hand resting against the small of my back, he guided me through the building and down the spiral staircase at the far end, pausing at the bottom to peruse the windowless but comfortably lit corridor in front of us. No matter what the time of day or night, it always looked the same down in the basement. I could only assume it had at one time been the servants' domain, the 'other' house downstairs; it was way too big for just storage rooms. Spensford Hall's rather modest facilities were nothing like the same size and consisted of just a disused pantry, now a storeroom for promotional nicknacks, and a wine cellar. Somehow it seemed incongruous that these underground rooms at Pulverton Manor had now become a playground for the rich.

'Tell me, Rebecca, if you could choose any room, where would you like to go today?'

'Well, the Shibari Room always catches my eye.'

'Interesting. I'm afraid my tastes and my skill set are a little more European than that. Where else?'

What would he like?

'I suppose there's always The Principal's Study.'

He looked amused.

'Do you think you require punishing? I assure you that punishment can be infinitely more varied and interesting than such blunt means as mere corporal chastisement; the mind is a far more powerful thing than that.' He thought for a moment. 'Perhaps on reflection, you're not ready for what either The Cell or The Electroshock Room has to offer. The latter tends to be better suited to shorter sessions of no more than two hours anyway, and The Cell is a little restricted for space. Very well, you shall have your wish: The Principal's Study it is.'

We made our way to the last door on the right and he

ushered me into the plush, heavy-draped room with its dark wood furniture, red leather upholstery and old-fashioned lamps. Over to one side sat the suede-covered vaulting horse over which I had bent a compliant and excited Svetlana on my first ever visit to the Aphrodite Rooms, but the centre of the space was commanded by a new addition, a substantial, rectangular frame with a number of attachment points and a row of metal rings along its top bar. I could immediately see at least some of the possibilities it afforded.

'A good choice. I think the suspension beam will do nicely.' Gordon walked around the wooden frame, tapping one finger against his lips, considering his options. 'Come over here, young lady. I suggest you might want to forego the shoes; you might be here a while. Keep the dress on for now.'

'Fair enough.'

He stopped, his expression turning serious.

'From now on, you are to call me sir. Do you understand?'

'Yes, sir.'

'Good.' He'd still made no attempt to touch me. Gordon nodded his head towards my feet. 'Shoes please, Miss Taylor.'

I dutifully complied, leaving my shoes at the side of the room while he fetched a set of black leather cuffs from the wall. He secured them around my wrists and ankles, checking that they had been buckled just tight enough, and pointed to the space in the middle of the frame.

'Stand over there, please.'

I did as I was told and he clipped me to straps anchored at the bottom corners and the furthest apart of the top rings, adjusting them until I was spread-eagled in the centre, helpless but still fully dressed. In that position, the tight skirt of my dress rode up above the tops of my thighs, exposing the cheeks of my scantily clad behind.

'Do you remember your safe words?'

'Yes, sir.'

'Very well. And just in case you are unable to speak for whatever reason, show me your safe signal.' I clicked the fingers of both hands. 'Good.'

Standing in close so he could inhale my perfume, he touched my hair and I nestled my face against his hand, enjoying the intimacy of it. But the tender moment was short-lived. He stepped back again, an air of formality returning to his demeanour.

'Remember, Miss Taylor: good things come to those who wait.'

Embellishing no further on his cryptic remark he walked away and left the room, closing the door behind him and leaving me bound and alone.

Really? Fuck!

I tugged at my restraints, rattling the metal rings above my head, but there was hardly any wiggle room. Since waiting was all I could do, I appeared to have no choice but to do just that. I don't know how long I remained there alone, immersed in my solitude and my thoughts, staring around me at the framed, sepia-tinted prints on the walls because, in the silence of the underground club, time had no meaning. It could have been ten minutes but it felt like half an hour before eventually, the door opened again.

'Oh, thank God you're b…'

But it wasn't Gordon; it was one of the men from the

bar who'd been so studiously ignoring me earlier. I'd seen him around, probably already fucked him at some point, but his name escaped me. Some things had become a bit of a blur. He slipped off the jacket of his dark suit and removed the cufflinks from his expensively tailored shirt, carefully placing them in one of the jacket pockets. Taking his time, he smoothed his jacket out and lay it on one of the leather sofas that lined the longest wall before rolling up the sleeves of his shirt.

'I'm afraid our mutual friend has been otherwise detained. In the light of his temporary absence, I will be keeping you entertained for the time being. I take it you have no objection to that?'

Seeing as I already qualified as a captive audience, what was the point in objecting?

'I suppose I don't have any other pressing engagements.'

He nodded tacitly but remained humourless despite my levity.

'I assure you I can be equally exacting, perhaps in some ways more so.' Standing behind me, he ran his hands down the undersides of both my raised arms and on down my body, following the curve of my waist until he found the hem of my dress and hooked his fingers underneath it, testing the material. 'This is all very nice, but I'd like to take a proper look at what's underneath if you don't mind.'

If I thought he was going to unzip me from the back, I was wrong. Two hands found the edge of the skirt and yanked apart, wrenching my dress open with a tearing sound as the rip travelled upwards. A second firm tug finished the job.

Bastard! Do you know how much that dress cost?

Back in the days when my mother had to care for my brother and me on her own, that amount of money would have fed the three of us for a month or more.

I kept my thoughts to myself, hanging my head so my hair would hide my annoyance while his hands traversed the smooth skin of my back.

'Lovely. Do you mark easily?'

'Not particularly.'

At least I had a good idea where he was going with this now. I wasn't going to get off lightly. After tearing through each sleeve to free what remained of my dress, he tossed the shredded garment to one side then turned his attention to my knickers, ripping them away from me in one sharp movement.

'That's better. Now we can see what we're dealing with.' He took hold of my hair and slowly bent my head back with one hand while feeling between my legs with the other, sinking his fingers into me to test my readiness. 'Mr Mackenzie has, however, been rather lax in leaving your hair down, which is something we shall have to remedy. We wouldn't want it getting in the way, now would we?'

'No, sir.'

He rubbed his fingertips together appreciatively and placed them between his lips, sampling the taste of me, then began plaiting my hair at the back, producing a hair tie from his pocket to finish the job. Finally, he took a handmade, leather flogger and a gag down from the wall.

'I'd like to say this will hurt me more than it will hurt you, Miss Taylor, but I'd be lying if I did and that would be a sign of poor character.' Cradling my jaw between his thumb and forefinger, he moved my head from side to side inspecting me. 'Shall we begin?'

-0-

By the time the man had done with me, I was beginning to feel it. Had it not been for my regular gym and swimming sessions, my legs would have been giving out and that would have placed even greater strain on my wrists, but braced in the frame I could lock my knees to support myself once he'd finished dishing out my 'punishment'. What first developed into a vigorous flogging was then followed by a relentless pounding from behind that left me a sobbing wreck. My nipples were still sore from where he'd been pinching them and grabbing at my breasts while he fucked me. He might not have been anywhere near as kinkily inventive as Gordon or shared his predilection for throttling a woman while fucking her, but Jesus, the man had ruthless stamina.

He dealt with the condom he had been wearing and dressed again without another word, leaving me suspended in the frame like a fly in a spider's web. With a final nod of acknowledgement in my direction, he left, and I found myself once again immersed in silence, drifting with only my thoughts for company.

What now? Am I going to receive a series of visitations like Scrooge?

I wasn't too far wide of the mark.

When they did eventually appear, the next people to arrive were a Japanese-looking couple in their thirties who had also been sitting in the bar, although they were now most definitely dressed for action in skintight latex fetish wear and came with a bag of their own toys. It was the woman who took the lead.

'Well now, my darling, I've been hearing a lot about you,' she said, caressing my throat with her long nails. 'I think it's about time we found out for ourselves just how adaptable you really are.' She gestured toward the bag. 'Masuo, I think you know what we need. We're going to do this one together.'

Masuo produced a strap-on from the bag and handed it to her. I'd seen worse. Nevertheless, I had a good idea what was coming my way and as it turned out, I was right. After they'd had their fill of teasing, I was treated to an enthusiastic rogering from the pair of them, one from in front and the other from behind, until my knees began to give way underneath me. The woman, in particular, seemed to take great delight in taking up the rear position and whispering into my ear what a filthy little whore I was while she fucked me in the arse with her plastic cock. Eventually, the pair of them took at least some pity on my situation and unclipped me from the frame before bending me over the desk, breathless and exhausted, to finish the job. Women are generally more tender than men, but not this one; she remained unemotional and quite without mercy. She, in particular, seemed to get a particular kick out of spitting on my face and calling me a worthless slut while her companion took his satisfaction from me in whatever manner best pleased them both.

It wasn't over, though, not by a long shot. After about the fourth or fifth visit from upstairs, I wasn't sure which, an audience to my ongoing test of endurance began to filter in, sitting around on the long leather sofas, drinks in hand and chatting while I was trussed up and used every which way I could imagine, along with a few others besides that I hadn't even considered, by a succession of people. They took turns to violate me however they wanted. Occasionally I was given a few sips of water but always returned to my position in the frame before the next person or group took their turn with me.

At one point, I was shackled and led blindfold to The Wet Room where I was strapped to a table and treated to the inevitable by a group of unknown men and women. I wasn't at that point particularly receptive to the fact that it was a first for me to be on the receiving end of a golden shower. Had the circumstances been right and my frame of mind better, I might have savoured the novelty of the situation. Instead, I let the whole experience, quite literally, wash over me. Afterwards, I was doused in cold water and allowed to dry off with a towel before being marched back to The Principal's Study.

Gordon had returned to watch but at no point moved to join in. He seemed almost disinterested. In the midst of everything else, I was left wrestling with the sense of anger and frustration that he hadn't even wanted me for himself. I felt abandoned, bereft. Was I really that worthless, just something to be passed around, a set of holes to be fucked, an object to be pissed on? I had more pride than to safeword them, though. I wasn't going to give them the satisfaction of knowing they had defeated me.

What are you doing to yourself?

But that was just it; I had done it to myself. What was more, where had Sadie been when I needed her? She would have responded with more fighting spirit.

When they finally released me, emotionally and

physically drained, the club was just getting into full swing. I was now almost invisible, somehow incidental to the goings-on of a typical Saturday night at the club. I scraped together my tattered clothing and picked up my shoes. There seemed little point attempting to put any of it on. I faced up to Gordon as he stood talking to the Japanese couple, in the hope that he would at least acknowledge my presence.

'I suppose you think that was funny, do you?'

He turned to face me, nursing his tumbler of whisky.

'Rebecca, funny doesn't come into it. Do I look like I'm laughing?'

Oh, so you're using my first name now, are you?

'I do recall telling you there are much more satisfying forms of punishment than the purely physical,' he continued, giving me the look of faint amusement that was now really starting to grate on me. It wasn't charming anymore; it was just smug and irritating.

'Well however you square this scenario in your head, consider our little arrangement terminated.'

Setting my jaw, I marched out of the room with what little dignity I could muster, trying not to let the stiffness show. Every muscle I possessed was now screaming at me but I wasn't going to show him how belittled I felt. I was hungry, I was thirsty, and I needed the toilet, but most of all I just needed to get out of there.

I ascended the spiral staircase and strode purposefully along the corridor toward reception, walking up to the counter as naked as the day I was born with my shoes and what remained of my clothes in my hand. Apart from a brief, questioning flicker, Tamzyn didn't bat an eyelid when I calmly asked for my room key.

I walked slowly and deliberately up the stairs and along the landing to my room, even though I felt like running. It was only when I closed the door behind me that my resolve fell apart. I dropped to the floor, fighting for breath as the tears began to flow: tears for the love I'd had snatched away from me by that selfish bitch, tears for the man I mistakenly thought loved me for who I was, and tears for my mother and what she was going through. They were hot, salty tears of anger, and loss, and emptiness, and loneliness, and guilt.

And the guilty tears stung the worst of all.

After vainly attempting to rinse away my own disgust under a steaming hot shower, I dressed in jeans, trainers, and a baggy top, and made to leave. I wore no makeup. My hair wasn't even fully dry. I didn't care. I just wanted to go home, to hold Poppy close and tell her everything was going to be alright.

On my way through the reception area, who should I encounter but Lana on her way to the Aphrodite Rooms, sweeping along like she owned the place? I, of course, owned more of it than she ever would, even if it wasn't something I ever capitalized upon. The less people who knew about how connected I was to Pulverton Manor, the better.

'Ah, there you are!' she announced, looking me up and down in my dishevelled state. 'I hardly recognised you. Aren't you here to play?'

I shook my head.

'No, I'm going home. Have fun.'

She waved one hand airily.

'Darling, I intend to. Next time, maybe?'

'Maybe.'

I watched her disappear in the direction of the club. A true friend would have taken the time to ask me what was going on. Instead, I finally began to see her for what she really was: shallow, selfish, and pleasure-seeking. In my present mood, I wanted no part of the club or her.

'Rebecca?'

I turned around to see Ryan emerging from the back office.

Of all the times to bump into each other, you have to see me like this! Why couldn't we have met each other earlier?

But then, of course, I'd spent most of the day tied up in the dungeon rooms downstairs being ravaged by strangers.

Oh God! What if he saw me on the security cameras?

The ground floor office behind reception was, after all, where the camera feeds went. My stomach lurched at the prospect of him witnessing my degradation. I felt ashamed, dirty.

What must you think of me?

Ryan showed no sign of having been aware of my ordeal, though. He certainly didn't seem to view me with the same revulsion I felt towards myself, but he did look concerned.

'What's up, Rebecca? You don't seem quite yourself.'

'I'm alright. Where's Linda?' I tried to put a brave front on it.

'She's having a rare night off. We're going to be busy after this in the lead up to the next Passion Flower event. Tamzyn's just finished her shift so I'm covering. Have you just arrived?'

'What, looking like this?'

He smiled gently.

'I'd call it au naturel. Reminds me of a young, wannabe musician I used to know before the world got a hold of her. It's refreshing.'

I shook my head.

'I just… I'm not in the mood to stay here tonight. I'm heading home.'

'If you want to talk, I'm a good listener. Linda did say your Mum's been going through it a bit.'

'No, I don't need to talk,' I said, unable to face the prospect of opening to him but still glad that he'd offered. Some wounds are just too raw to stand inspection. I could barely look him in the eye. 'I'm fine. I just want to go home to my own bed. I'll see you at the next Passion Flower event.'

Shit! Why did I say that?

Come to think of it, though, maybe a party event would be a better idea than the club for the time being, and I would get to see Ryan and Linda under better circumstances. There would be more wild enjoyment, less of the mind games, and fewer familiar faces, particularly the ones I'd rather not have to see. I could just have fun with it whether I chose to hook up with anyone or not.

Ryan nodded.

'Goodnight, then. If you do change your mind and you want to get anything off your chest or just yell and scream, I'm only a phone call away. Just remember that.'

'Thanks, Ryan. You're a good man, and it seems there aren't many of those left. Goodnight.'

I could feel him watching me leave. He knew I wasn't going to phone him to pour my heart out, although neither of us would admit it. How could I? My shame was mine and mine alone to bear.

CHAPTER THIRTEEN

'So what do you want to call it?' Mitchell sat back, regarding me enquiringly. 'I assume you're still content to release it under the name of just 'Rebecca'.'

I pulled a face.

'To be honest, I'm not in love with that as a banner but it's definitely turned out as more of a solo album than a band thing, and Taylor Made was just too cheesy. Over half the guitars on it are me, along with quite a bit of piano and all the vocals. I also wrote all of the songs, so it needs to have my name on it somehow. The title still definitely needs to be 'Shed This Skin', though, because it's all about the need to peel away the layers of the past, get back to the reality underneath, and move on. I can't help writing semi-autobiographically; it's what comes out.'

'It's very good; a much more mature offering, although I'm glad we kept a separate identity for it.'

'What about Ariva? What do they think?'

Mitchell gathered himself.

'I'll be totally honest with you. They don't, for the most part, like it. It's too original and different, which is giving their marketing people a headache. I get the feeling the publicity is going to be rather low key compared to what happens when the next Rebecca Taylor album eventually comes out because they'll put their energy behind what they know they can sell, particularly as the two albums are going to be released less than a year apart. Don't forget, record companies are marketing machines, not music enthusiasts. They don't give a damn about creativity. Truth be told, they regard this album as something of an indulgence, so I'm having to fight your corner here.' He paused for a moment. 'And then there's...'

'There's what?'

'Rebecca, how have you been keeping lately? I know you've been dealing with a lot.'

How is that relevant? It felt like he was avoiding the issue.

'I'm alright. Why?'

'There are certain quarters at Ariva that have raised eyebrows over rumours surrounding your private life. Lafontaine have expressed similar concerns so I get the feeling these rumours are quite widespread. People are talking, Rebecca.'

I shrugged my shoulders.

'They've always talked, ever since 'Come Inside' broke through. It's nothing new.'

'No, Rebecca, this is different and potentially damaging. I did warn you about your links with Linda Maloney and her business enterprises. There is talk that you've been frequenting her club. Please tell me it isn't true.'

Shit!

I hesitated, not knowing quite what to say, my mouth

opening and closing soundlessly. Should I lie about it or come clean? In the end, I didn't need to do either. Mitchell drew his own conclusions from my silence and placed his forehead against his palm with a deep sigh before rounding on me.

'Jesus, Rebecca, you're killing me here! What the bloody hell do you think you're playing at?' It wasn't the first time I'd heard him raise his voice, but I think it was the first time I think I'd ever heard him swear, and certainly at me. 'For Christ's sake, you're a high-profile public figure!'

'And what? Do you think I'm the only public figure who goes there? My private life is my business.'

Mitchell shook his head.

'No, it isn't; that's the problem. Selling people a fantasy through racy music is one thing but actually living like that is another. I'm not responsible for society's double standards, Rebecca, but make no mistake; careers can evaporate overnight as a result of them.'

He got out of his chair and paced over to the window, staring down at the busy, West End of London street scene below before continuing.

'I warned you, Rebecca, and now Ariva want to call a meeting with you to discuss your public image. Lafontaine are even threatening to pull the plug on the perfume if any scandal should threaten to tarnish their reputation, even if it did sell by the bucket load in the run-up to Christmas. They're touting your perfume as an upmarket brand, something alluring but classy, and they want to keep it that way. You are the selling point. A single mother frequenting S and M clubs, no matter how exclusive they are, and participating in God knows what with God knows who, doesn't come across with the kind of image they want to portray. If this sort of thing becomes public knowledge, and you know what the press can be like, then you could be finished. If rumours are flying around, you can bet your bottom dollar they've got their finger over the button, already itching to publish. All they need is some form of credible substantiation and they'll be all over you like a rash. The sort of press attention you've had to deal with in the past will seem like child's play by comparison. It's not about moral standards; it's about maintaining an air of the unattainable. If you're seen as too available then from Lafontaine's point of view, all you'll come across as is cheap rather than sexually appealing and that will be all the excuse they need to pull the plug. On the musical front, if you want to be taken more seriously as an artist then you're going completely the wrong way about it.'

I didn't really know what to say in my defence, and I wasn't going to open up a can of worms by asking about the details of the rumours that had been spreading. My imagination did a good enough job of filling in the blanks. Mitchell was right about the fickleness and the power of public opinion, and deep down I knew that, but some part of me still railed against it. Why should I be dictated to over how I lived my life? Whatever my choices had been, they were still my choices. Mine! Whether they turned out right or wrong I owned them, and that freedom wasn't something I was willing to give up lightly. Which was worse? The shackles into which I voluntarily placed myself on occasions or the shackles of public expectation?

Mitchell had always been the type to err on the side of

caution, so I was damned if I was going to let his fears dictate how I lived my life, and besides, I'd already given my word about going to the next Passion Flower event which was being held at some or other stately home in Wiltshire. If other people could have their fun, then why the fuck shouldn't I?

Perhaps the more pressing problem was the meeting with Ariva. Since everybody always seemed to have an unspoken agenda these days, I had to anticipate this would be no exception. Someone was going to try and use the rumours that had been circulating to turn the screws on me. I didn't want to have to go in there and tell a pack of lies to cover my tracks, even though I had no doubt that's what plenty of others would do, but total disclosure wasn't an option either. One way or the other, I was going to have to keep my wits about me.

-0-

Mitchell and I were ushered into a large, empty meeting room at Ariva's London headquarters. Its imposing lack of personality didn't do much for my confidence. I half expected they were going to shine a spotlight in my face and grill me for a confession of my sins, but I'd committed no crime and offended nothing other than a few people's sensibilities. Besides, what could they possibly know for sure about me? At least I had plausible deniability on my side.

Despite being glad I wasn't facing the inquisition on my own, I really didn't want to have to explain myself or put up a smokescreen to the record company in front of Mitchell, especially now he had some inkling of the truth.

I had no choice, though. Right now there was only us in the room; the others had yet to arrive. We sat awkwardly on one side of the long, boardroom table, waiting in unsettling silence while the clock behind us ticked ominously.

The door opened again and in stepped a man I thought I recognised, followed by an efficient-looking woman with a folder in her hand. I froze when it dawned on me who the man was: the Senior Vice President of Ariva Records. We hadn't exactly met, but I had seen him, although I was pretty sure he hadn't seen me at the time, at least I hoped so.

We stood to exchange pleasantries with them.

'Miss Taylor, pleased to meet you. I'm Gil Premmell and this is Amanda Brightman, our head of public relations,' he said in a softly spoken American accent that was already more familiar to me than it should have been. 'Please, take a seat.' At that moment, I was struggling to get a less than favourable image of him out of my head.

They sat down opposite us and Gil wasted no time getting to the point. His welcoming smile evaporated.

'Miss Taylor, we've called this meeting because there are matters of some concern which we would like to take the opportunity to address.'

'Oh?' I pretended to be politely surprised. 'And what might those be?'

He glanced across at Amanda, who nodded.

'Given the precariousness of the current market, it's important that the conduct of our artists is not at odds with the image required by their product. I'm afraid it has come to our attention that aspects of your private life are not compatible with the album you have been recording. In the light of that, and to protect our interests in this matter, our intention is not to release,' he turned over the top page and checked his notes for the title, ''Shed This Skin', and instead to focus on the next Rebecca Taylor record which I'm sure would be more in keeping with your expected output.' Gil couldn't resist a little self-satisfied and condescending smile.

I glanced across at the usually collected Mitchell. He looked dumbfounded. Even he hadn't expected them to use this as capital to avoid releasing the album altogether. This was a total sideswipe. I decided to get my counterpunch in first.

'So what you're saying without actually saying it is you hate the record and you're looking for an excuse not to bother with it, am I right?' I could barely contain my anger.

Ms Brightman entered the fray.

'Miss Taylor, you've been seen frequenting establishments which would be considered unsuitable for someone in your situation. I hardly think you're in a position to remonstrate.'

Her sneeringly dismissive tone instantly set my teeth on edge.

'And who told you that?'

'Where the information came from isn't relevant,' she replied smugly.

Oh yes, it fucking is!

I wanted to ram the arrogant bitch's teeth down her throat, but I knew she was just acting as the mouthpiece for the man by her side. He had to have found out somehow. He was, after all, an occasional visitor to

Pulverton Manor, and one of Linda's private clients. He might not have been a member of the club but maybe he knew people who were. They must have let something slip.

'I hardly think shelving a high budget album is in anybody's interests, let alone yours,' Mitchell countered, wading into the argument now he had recovered enough to gather himself, but Gil was ready for him.

'And we see no point putting good money after bad. It's purely a commercial decision, as I'm sure you understand.'

'So it is really about the record then. You're just using allegations about Rebecca's private life to ensure her quiet compliance.' Mitchell radiated quiet fury.

'Nevertheless, a decision is a decision.'

'And there's nothing we can do or say which would cause you to reconsider?'

Gil set his jaw and held Mitchell's gaze, waiting for him to be the one to break eye contact.

'No, I don't think there is.'

I had to try what I could or the last five months work into which I had poured my heart and soul would be for nothing. I might have kept the rights to the songs but I still had my hands tied by the terms of my contract.

'Mr Premmell, may I have a word with you?' I asked, trying to keep my voice steady.

'Shoot.'

'I mean in private.'

Gil raised one eyebrow but his superior manner showed no sign of cracking. He glanced across at the she-devil and nodded. Reluctantly, Amanda slid back her chair and glaring in my direction, got up from the table.

'You too, Mitchell,' I said.

He gave me a concerned look before heaving a sigh of resignation and getting up to join Amanda in leaving the room.

'I hope you know what you're doing,' he breathed on his way past.

'I'll be fine,' I assured him.

The door closed quietly behind the two retreating figures.

'Well, Miss Taylor? You have my attention.'

I stood, drawing my back straight, and fixed him with the same kind of stare he'd directed at Mitchell. I could feel Sadie padding up beside me and rubbing herself against my leg, digging her claws into the Axminster. She knew what was coming.

'Do you think it's wise to attempt to use my personal life as leverage to put weight behind your business decisions, especially given your own patterns of behaviour.'

He snorted.

'And what could you possibly know about me, Miss Taylor?'

'Well, I'm assuming you know about my visits to certain establishments because you go there yourself.'

Still he showed no sign of weakening.

'That's quite an assumption. You've got nothing.'

'Oh, I'm not assuming you go there; I know you go there. You see, I have my sources too.'

He looked momentarily startled but his poker face soon returned. Maybe he wasn't sure how much dirt I had on him but I had my quarry in my sights and I was lining up to take the kill shot. I still had my ace card to play. The last time I'd encountered Gil Premmell, he had been on the other side of a two way mirror, crawling on all fours with a dog tail sticking out of his arse and being led around the floor on a leash by Linda in domme wear. The pathetic apology for a man hadn't looked so fucking superior then.

'If you want to spread shit about me,' the words came out with as much quiet malice as I could muster, 'then I can spread some shit about you too...Fido.'

His eyes widened in terror and he stood up.

'How do you...?'

'Never mind how I know. All you need to concern yourself with is whether you really want to pull the trigger on this one because right now the gun is pointing more at you than it is at me. You have far more to lose than I do. What would your wife and all her precious friends think if they knew what a bad doggy you'd been? Hmm?'

Gil's jaw dropped but I wasn't finished, not by a long shot.

'Okay, so a few people get to think I'm even more of a slut than they already do. So what? I've built an image and a career on being sexually risqué, and you and your company have done very well out of it, but if people actually found out about what a pathetic little deviant you are underneath that respectable exterior of yours, where would you be? So I put it to you, it might be worth reconsidering your position because if you do, this all goes away and you get to keep your shallow little shell of a life in one piece without having to pay out a huge divorce settlement.' The tone of my voice softened to one of angelic sweetness. 'The alternative is, well, unthinkable really, because there's a trail of evidence, and you know there is.'

He scowled at me then eventually sagged into his chair again with a look of resignation.

'So what do you want? Name your terms.'

'I want you to release my album as originally planned, and I expect your full and wholehearted support. Afterwards, you'll get your Rebecca Taylor album that will continue to deliver what the fans want and make the kind of money you've come to expect, and we can all go back to playing happy families. Oh, and don't go thinking about retribution wherever you think I may or may not have got my information, because I will find out, and I will pull the pin on a public humiliation grenade you won't be coming back from.'

I leaned over the table with my hands pressing flat against the surface. Sadie hunched forward too, snarling at him.

'Pull another stunt like this again and I will finish you. Are we clear?'

'Abundantly.' He suddenly looked about three feet tall.

'Good. Shall we invite the others back in?'

Turning his head away, he waved his hand in submission.

'Do what you want.'

I opened the door and called Amanda and Mitchell back in. They sat down and looked first at each other, then the two of us in turn, waiting and wondering.

Gil was the first to speak.

'Rebecca and I have had a frank and honest discussion and I've come to the conclusion it would no longer be in the company's interests to withdraw from the release.'

Amanda stared at him in disbelief. I don't think Mitchell was much less surprised but considerably happier about the turnaround. Amanda opened her mouth to protest but Gil held up his hand.

'It's a decision.'

She shut it again.

-0-

Formalities over and the meeting concluded, Mitchell and I got into the back of the car that was to take us back to Sacker Management's offices, closing the doors and shutting out the wider world again. My faithful driver Derek slid into the front seat and took the wheel. Unable to contain himself any longer, Mitchell turned towards me.

'I don't know what the hell you said to Premmell, and perhaps I don't want to know, but I've never seen that man back down before; he's like a terrier in negotiations. Once he gets his teeth into something, there's usually no shaking him off.'

I smiled to myself. Mitchell had no idea how close his analogy was to the truth.

'It was a close thing,' I told him. 'I guess he's never had to face a tiger before.'

After the event, though, and now the adrenaline was starting to wear off, I was beginning to shake. I'd come within a hair's breadth of losing everything I'd spent the last few months working so hard for, but Sadie had stepped in to save the day. I doubted if left to my own devices I'd have had the fortitude to call Gil Premmell's bluff. Thank goodness for Linda's foresight when she insisted on giving me a view into that man's warped little world.

I looked down at my trembling hands and clenched them to still the nerves. I needed a drink.

CHAPTER FOURTEEN

As soon as I saw the venue, I knew it was going to be a big event. Passion Flower might not have had the run of the whole place but they didn't need to. One wing would be quite sufficient. A grand statement, its imposing, sandstone façade, reached at the end of a half-mile drive that led straight through the grounds, left no one in any doubt as to its importance. Spensford Hall seemed a trifling, provincial country home by comparison.

My sporty new Mercedes coupé, bought with some of the proceeds from the perfume, would have blended right in if I'd bothered to bring it. Instead, I employed Derek to take me there and back. It was a long drive and I didn't intend to stay all night. At least if Derek drove I didn't have to worry about having a couple of drinks. Linda's event was just a posh party as far as Derek was concerned. He didn't need to know the details since he wouldn't be going inside, and I knew he wouldn't be the kind of person to tell tales to the press or report anything back to Mitchell anyway. Better he drove me than someone I didn't know. Trust as a commodity was becoming rarer by the day.

We arrived along with a steady stream of other cars,

parking as directed alongside a Rolls Royce, and I leaned forward to place my hand on my driver's shoulder.

'Thank you, Derek. I've no idea what time this thing finishes, probably late, though.'

He glanced up to look at me in the mirror.

'Don't worry, miss; I've got the radio for company. Just text me when you're about to leave and I'll be ready and waiting.'

'Right, then! Wish me luck.'

I had no idea why I said that. Why should I need luck? After all, it was just a party, but some part of me still felt nervous. I put it down to my recent run-in with Gil Premmell, coupled with the events at the Aphrodite Rooms, and brushed any foreboding aside, telling myself not to be so stupid. I donned my silvery, feathered mask while Derek came round to open the door for me, and straightening my skirt, stepped out into the cool evening air. My dress wasn't particularly short or especially tight, but I still shivered slightly when the chill, evening air hit my legs.

Following other guests towards the entrance, I was greeted at the main door by another of Linda and Ryan's staff and shown through a vast, high-ceilinged hallway into a reception room where people had already begun assembling over drinks. Linda spotted me and waved, politely excusing herself from her conversation with a group of expensively turned-out revellers and sashaying over, drink in hand.

'Glad you could make it, sweetie. It's been a while since you made it to a Passion Flower event. Mind you, not too much has changed, except the clientele and the prices have kept on moving steadily upwards.' She grinned. 'Good girl, I see you remembered your mask.'

'Of course,' I said, tapping the side of my face. 'I came prepared.'

'Most of the events at least start off as masquerades although I think the masks tend to come off when the rest of the clothes do. I think it helps with the atmosphere, takes people out of themselves and lets them get past any nerves. It gives them licence to be who they want to be and throw the rule book out of the window, and the party certainly gets going quicker when there's a bit of the unknown about it. You can't beat that frisson of excitement at meeting all those mysterious and attractive strangers, can you?'

'I guess not.' Time had done nothing to change her tune.

I had to admit, the appeal of the lifestyle had somewhat lost its shine recently after the way things had gone at Pulverton Manor, but at that moment, caught up in the glamour of it all, I considered throwing caution to the wind again.

'Mind you,' Linda said, 'we've got ideas for an even bigger one in an eighteenth-century French chateau, all powdered wigs and mantua dresses, lace-up bodices, white faces and beauty spots. That one promises to be pretty special.'

'It all sounds a bit extravagant and unnecessary to me. What must that cost?'

Linda shrugged.

'I don't think cost is an object to most of our clients these days. Getting their rocks off is.'

Another idea came tumbling out of my mouth before my brain had time to question it.

'I would have thought that as you went up the power ladder it would be harder and harder to attract couples to events. After all, it is a man's world and women aren't generally invited to the top table.'

Linda snorted.

'I wouldn't be so sure about that. That's too convenient a generalisation. Admittedly there are quite a few of our paid female guests here today to ensure certain of our male clients are kept happy, but not perhaps as many as you might think. The world doesn't belong to men specifically, and it never has. There are circles within circles. The world doesn't even belong to those with just wealth, although they certainly are placed in a position of advantage. No, it belongs to the powerful and the influential, whether they happen to be men or women, and real power has nothing to do with paid employment; it's all about who's pulling the strings. There's a Venn diagram to be drawn here with a very small overlap at the centre.' She gave me a searching look. 'You're starting to sound like you have an axe to grind.'

And you don't?

'No, it's just... I had an encounter with Gil Premmell recently. You know, the VP of Ariva records, the one who likes to be treated like a dog?'

'I remember him. Not seen much of him lately.'

'Well, I wouldn't hold your breath in anticipation if I were you. He found out about my visits to the manor and tried to use it against me. He wanted to put my new album on ice but I threatened him right back and he soon changed his tune. I reckon it probably didn't take him long to work out where I got my inside information from but don't worry, he won't do anything; he wouldn't dare.

I told him I have evidence.'

Linda gave me a look of surprise.

'But you haven't, though!'

'You know that and I know that, but he doesn't. Sorry if I've cost you a client.'

Linda waved her hand in dismissal.

'Look around you. Does it look like I'm going to miss that worm's money? Some instinct told me you might need the inside scoop on him someday. Why do you think I made a point of showing you his private little antics? Anyway, listen, I'm going to have to circulate. You relax and have a good time. Don't sweat yourself over that little toad.' She checked over her shoulder, looking around. 'Ryan should be here somewhere. I need to catch up with him. Just chill and enjoy, sweetie.'

Alone again, for the time being, I watched her disappear back into the crowd as entertainers in fetish wear began to mingle, amusing small groups of guests with card tricks and illusions. Looking around, there appeared to be no one else I knew. I was either going to have to break out of my shell or it was going to be a short and disappointing evening. Maybe a drink or two would loosen me up. I accepted a glass of the inevitable chilled champagne from a passing tray and downed it quickly. I beckoned him back and replacing the empty glass with a smile of apology to the waiter, took another.

'Sorry about that; I was thirsty.'

'That's quite alright, Miss Taylor,' came the reply.

So the mask isn't all that much of a disguise, then. Maybe he also worked at Pulverton Manor and knew me from there. In their identical uniforms, the staff all looked much alike, which I suspected was rather the point. They were meant to be available but invisible.

If I had actually succeeded in remaining anonymous, maybe some of the guests would think I was one of the escorts whose job it was to keep any single guests entertained. It was Linda's mission to ensure that no one got sidelined and left unsatisfied. Now I was aware of it and knew what to look for, I could make out a few well-presented and attractive men and women homing in on their targets. One or two of them I might even have recognised from previous events or from the club. They moved with studied assurance, a sense of purpose not shared by the other guests, and outwardly at least, displayed a level of inner confidence I wished I felt myself. I wondered if Linda had somebody lined up for me, but somehow I think she knew I wasn't inclined towards 'professional engagements'.

The idea was starting to warm on me, though. At least a 'paid guest' would be more concerned with the pleasure and wellbeing of their respective target rather than simply taking pleasure from or humiliating others like Gordon and his cronies had done at the Aphrodite Rooms. Maybe I could see the merit in it. They may have been paid to be there but at least there was a certain kind of honesty and decency about the transaction.

'All on your own?'

I turned to face the voice. It was quite well-spoken, but the face told me he was not one of Linda's escorts; he was a good ten years older than any of them and not exactly in the same finely honed shape. Being quite tall and broad, the extra weight didn't seem to hamper him. Nevertheless, he had a pleasant enough smile and looked expensively dressed.

'For the moment,' I said. 'What about you?'

'Oh, just waiting to see what the evening brings. The name's Tony.'

'Becca. So is this your first event?'

His smirk gave him away.

'Not exactly. I've been to a couple of Passion Flower events but I think this is probably one of the biggest. And you?'

'About the same.' I wasn't about to mention the club.

We talked for a while until Linda made announcements about where the playrooms were and what time they would be opening. The dancing was about to start, which apparently included a floor show to get people in the mood. Given the entertainment at previous events, I had a good idea what that was likely to involve. Attentive enough though my present company was, his conversation was rather one-dimensional, and that dimension was mostly himself. I would rather have caught up with Ryan for the opportunity to talk, but there was no sign of him and besides which, he was probably busy anyway. At least I wasn't alone.

We made our way through to the ballroom and Tony fetched another couple of drinks from the bar. I thanked him, of course, and couldn't really refuse when he asked me to dance. After another half hour, the floor was cleared and a large plastic sheet laid down in the centre.

Okay, I'm not too sure where this is going but I can hazard a guess.

As it turned out, my guess wasn't too far off the mark. The floor show involved two men and two women, all dressed in little more than token clothing that didn't remain on for long anyway, and liberal quantities of body oil. How they managed to keep hold of each other remained something of a mystery. It must have been like trying to grapple with a wet bar of soap, but somehow they managed it and the ensuing, frantic, four-way orgy of athletic fucking certainly hit the spot with its audience; there was no denying its effect on all the partygoers who stood around watching with glasses in their hands. Tony looked on hungrily, but the attraction was wearing a little thin for me.

I could see the audiences body language subtly alter as layer by layer they shed their inhibitions, aided no doubt by the entertainment and the application of alcohol. My head was starting to swim a little. It wasn't normally this bad after only three drinks. To be honest, I didn't feel a hundred per cent.

'Fancy heading for one of the playrooms,' Tony asked, leaning in to shout over the accompanying music.

'I might hold off,' I told him. 'See how I feel.'

He nodded.

'Sure.'

Once the dance floor had been cleared again and it had been returned to its original intended purpose, the difference in people's behaviour became clear. The dancing began to involve a lot more physical contact, any earlier reserve having been put to one side. Small groups of people began to disappear off in the direction of the playrooms but in all honesty, I wasn't that interested. The whole experience suddenly seemed hollow. I would rather have sat and had a good chin wag over a cup of tea with friends. My companion's conversation hardly sparkled and truth be told I wasn't that attracted to him. Somewhere in the back of my mind was the thought that I could be snuggled up with Poppy, having a long overdue catch up with Jayne and Sophie or an evening of wine, piano, and tarot cards with Janine and Alan, perhaps sharing their bed at the end of it. Instead, I was mixing with people I felt I shared nothing in common with.

Actually, what am I doing here?

The wooziness and the ringing in my ears weren't helping.

'Do you want another drink?' he asked.

I shook my head.

'Thank you, but no. Actually, I'm not feeling too great. I might just head home.'

He hesitated a moment before giving me a tight-lipped smile.

'Of course.'

I thanked him again for his company and made back towards the entrance, certain that I'd seen a sign for the ladies on my way in. I could do with a pee and the opportunity to clear my head before the long journey home. On my way, I looked around. I could see no sign of Linda or Ryan as I wove through the revellers. I would have liked to say goodbye before I left but the swimming in my head left me little choice.

Ah, there it is!

Crossing the now deserted entrance hall, I spotted the door for the bathroom and made my way inside. Apart from myself, it appeared to be empty. Maybe there were other facilities closer to the playrooms. In a place this size, it wouldn't have surprised me. Leaning against the edge of the polished granite countertop I removed my mask and stared at my own reflection in the mirror, trying to steady my breathing. Why did I feel so peculiar? I looked alright, or at least I thought so; my vision kept drifting in and out of focus.

When I heard the door opening I paid it little heed, but the footsteps quickly crossing the floor soon brought my attention sharply back into the moment. I turned just in time to see Tony bearing down on me, his face set into an angry snarl, hardly recognisable as the man I'd been speaking to for the last hour. He grabbed my jaw and practically lifting me off my feet, backed me into the wall, slamming my back against the cold travertine.

'So you thought you'd just walk away from me, did you? And after I'd been so nice to you too, you fucking bitch!'

Before I could say anything a stinging blow from the back of his hand across my cheek caught me off guard and sent me reeling.

'You don't get to turn me down. No one does that. Fucking prick tease!' He was so close now I could feel his hot breath on my face, flecks of spittle landing on my skin from the corner of his twisted mouth. 'People don't come to a do like this just to lead a man on and then say no, and certainly not someone like you. Oh, I know who you are, you fucking slut. Everybody knows who you are and *what* you are.'

Two large hands gripped my shoulders and pressed downwards, forcing me to my knees. In my current state, I could offer little resistance.

'I'll show you what you're good for,' he snarled, grabbing my hair with one hand while reaching for his zip with the other. 'It's a shame I never got the chance to do what I really wanted. I knew I should have given you a bit more in your drink. Well, you can suck my cock like the whore you are, and then I'm going to fuck you ragged you filthy little cunt.' Another blow caught me across the side of my face. 'And don't ever think about breathing a word because no one's going to believe a cheap little slut like you anyway.' He reached for his cock and shoved it in my face. I pressed my lips tightly together and turned my head away but he raised his fist again. 'Now be a good little girl and stick it in your mouth or else I'm going to make it worse for you. Right now, nothing would give me greater pleasure than working you over like the stuck up bitch that you are.'

Any other time I would have fought him to my last breath, but my head was spinning and every movement made me feel like my arms and legs were made of lead.

He grabbed my head and was just about to force himself into my mouth when the door burst open again, and before he could react, my assailant was propelled backwards at great speed by two burly, black-suited security men. Behind them, I could see a mortified Linda, high heels clutched tightly in her hand and wide-eyed with shock, and just behind her an equally horrified Ryan, righteous anger taking over as he surveyed the scene in front of him. They rushed over to where I knelt, crumpled on the floor while the security men manhandled my assailant to the far wall and pinned him there.

'Oh my God! Sweetie, are you alright? What did that bastard do to you?' Linda cradled my face, looking as if she was about to burst into tears which in itself was a rarity; having never been given to outward displays of emotion.

I waved them both away, struggling to my feet. A

trickle of blood had run down from my nose and into my mouth. I could taste its metallic taint when I pressed my tongue against the back of my teeth. At least they all seemed to still be there even if everything stung like a bitch. The whole of my face felt stiff.

'Apparently, nothing I don't deserve,' I sneered, wiping away a smear of blood with the back of my hand.

Ryan turned his attention towards Tony, ice-cold formality taking over.

'I think it's safe to say you have considerably outstayed your welcome, Mr Holbrook. We'll let the police deal with this matter from here.'

Shit! No!

That would be nothing short of disastrous. The adverse publicity would do them no favours but it would ruin me! I couldn't have the police and the papers all over this; they'd have a fucking field day. For their various reasons, Mitchell, Ariva, and Lafontaine would all wash their hands of me whether I was at fault or not.

'No!' I insisted, standing up as straight as I could. 'I can't let you do that, Ryan.'

'But…'

'No. No police. No press.'

'You can't seriously let him get away with this,' he protested, staring my way but gesturing in Holbrook's direction. 'There's a potential list of charges here as long as your arm.'

'I said no!' The words came out with a fierceness which seemed to come from my gut. They reverberated off the stone tiles.

Ryan stood thinking for a moment, curling his fists, trying to decide whether to heed my wishes, throw the book at Holbrook, or just punch the fucker while the security men held him. Eventually, he appeared to come to a decision and pointed up at a tiny security camera in the corner of the ceiling. I hadn't even noticed it before, but then I'd had no reason to look for it when I came in.

'You see that,' he said, stepping forward so he was right up in Holbrook's face. 'That's recorded everything. Not that I agree with it or that you deserve it, but I'm reluctantly going to respect Rebecca's wishes. You can consider yourself very lucky to be walking out of here because if it was down to me, I'd break both of your fucking legs you worthless piece of shit. You can consider your welcome at Passion Flower events and any events by similar organisers well and truly rescinded. If I were you, I wouldn't make the mistake of thinking we don't share information on undesirable guests. You will never attend any events like this again.'

Holbrook pulled his arms free of the security men and drew himself to his full height, speaking as if he had a plum in his mouth.

'Who the hell do you think you are? You're a nobody. Don't you know who I am?'

Ryan smiled inscrutably, unfazed by the man's attempt at bluster.

'Oh, we know exactly who you are, Mr Holbrook. We know far more than you think about all our clients. Don't go thinking you're untouchable here. We've got everything we need to ruin you and your political aspirations if you're stupid enough not to realise when you're getting off lightly, and in my opinion, you are... far too lightly.' Ryan glanced across at me again. 'Are you absolutely sure you don't want to press charges? I really think you should.'

I shook my head. If I had a gun in my hand I'd have shot the fucker right then and there given the hatred that was boiling up inside me, but I had to put self-preservation first. I could still think clearly enough to realise that much, despite my brain currently feeling like it was made of marshmallow. It was like trying to think through fog.

'It's complicated. I have my reasons. Just get this bastard out of my sight.' Not wanting to make eye contact with Holbrook I waved my hand in his approximate direction, still staring down at the floor.

Ryan resigned himself to his course of action and stepped back to address the security men with a knowing glance.

'Gentlemen, kindly see to it that Mr Holbrook leaves the premises without any fuss and that he comes to no harm in the process. I would hate to think of him hurting himself while in our care.' He stepped over for a brief but quiet exchange with the man-mountain on the left.

'Yes, Mr Maloney. With pleasure!' He seemed to relish the prospect of ejecting their charge in no uncertain terms. They both grinned and grabbing an arm each, forcibly marched Holbrook out of the room.

'Right, I think we need to get you cleaned up, sweetie.' Linda had taken charge again now the odious man had been removed from the equation. 'There's a full first-aid kit in the event hub. Let's get you out of here and check you over properly.'

'I feel like I might be about to throw up first,' I told her. 'I don't know if it's just the shock or what he slipped into my drink. He practically admitted to drugging me. I think he was actually proud of it.'

Once again, Linda and Ryan's faces registered shock.

'And you let that bastard go?' Linda asked. 'I still think we should have nailed him to the wall.' She shook her head. 'What's the world coming to when it's more trouble for you than it's worth to ensure he gets his just deserts?'

Leaning over the sink, I could feel a wave of nausea rising, retching a couple of times before I vomited up what little I had in my stomach. I ran the tap to wash out my mouth and clean the blood off my face while Ryan fetched a towel.

'Well, tonight hasn't turned into quite the glamorous evening I was expecting.' I did my best to make light of it all. 'I didn't realise you had CCTV at events as well as at the club.'

'We didn't back when we started out,' a still serious Ryan admitted. 'These days we make sure of it. Thankfully this venue has its own systems already installed, but we can also set up temporary ones if needed. We don't take chances, and it was just as well. If we didn't have security manning the cameras at all times he might have...' Ryan's voice trailed away as his emotions finally got the better of him. 'I'm so sorry. This shouldn't have happened. I'd like to wring that slimy, arrogant bastard's neck.'

'It's not your fault,' I assured him. 'You've always had my back, both of you.'

On our way to the evening's centre of operations, Linda stopped a passing staff member. He kept glancing across at me but Linda drew his attention back with a few clicks of her fingers.

'Owen, I need you to seal off the ladies toilet and get two people to help you clean up. I want that bathroom spotless before anyone else goes in there. Got me?'

'Yes, Miss Maloney.' He scurried off to carry out her instructions.

Linda sat me down in the office and cleaned me up while Ryan checked the cameras.

'Oh, honey!' she soothed. 'He really went for it, didn't he? You're going to be nursing some nasty bruises for a few days.'

'Well that's Anthony Holbrook off the premises,' Ryan looked up from the screen in front of him, 'and now we've got clearly filmed evidence of him leaving in one unharmed piece just in case he wants to make trouble. He might try to pretend we took matters into our own hands and then concocted stories about him if anything does come out. I wouldn't put it past him.'

'I'm sorry,' I said. 'I appear to be making you some powerful enemies.'

Ryan quickly came over and knelt, taking my hands in his.

'Promise me one thing. I want you to stop apologising for something that was not your fault. He attacked you, not the other way around. There was no excuse.' He paused, looking reflective. 'It's not the first time you've felt responsible for someone else's unreasonable behaviour, is it?'

'What do you mean?' I asked, beginning to tear up.

'You remember when that awful bitch Samantha said horrible things about you at the garden party your folks threw?'

I nodded. It was a long time ago but I remembered

alright. She hadn't exactly been my favourite girlfriend of his. Ryan's hands remained clasped tightly around mine.

'You did nothing wrong then and you've done nothing wrong now, so stop blaming yourself.'

-0-

By the time I left to go home I had dried my eyes and cleaned myself up as best I could, but Derek still looked shocked when he saw me stumbling over to the car, held up by Linda with her arm around my shoulders. The party was still in full swing and would be until the small hours. In my muddled state, I hadn't had the presence of mind to message him I was leaving.

'Take good care of her,' Linda instructed. 'She's still a bit shaken.'

For a moment, he stared at us in disbelief.

'Is this anything to do with the gentleman I saw leaving earlier?' Derek asked, rushing over to assist.

'Trust me; that was no gentleman,' she assured him. 'And yes, it is. I think Rebecca just wants to go home now. She's had a bit of a rough time of it.'

'I can see that. Jesus, you look like you've been hit by a bus, Miss Taylor.'

'Thanks!' I said in an attempt at mock indignation.

I was in no mood to recount the evening's events, though. I just wanted to block the whole thing out.

'Thanks for your concern, Derek, but I'd rather not talk about it if that's alright.'

He nodded his acceptance.

Linda waved us off, and I remained by the window the whole journey home, staring blankly out through the glass. I hardly said a word and even asked Derek to turn off the music that was playing softly in the background. I just wanted to be left alone with my thoughts.

When we finally arrived home, I wished him goodnight and let myself in. Instead of going straight to my room, I headed along the landing to the nursery and quietly opened the door. Poppy lay sleeping peacefully, her breathing slow and even. I wanted to hold her and kiss her, but not wishing to wake her up I pulled a blanket out of the cupboard and wrapped it around me. I curled up on the floor beside the cot, rocking backwards and forwards and sobbing myself to sleep.

A jumble of voices and images assault me, warped and twisted faces leering out of the darkness: a figure with a tumbler of whisky in his hand; the sneering face of an Asian woman standing over me; Gil Premmell sitting back in his chair with a look of smug superiority; the hateful face of Anthony Holbrook; and worst of all, a disappointed Mitchell Sacker.

'Everybody knows who you are and what you are... There are much more satisfying forms of punishment than the purely physical... Jesus, Rebecca! What the bloody hell do you think you're playing at?'

Waking in the first rays of morning, I found Poppy standing in her cot, looking calmly down at me with her little fingers curled around the bars. I slowly hauled myself up, unsure whether I felt stiff from my treatment at the hands of Holbrook, or from several hours spent lying on the floor. It was probably both. She reached her hands out to me and I scooped her up in my arms, tears beginning to roll down my face, stinging against my bruised cheeks.

'It's alright, darling; I'm here. I promise to be a better mummy from now on,' I told her as she intercepted a droplet with her fingertip, her lip trembling as if in imitation of my own.

Poppy flung her arms around my neck and held me tight.

'Mummy,' she said.

CHAPTER FIFTEEN

'Oh my God! What happened to you?'

I should have known Francesca would fuss when she saw the state I was in. She reached out her hand to touch my face but I brushed it aside. I couldn't handle talking about it. How could I put my desolation into words?

'Some arsehole is what happened to me' I said, turning away slightly. 'Let's just say the evening didn't go as expected. It's not as bad as it looks.'

She stared at me and went to open her mouth, but perhaps decided against enquiring too far. My expression must have told her I wasn't ready to share any more information than I already had.

'Breakfast?' she asked, struggling to find something suitable to say and instead resorting to her usual offer of food. I shook my head.

'Thanks, Francesca, but I'm not in the mood. I might have something later. Karina's taking Poppy out for some fresh air so I'm going for a swim in a minute.'

Maybe it would clear my head and ease the aching in my muscles. Traces of whatever Holbrook had slipped into my drink must have remained in my system; I still didn't feel right.

'Well at least have a cup of tea first,' she insisted.

I gave in. It might placate her enough to keep her off my back.

Once Francesca had been satisfied that I was in no immediate danger or distress, I sloped off to the pool room. Standing at the water's edge, I stared down at the little ripples on its surface then removed one trainer and dipped my big toe in. I swirled it around, hypnotised by random reflections from the overhead lighting as the liquid moved. My mind wandered off at a tangent. Maybe the water would wash away the feelings, purge me of the stain that spread across my skin like an invisible tattoo that spelt out one single, ugly word: whore.

Is that all people see me as? A sex object?

Couldn't I be more than that, musically or otherwise? Surely nothing I had done negated my value as a human being, no matter how outlandish it might have been or who I'd done it with. None of us is ever defined by just one thing. Anyway, why shouldn't I enjoy sex? Everybody else seemed to.

But perhaps, deep down, the trouble was I wasn't enjoying the sex any more. It was no longer what liberated me, my escape, but one more item in the long list of things that enslaved: a cage with invisible bars. As long as I went through the motions with nothing else of any worth behind it, it had become a hollow, meaningless act, an attempt to fill an unfillable void, to replace what could not be replaced. More than ever, I had to reinvent myself, to use the new album to make a statement. Quite literally, I needed to shed this skin.

I removed the other shoe and slipped out of my jeans.

I couldn't even be bothered to change into a swimsuit; I just jumped feet first into the deep end, still wearing my tee shirt and underwear, and let the water envelop me, taking me under. Bubbles rose around me and burst above my head until I was finally surrounded by blissful silence: no nagging voices, no demands, no arbitrary condemnation by those who have no right to pass sentence, just silence.

In my mind's eye, I could see Janine's hand turning over a tarot card on which a female figure held aloft a sword and scales. Judgement may have been passed, but it bore little semblance to justice. Maybe such fairness is one of those ideals we cling to. It has little to do with reality; the world and how it works gets in the way.

I opened my eyes and looked around at my aquatic underworld, ripples of light dancing across the pale blue tiles. It would be so easy to leave everything behind, to release all the air in my lungs and drift into unconsciousness, let the water take away the pain. For a moment I was tempted, but a little face with a mess of dark hair and the bluest eyes looked up at me with such helpless innocence. 'Mummy,' she said, and I knew I couldn't. I needed to fight, for her sake as well as mine. I had to redouble my efforts, work even harder, find my place again. I owed it to her, to my family, to the band, and everyone else who had ever believed in me. Appealing though oblivion was, taking the easy way out would have been an act of pure selfishness. Giving up was not an option.

But I was faced with an inevitable choice. As much as it hurt to do it, I had to distance myself from the club and from that world. Of course, it meant I would hardly get the opportunity to see Linda or Ryan, but they were always working anyway. They had sold their souls to their work just as I had done to mine. Maybe we weren't so far apart after all. None of us is truly in charge of our own destiny because even freedom comes at a price. We are all slaves to something.

Becoming aware of the burning sensation in my lungs as my body increasingly struggled for oxygen, I launched from the bottom of the pool and fought my way back to the surface, hauling myself out of the water and lying, dripping, on the cold tiles, taking big gulps of air while my breathing returned to normal.

Somehow I had to find my way out of this dark place and back to the light. Music had always been my salvation. It could be again. It had to be.

-0-

'Well,' Mitchell shuffled uncomfortably, 'the first reviews are in.'

'And?'

'I'll be honest with you, it's a mixed bag. The new album seems to be like marmite; they either love it or hate it. In general, serious music magazines are more complimentary while the popular press has been somewhat less favourable.'

I sighed, sagging into the chair with an air of resignation.

'Go on, you might as well hit me with it.' Even the phrase felt awkward under the circumstances. Thankfully the bruises had mostly faded. I'd hidden away and made my excuses to avoid having to face anybody too soon.

The real scars the experience left behind were the ones no one could see, not even me. Nevertheless, Penny had given me a few searching looks when I came into the office, so I fobbed her off with a story about walking into a door, and despite being indoors decided to keep my sunglasses on.

Mitchell steeled himself, trying to maintain a cheery disposition.

'Alright, let's start at the positive end of the scale.'

He picked up one of the magazines off his desk, and locating the article via a tab attached to the appropriate page, flicked it open. He cleared his throat.

'Rebecca Taylor the artist comes of age.'

He glanced at me through his little, round glasses, in the hope of gauging my initial reaction.

'We've been waiting a long time for this album, not just since her last output but for the whole of her career so far, although this apparent side project arrived in the review pile with little fanfare and none of the previous accompanying hype. It turned out to be far more than just a pleasant surprise. Rebecca Taylor (aka Rebecca) has finally shown us the depth and maturity we all knew she was capable of. Gone is the glamour and glitz of A Suitcase of Diamonds to be replaced by a much more thoughtful and reflective collection of songs. They cover a smorgasbord of styles and moods ranging from the sultry yet strangely uplifting acoustic stomp of Black Roses to the soul-baring vocals and orchestral sweep of the title track, Shed This Skin, via the defiant Never Hurt Me Again. Rebecca Taylor's voice has never been in finer form or displayed such raw, emotional depth. The startlingly original songs just keep coming, each a perfectly self-contained stylistic vignette: Return to Earth, Blood of my Blood, Walking Away, Heart on my Sleeve, Waiting for the Sun to Rise, Ghosts, and my personal favourite, One More Dollar, which despite its cryptic lyrics appears to be a fairly damning indictment of the music industry as a whole. Perhaps this at least partly explains why an album by an award-winning artist supposedly at the top of her game has received so little attention prior to its release. Other highlights include the upbeat You've Made Your Bed (So You Can Lie in It), No Sign of Life, and perhaps the more familiar tongue-in-cheek double-entendres of Tie Me Down.'

Up until this point, I hadn't made a sound. Mitchell looked up to check that I was still listening before returning to the page. I was. Intently.

'That said,' he continued, 'apart from the strangely catchy Black Roses which I suspect is going to be a bit of a grower, none of the songs is overtly commercial. There doesn't seem to be any obvious chart material designed to suit the current rather formulaic climate. Instead, this is a bravely individualistic collection of thirteen songs that highlight Rebecca Taylor's many talents, as a songwriter, singer, guitarist, and even as a pianist. Except for the input of a handful of top session musicians, much of the album appears to be her own work. The passion and the integrity behind it shine through. Forget what you read about her private life in the gossip columns. If you want to get to know the real Rebecca Taylor, just sit back and soak up the atmosphere of this sixty-five-minute collection. Complex, varied and satisfyingly rich, it may not grab you at the first listen but stick with it. This isn't bubble gum pop that loses its flavour after the first couple of plays through, not that Rebecca's music ever has been. Instead, this is an album to savour.'

Mitchell looked up at me and I found myself nodding.

'So far, so good. I'd say that one got the memo.'

He winced.

'Yes, but then there's this, and I'm afraid it's far more typical.' He picked up one of the newspapers in front of him. 'This one went out under the heading 'Where did Rebecca Taylor go?''

Mitchell straightened his glasses and cleared his throat again.

'Since disappearing from the charts over a year ago, everything has gone rather quiet from Rebecca Taylor. Then, out of nowhere, and without even a lead single, comes Shed This Skin, an odd assortment of over-serious, dreary tunes which has none of the energy and excitement of her previous records. Apart from an attempt at humour with Tie Me Down, and despite some expensive-sounding production, it's just dull. Even the title track, Shed This Skin, sounds like an unholy union between Elton John and Pink Floyd that grows by the end into a wall of orchestral noise. There's nothing here that makes you want to get up and dance, no obvious crowd-pleasers, none of the feel-good factor that made Come Inside and Devil on my Shoulder so irresistible. Only time will tell whether the bubble has burst for the queen of naughtiness because this is a long way from what anyone would have expected. She used to be entertaining and sexy. She used to be fun. Come back Rebecca Taylor, all is forgiven.'

Mitchell put the paper down and I puffed out my cheeks.

'I guess they didn't like it, then.'

'I'm afraid not. It seems to be a love/hate thing depending on people's expectations. Of course, it wouldn't be the first time critics have initially slammed something that turned out to be a huge success; just look at what happened to Bohemian Rhapsody. It was a rare enough example of true individuality in its day, though, a bold and commercially risky move, and that's become even rarer in the modern age, especially from an established artist with a lot to lose. Perhaps it's just as well we insulated ourselves from any backlash. Of course, I'm sure you realise this makes it all the more imperative to give your existing fans more of what they want. But as well as doing our best to promote an album Ariva are putting none of their own weight behind, we really need to get another Rebecca Taylor album in the can before the tour commences.'

'What's the initial response to the tour so far?' I asked, but Mitchell shook his head.

'Ticket sales for even the bigger gigs have been slower than I'd hoped. It hasn't taken long for up and coming artists to begin stealing your thunder. You may only be into your mid-twenties but you're no longer the new kid on the block any more. We're already committed to some of the larger concerts at the end of the European leg, but I think we may have to start by playing some smaller venues and build up. The promoters are, to put it mildly, a little nervous. In the meantime, your TV appearances are going to be crucial to turning things around. I've got you booked onto Friday Night Live with Phil Cross to coincide with the release of Black Roses. That's the one and only single Ariva are committing to. As I'm sure you're aware by now, there are no plans to make a video for it at the moment, and even if there were, there wouldn't be enough time to do it any real justice. On the plus side, and perhaps bizarrely, Whispered Scream are planning to promote the song you recorded with them as a single. Their management has approached us about shooting a video with you, so you should at least get some exposure on the rock channels. Your impromptu recording session may have turned out to be a blessing in disguise after all.'

Mitchell settled into his high-backed swivel chair and resting his elbows on the padded arms, raised his hands in front of him.

'The next few months are going to be make or break, so buckle up, buttercup; it's going to be a bumpy ride.'

CHAPTER SIXTEEN

Rafael gave me a surprised look.

'So you're saying you want us all to contribute equally to the next album?'

I nodded my head. We'd just finished throwing some ideas around for the next few songs and a coffee break in the vestibule of the studio had turned into a kind of impromptu band meeting.

'Yes, why not? You've all written or co-written some of the songs on previous albums and when it comes to the details, we work collectively. You all know the style, the feel of what we do, inside out. The record company wants more of the same and this album needs energy. It needs a fire in its belly that I'm just not able to achieve on my own; Shed This Skin has proven that. Left to my own devices it produces a very different vibe and it's given me a different appreciation of what happens when we all play together. It might sound strange but the way things have evolved, Rebecca Taylor is more of a band and not just one person, and that band is collectively greater than the sum of its parts. I want you all to have your input. For all our sakes, when we go out on the road with these new songs we've got to smash it. With the tour being critical to how any new songs are received, it's going to have to be all about the live energy.'

Helena put down her coffee.

'You're serious, aren't you? You realise that with less of the songwriting credits your income is going to drop.'

I shook my head.

'Only proportionally. It's not just about me; that's what I'm trying to say. I'll tell you something, I'd rather have a smaller proportion of a bigger success rather than be the queen of nothing, and what we've always had together is a certain undefinable chemistry. That's what we need to capture on this new record, even if it means abandoning or re-recording some of the stuff we've already done. Shed This Skin was an album I needed to get out of my system and I can't thank you all enough for your patience with that, but this next record has to be all about us. I want some of that magic back. Why shouldn't all of you get your share of the credit? Besides, I'm going to be too busy trying to make a success out of the solo album to do all the rest of the songwriting, so even when I'm not around we need to be keeping the studio here at Spensford Hall busy. Steve is primed and ready to go on the production side. He's still on board. What do you think, Alex?'

He'd been very quiet up to now, but then that was nothing unusual. Offstage, without the roar of the crowd in his ears, he could be so self-effacing.

'I've got about half a dozen songs already up my sleeve but I didn't want to push my luck with too many of them. We can give some of them a go and see what you think.'

Daniel gave us all his infectious grin.

'And maybe we can rope in some more touches of the stuff Helena and I listened to on our travels. You know, get a bit of that belly dancing influence in there.'

Helena glanced at him out of the corner of her eye but despite pursing her lips, couldn't help the beginnings of a smile.

'That's settled, then,' I said. 'It's good to have the family back together. It's lonely working on my own; I've missed you.'

We were all in the middle of a group hug when Francesca came in.

'Sorry to interrupt, Rebecca, but Guy's here. I thought you might want to see Poppy off, seeing as she's going to be with her dad for a couple of days.'

'Thanks, Francesca. I'll see you guys in a few minutes.'

I followed Francesca out of the studio and along the ground floor corridor of the house. Guy was already waiting for me in the kitchen.

'I hope you don't mind me coming in. I just thought it would be good to catch up before Poppy comes with me.' He stopped and gave me a frown. 'What happened to your eye?'

Not you as well!

'It's nothing,' I told him, 'just a minor argument with the edge of a door. How are you?' I enquired, doing my best to keep everything calm and civil.

'Oh, you know, fair to middling. No new films on the horizon but they have finally decided to make a third series of Hidden Agenda, so that's okay.'

'And how's Anna?'

He stared at the floor with his hands in his pockets, shuffling one foot.

'I, um... I wouldn't know. She started a new film and now she's seeing one of her co-stars. You were right about her all along.'

'I hate to say I told you so. I could tell what she was like from a mile off. It's just a shame you couldn't.'

He looked up again.

'I don't need you to tell me what an idiot I've been. I really fucked up, didn't I?'

'Yes. Yes, you did.'

I remained impassive but Guy's face cracked into the beginnings of a smile.

'Okay, don't sugar coat it. Don't you hold back on me now.' A thought appeared to cross his mind and he became more serious again. 'You know not a day goes by when I don't regret the way things turned out. We had a good thing going, an amazing thing actually, and I totally blew it. I guess you never really understand what you've got till it's gone.'

Where are you going with this?

'I guess not,' I replied.

He took a step closer.

'Perhaps it's not too late for us. Maybe we could try again for Poppy's sake. Things could be good again for all of us if we could find our way back to that.'

Oh, that's where.

I kept my cool. In fact, my voice remained icily clear, as did my thinking.

'Guy, in case you've forgotten, I threw you out because underneath that charming exterior of yours you're a lying, faithless, money-grabbing, selfish scumbag who sold our relationship and our family life down the river for the sake of an easy screw and what you thought might be a good career move.' He looked completely taken aback, but I wasn't about to weaken. 'I haven't forgotten your general attitude towards people you didn't think were important to your ladder of progress, people you should have had the good sense and decency to treat with more respect, and I'm including Emily and Francesca in that, amongst others. And now, just because Anna has dumped you for the next stepping stone in her own career, you think you can revert back to plan A, waltz back in here and pick up where we left off. Well, you can think again. Hell will freeze over long before I open my arms, my legs, or my life up to you again. My self-respect may have taken a few knocks lately but I haven't abandoned it completely.'

His mouth opened and closed but no words came out at first. Then he flushed with anger.

'I'd have thought you'd have leapt at the chance to regain some respectability. Have you any idea what some people have been saying about you lately? Your reputation's not exactly in glowing good health.'

Oh, so now we see the real Guy Draper!

'So you thought you'd try and wheedle your way back in while I was at a low ebb, is that it? You're so fucking predictable, Guy. You must think I was born yesterday. Well, I've got two words for you, and the second one is 'off'. I suggest you spend some quality time with Poppy instead of wasting it by coming on to me. Maybe she can teach you how to be a better human being.'

Karina came in, holding Poppy's hand as she toddled along beside her. Perhaps it was a good thing I'd managed to keep my voice down, albeit only just. Poppy's face lit up, and letting go of Karina's hand she ran over to Guy. He crouched down to enfold her in his arms.

'By the way,' I told him, 'your daughter said her first proper words a few days ago, so my advice is to be careful what you say from now on unless you want to have it repeated back to you, or worse still, to me.'

He nodded his acquiescence.

On the one hand, I felt like I was being a bit harsh with him. On the other, some part of me knew he deserved it. I could never trust him again, not like before, and after my recent experiences, I had to wonder whether I ever wanted to trust anyone that way again.

Lonely as it might have been, I had my career to focus on. If it meant living a solitary existence then so be it; better that than allowing myself to be used over and over again in different ways. I had my band and I had my family. The next few months would see me locked away in the studio for the most part while we finished recording the next album and then we had several videos to film and a tour to rehearse for. The last thing I needed was any other distraction, and that included relationships. I had to set my emotions to one side and concentrate on rebuilding the future Guy had so nearly stolen away from me.

As it turned out, that was going to be easier said than done. My greatest enemy would turn out to be the one person I could not escape.

CHAPTER SEVENTEEN

'So give me the rundown,' I said. 'What's happening and when?'

We had just finished a soundcheck and rehearsal for the live performance. It was a slightly bigger stage than before, in a new TV studio with a different set. However, Phil Cross remained his usual, animated self.

'Well, as you know, we're devoting a bit more time to the interview with you today than the last time you were on the show, so we're keeping the previous two interviews a bit shorter to allow for it before you play the show out. I still don't like to over-script things but I get the feeling there will be plenty to talk about.'

Yes, I'm sure there will.

'Hopefully. I'll try not to disappoint,' I said.

Phil shot me an incredulous look.

'If it's anything like the last time you were here, I don't think that's likely. It's a different band, though, isn't it? I don't recognise the faces.'

'For the latest album, yes. All the usual suspects will be back with me in time for the tour.' I filled him in on the background and he listened carefully.

'Good. Well, make yourself comfortable in the Green

Room. We've still got a couple of hours before we film the show. It's all done near enough in real time, except for a bit of tidying up in the edits before broadcast. The station won't let the show actually go out live any more, not since…'

'Oh, God! It wasn't what I said last time, was it?' The thought made me cringe. I still couldn't believe I had not just used the F-word but used it in its proper context, live on TV, and only just after the watershed.

'No, not that! That was funny,' he insisted, chuckling at the thought. 'The network almost pulled the plug when Nell Grayling came on here during the last series. She totally froze out the interview before turning abusive. I still think she was on something, although we had no proof. Either way, the woman needs help.'

Come to think of it, I remembered all the furore about her going off the rails. I think I'd been pregnant with Poppy at the time. Now I was beginning to understand what holding on by your fingernails felt like, even if I hadn't exactly taken a shine to Nell on a personal level.

'We've met, well at least sort of, at the UK Music Awards, the night you were hosting. I can't say I know her that well,' I admitted.

'Oh, and while we're on the subject of awkwardness, are there any topics that are off-limits?' he asked. 'If I asked you about Guy it would be your chance to set the record straight. He's taken the opportunity to tell his side of the story but you've said very little publicly.'

He would be keen enough to save face. You want the real truth, do you?

'I'll tell you what I can,' I said. 'I don't want to enter into a mud-slinging match. At the end of the day, we're both still my daughter's parents. What's between us is between us.'

He nodded appreciatively.

'That's fair enough. I am going to ask some fairly searching questions, though. The public won't forgive me if I don't. They've been itching for this interview for a long time.'

Something told me this wasn't going to be just a repeat of the light-hearted teasing that went on the last time we met. But that was what I wanted, wasn't it? The chance to be taken more seriously?

Phil excused himself and went off to find his other guests while I retreated to my dressing room to prepare for the show. My stylist Trudi was waiting for me, already unpacking her stuff. The TV studio had their own makeup and wardrobe people but I always insisted on bringing Trudi regardless. It was certainly nice to have the moral support from a friendly, non-judgemental face.

'Hi, Rebecca, how are you?' she asked, lifting the lid on her makeup kit.

'Oh, you know,' I said noncommittally. Confessional though time spent in the dressing room can often be, I still wasn't about to share my innermost thoughts and feelings, even with Trudi. I could barely face them myself. 'Alright, I suppose. A bit nervous. There's so much riding on making a good impression with the new single.'

She looked surprised at my reticence.

'You'll smash it; you always do.'

'Oh, it's not me; it's the others.'

'What? The band?' She asked, a little shocked.

'No, they're professionals; I've got no worries about them. It's people's reactions I'm concerned about. You'd be surprised how many people are just waiting for me to fail. The bigger you get, the more they want to shoot you down, and too many people already think I'm just a stupid tart who only sings songs about shagging. On one level, that's all they want me to be; I suppose it's what they've become used to. On another, they want to find excuses to condemn me for it. I can't win.'

She tapped the back of the chair.

'Come and sit down. There's not much I can do about the other stuff but if you're going out to face the firing squad, at least I can make sure you look good doing it.'

I plonked myself down in front of the ubiquitous mirror ringed with lights which inhabits every dressing room everywhere while Trudi worked her magic. She managed to make me look more attractive than I felt. That fucker Holbrook had really screwed over my inner confidence but I hoped the performer in me would somehow take control. In my present state of mind, Sadie seemed to be around less and less, so I could hardly rely on her presence to buoy me up.

Most female pop stars, and already younger ones than me, had taken to wearing increasingly skimpy outfits as they vied with each other for public attention, but I'd deliberately gone for an ensemble that covered me up. The sex siren image wouldn't have been right for the song and besides, whether I sold any records or not, I needed to show a different Rebecca Taylor to the one everybody thought they knew. The trouser suit and top we had picked out for me with its applique flowers that wound their way down the sides would be smart and sleek, just the kind of 'together' image I needed. I wished I felt as together underneath the painted surface. Maybe a drink beforehand would shake off the nerves and loosen me up. If it was anything like last time, they kept a well-stocked bar in the Green Room.

To my disappointment, it turned out the bar had been dispensed with in the wake of Nell's disastrous appearance on the show. It only stocked soft drinks, tea, and coffee these days so that was that idea out of the window. Without my own band for company, I sat and waited, fidgeting, until the other guests came in. They were typical of the usual mix of actors, comics, and sports celebrities: no one I knew especially well, although I had once briefly met Lionel Macej through my brother's footballing connections. He'd become quite the darling of the talk shows since winning Player of the Year.

The other guest, Sandra Mulligan, had made quite a name for herself on the comedy circuit. Her particular brand of homely filth usually made me laugh whenever she appeared on the telly. She managed to come out with the most risqué humour but did it with a ditzy girlishness no one could take offence at, despite saying things that were far more sexually graphic than anything I'd ever dare come out with in public. A different set of rules and expectations applied since I was treated as a sex symbol and she had become almost the opposite of one. In a way, I envied her. Like many comics, though, she wasn't the same barrel of laughs behind the scenes. She paced, self-absorbed, looking a little nervous and agitated before she went on. Like all of us, she'd learned to turn it on for the cameras when the occasion demanded. I watched her via the large screen on the wall of the Green Room. As soon as she stepped out in front of the audience, the Sandra everybody knew appeared and the show got off to a great start.

Lionel was up next. Sport never had interested me much, but he had more to say for himself than most footballers. Successful as he was on the pitch, my brother Rob would have been useless as a chat show guest. Getting anything other than a few sentences out of him had always been a challenge. I could understand why Lionel had become a talk show favourite, despite hardly speaking a word of English when he first transferred to a British club. He'd come a long way.

Then it came to my turn. Having been miked up in readiness, I waited out of sight for my cue while Phil introduced me.

'Ladies and gentlemen, I'd like you to welcome our third and final guest of the evening, a young lady who has so far sold in excess of forty million records, including over eleven million albums, and reached number one in the singles charts of forty-three countries. For the last two years since she took time out to have her daughter, she's barely been out of the news but rarely in the public eye. Well, she's back, with a new album and a whole new sound so everybody please put your hands together for the beautiful, the talented, Rebecca Taylor.'

I stepped out in front of the studio audience accompanied by Bliss, one of the singles from A Suitcase of Diamonds and still a good song despite my no longer sharing its relentlessly positive sentiment. I'd been feeling all loved-up when I wrote it, and look how that turned out! Phil kissed me on the cheek before I took my place on the sofa beside his desk.

The applause died gradually away.

'I must say what a pleasure it is to have you back on

the show, and congratulations on the new album. You've obviously been busy behind the scenes.'

I settled into the upholstery and leaned forward with my legs crossed and my hands resting on top of my knees.

'Thank you, Phil. Yes, I have. I think it's safe to say there hasn't been a dull moment,' I replied with the beginnings of a chuckle.

'This new album is quite a departure from your earlier records, though. What brought that about?' Phil wasn't wasting any time getting to the meat of the interview.

'Firstly, don't get me wrong; I'm very proud of the three albums I've done prior to this one. They've obviously been very successful and they captured where I was coming from at the time, but I felt like I needed to explore different things musically, to rediscover who Rebecca Taylor is and what she is capable of. It was something of a personal and musical journey. I wanted to make music that moves people, something they could experience in the same, all-encompassing way I do.'

'It sounds like the making of this album has been a very personal experience.'

'Definitely. For me, the difference between good music and great music is that it can be such a completely immersive experience rather than just an enjoyable one. When you get it really right, there's literally no barrier, no separation between the music and the listener. There are artists out there who gave me goosebumps the first time I heard them and still do. You don't so much listen to their records as absorb them into the very fabric of your being, and it's always felt like a privilege to be able to experience them whenever that happens. It makes you feel so alive, so connected. If anyone out there has never been so overwhelmed they've been moved to tears by the intensity of what they're being exposed to then they've not listened to the right stuff yet. I wouldn't be so arrogant as to put myself up there with the greats but that's the kind of effect I wanted to have on people. It was something to aim for. Besides, there's no point repeating myself, just trying to imitate what's gone before. Life moves on. I've moved on. I guess that's the difference between being an artist and being an entertainer.'

'How do you mean?' Phil looked genuinely baffled, as if it had never occurred to him they weren't the same thing.

'An entertainer gives an audience what they think the audience wants and for many, that's enough, but an artist makes it their mission to take people somewhere they never expected to go. An artist leads, whereas an entertainer merely follows. That doesn't mean I don't set out to be entertaining but I always intended to be an artist, not just an entertainer.

'You started quite young making music, didn't you?'

'Oh yeah! Music has been my life since I could walk and talk. People forget I was only eighteen when Come Inside came out. In my own way, I was still quite naive back then, but life in the music industry soon knocks that out of you. I'm still only twenty-four but there are times when I feel a lot older. I had to do a lot of growing up very quickly and although I still love those records, I don't want to stand still creatively. It would be too easy to keep repeating a formula, which to be honest is what record companies and marketing people would have me do, but I'm not in this for the money; I'm in it for the music. I always have been.'

Phil appeared to seize the opportunity to dig deeper.

'I take it you're not always the music industry's biggest fan. You have, after all, been quite outspoken at times.'

He sat back in his chair as if inviting me to carry on speaking, or was he handing me enough rope to hang myself? I wasn't entirely sure, but I was too in the flow of my thoughts to stop, regardless.

'You could say that. It's always been pretty cutthroat, but at some point in the past, the music business transformed into the music industry. That's when it lost it's soul because when corporate interests took over and when respect for genuinely creative people got lost, their influence went with it. These days it's driven from the top down and not from the bottom up, much to the detriment of creativity. I hope one day music gets it's soul back. Until then, people like me just have to keep chipping away at it until eventually the edifice crumbles and people start to appreciate music at the grassroots level again. It's still out there if you look hard enough, but that's the point; people need to seek it out rather than sitting around passively while being told what to like.'

I could hear a little intake of breath from parts of the audience. Maybe some of them had taken my words personally. It wasn't intended that way.

'Going back to what you said earlier,' Phil continued, 'and speaking of moving on, quite a lot has changed in your life since the last time you were here. How much do you think that impacts the music you make?'

'Oh, loads. Motherhood can't help but change you. Everything seems so much more multi-dimensional. I feel the world more deeply, both its pain and its joy because I've started to experience things differently through my daughter's eyes. Everything has consequences, and not just things directly involving me but things around me. A friend of mine was being stalked by an ex-boyfriend and I became embroiled in all the drama around that. My mother's been ill too. She's been undergoing treatment for breast cancer for the last few months and thankfully she seems to have turned a corner, but it's not been easy on any of us. I've had to do a lot of growing up and a lot of toughening up. It's been a difficult time.'

Phil looked quite surprised at my revelations. Obviously, none of this had appeared in his researcher's notes. If he wanted to keep his interviews real, he had just succeeded. For a moment he appeared to be rethinking what he was going to say next.

'I'm... I'm sorry to hear about your mother. As far as I'm aware, that's something that hasn't been public knowledge. Am I right?'

'Yes. It's family, and I try to keep their business out of the public eye. I didn't want to say anything until we were out of the woods but fingers crossed, we're just waiting for the all-clear.'

'And I imagine when you talk about it being a difficult year, you were also referring to your much publicised split with Guy Draper.'

At least Phil had warned me that would come up. Thankfully, I was ready for it.

'Amongst other things. We may not be together any more, but we're still Poppy's parents. I wouldn't want her to lose out on having a good relationship with her dad, and Guy dotes on her.'

'Since the split, there have been a lot of rumours about what happened and about your private life. Is there anything you'd have to say about those?'

I resisted the urge to roll my eyes.

Here goes nothing.

'We broke up because Guy found somebody else. It's as simple as that. The fact that they're no longer together is neither here nor there. From my point of view, we were either going to have an honest relationship as equals or not at all. I guess he wasn't reading from the same script. As far as my private life goes, depending on which gossip column you happen to be reading at the time I'm apparently either a party animal or a recluse. It would be nice if they made up their minds so I knew who I was supposed to be.'

I couldn't resist a self-satisfied little smile while Phil appeared to be somewhat wrongfooted. My words might have sounded sarcastic, but sometimes attack is the best form of defence.

'I'm afraid the reality isn't as newsworthy as either of those things,' I continued while Phil struggled to find his next words. 'It never is. I've devoted myself to making music and being a mother, and that doesn't make for particularly interesting headlines. There have always been lots of stories about my private life so I wouldn't believe everything you hear.'

Phil appeared to have found his thread again.

'You do appear to be working hard to play down your earlier image, though.'

'I've just evolved, that's all. Why can't a woman be professional, and creative, and a good mother, as well as sensual, seductive and uninhibited? These things are not mutually exclusive. The problem with making a sex object out of somebody is it doesn't reflect the whole person; it's just a one-dimensional snapshot.'

'This sounds like Rebecca Taylor the feminist speaking.'

I know he didn't mean it negatively, but Phil's line of questioning was starting to irritate me. It shouldn't but it did. It was as if he'd suddenly come to represent everything I was railing against.

'No, it's just Rebecca Taylor the human being speaking. I've always thought people are more complicated creatures than that. You can't define anyone by their sexuality alone. In fact, if you're looking to judge someone's true worth, it probably ranks alongside how much money they make as one of the least useful measures.'

'So are you denying what's been said about you?'

'I'm afraid you're going to have to be a bit more specific. Which of the many rumours about my personal life that have circulated over the last few years are you referring to?' I could feel myself bristling but I tried to maintain my smile. This portion of the interview was beginning to feel like raking nails down a chalkboard.

Phil hesitated for a moment.

'It's been rumoured that you've frequented some rather colourful clubs, for instance, and that your personal life is somewhat less than conventional.'

Shit! He's going to try and pin me down on this.

I was going to have to fight fire with fire. Outright denial would achieve nothing. Perhaps it was better to take the wind out of the critics' sails.

'You mean fetish clubs and the like? So what? There's

no law against it. It's the age-old debate about whether life imitates art or art imitates life. Every artist needs to do their research. I'll be expected to keep up the sexy image and themes for the next Rebecca Taylor album which we've already started recording and which we want to complete before I go on tour early next year. You can't make an omelette without breaking eggs. That was what was so nice about the new album, because I had the freedom to do something completely out of the box, so people will see other sides to my music, but fans of the earlier albums needn't worry; there'll be plenty more of what they already enjoy on the next one.'

Hopefully, that would be enough to placate them.

'So I guess that brings us quite neatly back round to your new album...'

Thank fuck we didn't have to go any deeper. Neatly sidestepped, Rebecca!

He held up a copy in the direction of the camera.

'...which is titled Shed This Skin and credits you as Rebecca, not as Rebecca Taylor, which makes more sense now in the light of what you've been saying. It's out now and I believe you're going to be playing your new single from it for us tonight, completely live.'

I confirmed that I was.

'A little birdy once told me that you hate miming to music,' he continued. 'I know you usually insist on playing live and will be tonight.'

'It's true. Even in TV studios, I'd much rather play fully live than simply sing or mime over a backing track. It happens more than most people realise, but an audience deserves a real performance, not just a bunch of dance moves. It's more raw, more real, and that's the artist I've always wanted to be. I won't use autotune either; it stifles all the nuances of a vocal performance. Keeping pitch has never been an issue for me anyway, as long as I can hear what I'm doing properly. There are some tracks on previous albums where I only sing, which frees me up to concentrate on the vocals anyway, but on this album I played as many of the instruments as possible too. I didn't learn to play half a dozen instruments only to stand up in front of an audience and pretend; it doesn't feel honest. Making videos is different. Everybody knows it's not a live performance; it's a visual enhancement of the record.'

'So what's the new single?'

At least we were now back on more conventional ground.

'It's called Black Roses. It's a kind of bittersweet song about love and loss. Although it's upbeat and trying to be cheerful, it's also tinged with sadness. I think songs like that are much more powerful than just ones about how wonderful love is or how miserable we are when things go wrong. Life is full of mixed emotions. It's messy. It can be beautiful and it can be painful too. That's what I wanted to capture.'

'Having heard it earlier on, the lyrics are, as always, very vivid.'

'Thank you. That's just how they come out. I've always had a very visual imagination. For me, imagination and reality often blend into one. In my head, I see music in colours too.'

Phil looked a bit confused so I explained myself.

'It might sound strange but that's just how my head works. It's something I've always naturally done.

Apparently, it happens when auditory and visual responses cross over in the brain. At first, I naturally thought everybody must be like me and to be honest, it came as a bit of a surprise to me when I first discovered other people don't all hear music the same way. I was still quite young at the time so I then thought I must be the only one it happens to, but I discovered much later on it's a known thing and it's called chromesthesia. Understandably, it's more common amongst musicians than it is with the rest of the population.'

Phil turned to face the audience for a moment with a wide-eyed expression.

'And that's what I love about this job; you learn something new and interesting every day. Well, Rebecca, on behalf of everybody here I'd like to thank you for coming back on the show. I think we've all seen new sides to you we only usually get glimpses of, so it's been a revealing talk.' He stood up and gestured towards the performance area. 'So if you'd like to take your place over on the stage, we're looking forward to hearing the new single.'

I sauntered over to join the other musicians while Phil completed his introductions to camera.

'So, ladies and gents, without further ado and to play us out for tonight's show, we have the still equally lovely but rather different Rebecca with her brilliant new single, Black Roses.'

I popped the monitor earpiece into place while the band readied themselves. An assistant handed me my acoustic guitar and I steadied my hands, resting a plectrum between my thumb and forefinger. This was it. This was the moment: make or break.

The click track in my ear counted us in and we struck up the opening chords, settling into the song's four-on-the-floor, upbeat groove. The main guitar part, strummed on the acoustic, was mine to play while the two other guitarists behind me would add further rhythmic accents and clean-sounding lead parts later on in the song. For now, it was basically, me, a guitar, and the drums: simple and direct, nothing fancy.

You promised me the moon and stars
Said it would last forever
Gave you my heart and here we are
An eternity of never

We watched the flowers bloom and grow
Raised our faces to the sunlight
The clouds rolled in but even so
I thought that we'd be alright

I looked out at the sea of impassive faces in front of me. Apart from the odd murmur of surprise, the audience hadn't reacted as openly as I had expected at the start of the interview and not much had changed yet. Neither the song nor the interview appeared to have been what they were expecting. I dug in for the final part of the verse. Maybe they would get into it more as the song went on. I could only hope.

As long as I could hold your hand
We could walk through the garden together
But dreams we made were built on sand
And I know...all that's left is black roses

As well as one or two feet tapping, the occasional head was beginning to nod in time with the beat. Perhaps there was hope yet.

I wish I could go back in time
To the moment that I met you
And whisper warnings in my ear
Why did I trust you?

There was a time that winning smile
Played tunes upon my heart
But now it seems that all the while
You only played your part

Sometimes the world is not how we would want it to be
Sometimes the surface is all that we can see
Now how my heart it breaks for you and me
And I know…all that's left is black roses

By the time we got to the instrumental break, I could see smiles beginning to break out amongst the audience. Hands were already tapping against thighs. Others were just listening, paying more attention to the lyrics and the melody. I hadn't expected a rapturous reception, so at least the response was positive. Encouraged, I pressed on as more of the backing instruments joined in.

The seeds we sowed in better times
They fell on stony ground
Where once a garden should have been
There is no green around

At the end of the song, the audience broke out into applause. Some of them looked genuinely touched by what they had just been listening to.

'Well, ladies and gentlemen, that just about wraps up tonight's show. I'd like to thank my guests, Sandra Mulligan, Lionel Macej, and of course the lovely and always surprising Rebecca Taylor. We'll be back next week with more fabulous guests but in the meantime, I wish you all goodnight.'

The credits rolled before the audience departed, leaving the crew to pack up our equipment. I thanked the band before returning to my dressing room and flopping down in the chair.

'How do you think it went?' I asked Trudi. 'Go on, you can be honest with me.'

She hesitated, choosing her words.

'It's a really nice song.' She pinched her face in slightly. 'Do I think it's going to be as big a hit as Devil on my Shoulder? No, but then even the biggest artists only get one or two songs that successful in an entire career. If it's more the kind of music you want to make, then fair enough. I suppose it'll appeal to a more mature audience but it will take time to win them over. Sorry if you think I'm overstepping.'

I shook my head.

'No. I did ask.'

To be honest, I trusted her candid opinions. I guessed she was right too. I don't know what I'd been hoping for from the show. After my first flush of success, everything had seemed so easy. I'd hardly stopped to think about what I was doing. Maybe that was the secret: not thinking too much. I'd been young and reckless enough not to consider failure an option, leaving all the tactics to Mitchell. Now I found myself overthinking everything and it felt like wading through treacle. At least after this interview, I stood a better chance of being seen as something more than just a sex object. Sexy was the last thing I felt.

Derek was ready and waiting at the back entrance of the studio when I left.

'Home then, miss?' he asked, holding the door open for me.

I wasn't ready for that yet. I needed that drink I'd promised myself earlier, something to switch off the nagging voices of doubt that plagued my head.

'Actually, Derek, I wouldn't mind finding a quiet bar somewhere. I could do with the chance to wind down a bit and there's no rush to get home, is there?'

CHAPTER EIGHTEEN

Between the phone and the front door, things didn't stop all morning, and given the makings of a hangover I'd started the day with, my day wasn't improving either. Poppy began the day in a grizzly mood too and was still craving my attention when the phone rang for the first time. I handed her over to Karina.

'She wants her Mummy,' Karina insisted.

'Well her Mummy has things to do. Just deal with it, will you!'

Karina gave me an injured look but I just wasn't in the right space for either Poppy's neediness or Karina's remonstrations. She said nothing else but nodded her head and took Poppy out of the room while I answered the call.

'Rebecca.'

'Hi, Mitchell, what gives? I take it you've seen the interview.'

'I have.'

'And?'

'I've also seen the aftermath in the press and online. Did you really have to go and confirm the rumours about some of the places you've frequented? Do you have any idea of the feeding frenzy you've started?'

Really? Out of all the things I said in the interview that was the one thing everybody latched onto?

It seemed I couldn't win.

'I suppose you're going to enlighten me,' I said, resigned to another of Mitchell's lectures. 'I thought I dealt with it quite well, putting it all down to research.'

'And if you think they swallowed that explanation, think again.' Mitchell sighed. 'At least if anything does come out as confirmed, they can't say you lied to cover your tracks. It's just…'

'It's just what?'

'I just wish you didn't sail so close to the wind all the time. You might thrive on pushing things to the limit, but you're shredding my nerves here. I try to navigate a path through treacherous waters and you insist on aiming for the rocks.'

I sat down on a kitchen stool, rubbing the heel of one hand against my forehead. I wished this fucking headache would go away.

'What was I supposed to do? Act all whiter than white? It wouldn't ring true. I gave them just enough of the truth to keep them off my back. Anyway, more importantly, what do they make of the song?'

I could sense him settling into his chair on the other end of the line. I had a feeling this was going to be one of his long haul sermons.

'It went down well enough, but I don't think it's setting the world on fire. It's not what people expect from you so they don't know how to react. Something tells me this album's going to be a slow burn so you'd better press on with the next round of recordings. We can't afford for your existing fans to drift away.'

I confirmed that we were already well underway; conveniently omitting to mention that for much of it we were going back to the drawing board but explaining how the intention was to give the album more of the feel and energy of a live performance. We needed material that was going to blow an audience out of the water on tour, and it had to be right. If it wasn't, the game would be over. In the rock world, a longer career with ups and downs was to be expected, but in the more transient pop world, there was no coming back from a commercial flop. As far as I was concerned, though, I didn't quite fit into either camp.

It was definitely true that the younger the audience, the shorter their attention span and the quicker you can become yesterday's news. I was at that awkward phase in my career of being neither new enough to be the latest thing nor established enough to be sure that no matter what I did, there would always be a fan base loyal enough to fall back on.

I hadn't long been off the phone from Mitchell and was looking through the kitchen cupboard for some paracetamol to help with my headache when Jeff arrived and let himself in.

'Oh!' I said, looking around at him. 'I didn't know you were planning to come over.'

'I wasn't,' Jeff's serious expression didn't drop, 'but after your TV interview I thought it might be important to clear a few things up before you make any more public announcements.'

'Okay.' His opening gambit didn't sound positive; our uneasy truce was beginning to feel a little shaky already.

Jeff indicated towards one of the kitchen stools. I sat down and he parked himself next to me, placing his hand over mine.

'Look, I know your Mum's been keen to play the whole thing down with her cancer treatment but the truth is it's too early to start drawing any conclusions about whether she's in the clear yet, and definitely too early to say so publicly. I wish you'd talked to me first.'

'But I thought…'

'Yes, I know you thought it was all behind us, and it still might be, but it also might not. Avril's always ready to look on the sunny side and I don't want to take that away from her; it's what's kept her going through all the treatment. Yes, she's feeling better, and yes, her hair's beginning to grow back, but we can't say for sure whether it's totally behind her yet. I need you to promise me you're not going to say anything else in public; it just adds pressure to an already delicate situation, and your mum doesn't need that.'

'But she said…'

'Yes, I know what she said. She's made a lifetime habit of playing things down and being strong for everybody else's sake. I don't think she's ever shared the full details of what happened with your father either, and from what I can make out, probably for good reason. Just promise me you'll keep any further information about what's happening with your mum inside the family. I know the public wants to know all about you and you need to keep on feeding the publicity beast. Believe me, I know what that does to people; I've spent long enough around it, but your mother doesn't need the ups and downs of her health spread all over the media.'

I promised him I'd keep anything further out of the public domain. Jeff nodded and let out a long breath. He looked tired and drawn, a long way from the force of boundless energy and drive I'd first encountered in my early teens. Mum's illness had obviously taken its toll on him too.

'While you're here, why don't you go through and spend some time with Poppy?' I suggested. 'You know how she loves her granddad.'

A sucker for the men in her life, just like I've been.

Jeff seemed to agree some time with Poppy was a good idea. I'd just made him a cup of tea when my phone rang again. I could see at a glance it was Linda on the line. I really didn't want to face Linda's razor-sharp insights; she knew me too well, but I could hardly ignore the call. I sent Jeff through with his tea and picked up.

'Hey, sweetie!' Linda sounded unnaturally cheerful. 'How's it going?'

'Oh, you know. It's going,' I said noncommittally.

'I've been missing you. You haven't been around much lately.'

'It's just work. There's been a lot going on.'

Linda hesitated for a moment.

'Are you sure that's all it is?'

'Of course!' I wasn't certain how convincing it sounded.

'You aren't returning my messages. I wanted to make sure you're alright.'

'As alright as someone who's been drugged and attacked by a fucking slimeball can be.'

'In other words, no. I knew it. Sweetie, talk to me.'

'I don't... I don't want to talk about it. I just want to

put it all behind me and get on with putting my life back together. Look, you've chosen your path in life, and that's all very well. I've chosen mine, too, and it's just not compatible with yours. You got me into the lifestyle and involved me in the business. It's introduced me to so many things I'm grateful for, but if it hadn't been for all that, I'd never have met that fucking creep and all the other pervs in the club who used me as a pawn in their little power games.'

'Listen, about that…'

'And then you wonder why I'm keeping my distance. I've got pressure coming from every angle, a reputation that's shot to shit, a career to try and pull back from the edge, and you wonder why you're not seeing me.'

'I did try to warn you about certain individuals in the club but you wouldn't listen. You have to go in with your eyes open.'

'Well, they've been opened now. Frankly, that's the least of my problems. I'm not pulling my money out unless you'd rather I did that, but I can't be involved with that world any more. I'm sick of it. I'm sick of feeling empty and used, and caught up in the middle of it all.' By now the tears were flowing down my face: hot tears of anger and frustration, along with a dozen other pent up thoughts and emotions that had finally bubbled up to the surface. 'I just… I just wanted to be loved, loved for who I am and not desired for what some people think I am. Is that so wrong?'

'But you are loved. There are people around you who love you for exactly who you are. I just think you're losing sight of that. You've got friends.'

'Your kind of friends? The ones you casually fuck, is

that it?'

'It's not about sex. You've got family. You've got friends that care. Janine's worried about you and I agree with her whether her concerns came from the cards or not.'

I had an absentee father, a mother who might take a turn for the worse at any moment, and a child I never planned for or expected whose father I could no longer stand the sight of. Most of my friends were either friends with benefits or a handful of old school comrades who could still barely contain their jealousy over my current life. In my own way, I envied theirs. At least they didn't live their whole lives under a microscope. My frustration boiled over, spilling out into the conversation and injecting itself down the phone line like a shot of venom.

'So, what, now you're saying sex is not the answer? You. You're actually saying that: the woman who avoids relationships because they're too complicated, the woman who wouldn't know what emotional commitment was if it hit her over the head, the woman who's never been in love, whose every relationship has its foundation in sexuality. You.'

Linda remained silent on the other end of the line, reeling.

'I've been in love,' she said eventually in a quiet, even voice, 'more than once if you must know, but I knew it was never meant to be. Life isn't always fair.'

'Who? You never said.'

'No I didn't, did I,' she sniffed, the bitter irony in her voice now unmistakeable.

'And that's another thing. I'm sick of all your fucking secrets and your casual brush-offs and your cryptic shit. It does my head in. I don't need all that right now; there's enough to deal with already. I didn't want to say this but I think I just need my own space for a while to get on with my job and set my head straight.'

'If you're sure that's the way forward. Personally, I think you're going about this the wrong way. You've always tended to shut yourself off and that's not healthy.'

'Well, I am sure. I just need some time away from everything to get my shit straightened out and my career back on track.'

'Rebecca, I…'

Suddenly, I'd had enough of this conversation.

'I'll call you.'

I pressed the screen to end the call with quivering hands. I'd just cut off the one person who understood me more than anyone else in the world but I couldn't deal with her fucked-up world anymore. Enough was enough. She knew I wasn't going to call her back, and I knew it too, but at that moment it felt like the only way.

CHAPTER NINETEEN

We made the rest of the album remarkably quickly. I guess nothing focuses people like a deadline. For me, it was a welcome release, something to pour myself into which provided an escape from having to deal with all the other things going on in my head. If it meant shutting out the world and living like a hermit, then so be it.

Besides, if I wanted to be judged differently, then perhaps it was better to be seen as remote rather than overly available. If all people wanted me to be was a sex object and yet they persisted in condemning me for it, I had a steep climb ahead of me. When all else failed, I still had my music. It remained my one constant.

I kept myself to my band and its immediate circle. I no longer missed sex anyway; for one reason or another, all the joy had been sucked right out of it. It had just become something empty, passionless, a mechanical act that, like a drug, provided only a fleeting distraction from the emptiness inside. Just like a recovering junkie, I wanted to prove to myself that I didn't need it. I wasn't particularly conscious of it at the time, but even Sadie had faded into the distance. Her presence or lack of it seemed less and less important to me with every passing day. If she had abandoned me too, I was just going to have to do this on my own.

Despite receiving messages from Linda every so often, I didn't answer them. I couldn't bring myself to. Eventually, they became less and less frequent. For pretty much the same reasons, I kept my distance from Janine and maintained only occasional contact with Jayne and Sophie.

Sophie's court case had come up and thankfully it looked like Brett would be spending some time behind bars, although, in all honesty, for too short a stretch. As I suspected he would, he presented himself as a model citizen and with time off for good behaviour he probably wouldn't serve much of a sentence.

At least there had been enough solid evidence to secure a conviction; Three Rs Security had made sure of that. By bringing them in I had more than done my part to help. With a prison record to his name now, there was no way he would be going back to work as a detective either. Given my commitments, I told myself I was simply too busy to get involved any further.

Focus, Rebecca, that's the key.

Occasionally the band came out of hiding, though. We broke the ice in advance of the upcoming tour with a secret gig to an invited audience of fans and carefully selected press. It gave us a chance to try out new material for the first time on a limited number of people, iron out any issues we hadn't nailed in rehearsal, and also to blow the cobwebs off of songs we hadn't played in front of an audience for some time. Knowing the notes is one thing; performing them is always another. It's often said one gig is worth ten rehearsals and on this occasion, it was certainly true. We all came away with some tweaks we wanted to make plus a few ideas to improve the staging. Everything came out sharper as a result. On the whole, it generated a positive buzz of expectation for the new record too.

We worked long days to complete the recording sessions. By the time I emerged from the studio at the end of the day, Francesca had usually long since gone home and Karina had been left to amuse Poppy by herself. I missed my time with my daughter, but there was a job to do and that was that.

Francesca usually had food prepared ready, but to be honest, I didn't feel much like it by the time I finished up in the studio. I needed to be careful about my weight anyway. The band's collective liking for pizza coupled with eating at odd hours wasn't doing me any good so I tended to abstain. They would often go out to eat at the end of the day's recording but I remained at home.

Once Steve and the band left the studio, I was more in the mood for a shower followed by some gin and tonic or a bottle of wine anyway. After a few hours winding down, I would eventually drag myself off to bed only to get up and do it all again the next day. The sessions were intense but we worked fast, perhaps not quite as fast as when we recorded my first album but it was different back then; we'd been gigging the songs for months. This time, given the fact that we had the luxury of our own studio, we were creating as we went. It was a much more organic band vibe, but that was what we wanted. Capturing a spark of creativity is rarely something that happens by accident. It takes long hours and hard work to make complex arrangements sound spontaneous;

that's the illusion of making records.

It must have been around the end of the recording sessions and just before we went straight into mixing everything that I had to let Marie, my personal trainer, go. Even though staying in shape to cope with the rigours of the upcoming tour was a necessity, I was becoming less and less into my sessions with her and I certainly wasn't about to take her sanctimonious crap about not looking after myself.

Who the hell does she think she is? My mother? A dietician? An AA counsellor?

When, how, and what I chose to eat and drink was frankly no concern of hers. From now on, I told myself, I could take care of my own exercise routine. I didn't need her bending my ear. I got enough shit out there in the wider world without having to put up with it in my own home.

Once the album was finished we went straight on to the preparations and rehearsals for the tour, including how we were going to light everything and stage the songs for all the different sizes of venue we were going to encounter, from some pretty modest two-thousand-seater venues early on to the larger arena gigs which were mostly scheduled for later in the tour. Knowing we weren't going to be around for long, we also crammed in the shooting of footage for the videos that had been scheduled to accompany the two proposed singles. There was no time to dwell, which from my point of view was a blessing; it saved me from myself.

Ticket sales had been slow, though. Unless they picked up, we would be lucky to do much more than cover the cost of taking a show across so much of the globe, but a commitment was a commitment and we had to honour it. If we pulled out of a tour for a second time, the promoters were going to crucify us; we'd be lucky to ever gig again, so, on we ploughed. I barely had time to look at how Black Roses had been doing in the charts. Perhaps I didn't want to know; Mitchell had gone rather quiet about it and the press wasn't exactly bashing the door down for interviews. He did say the album was selling steadily, though, so it wasn't all bad news.

Our bigger concern was getting everything ready for the road. By January, once we'd stopped for a Christmas break, there was little time to think about anything else. Most of our previous road crew had been reassembled, although there were some new faces to replace those who had moved on to other commitments. In a team of over forty people, some were always coming and going anyway and never more so than in between tours. At least we still had the same road manager, Clive Dunsmore, who had been busy coordinating transport, hotels, and other logistics for months, dovetailing his work with Mitchell, who still kept a tight grip on the business and the creative side.

Before the tour got underway in the spring, I took a couple of days out to spend time with Poppy, who by now was into everything and accumulating new words by the day. Karina definitely had her work cut out.

The plan was to ease ourselves in gently with a series of smaller UK dates first. Even then I had no idea how bad the pain of being away from Poppy for weeks at a time was going to be, but the tour could wait no longer; I had a career that would require all of my time, energy, and focus to secure all our futures. What choice was there?

The album wasn't out yet, and wouldn't be for at least another couple of months, so at least for the start of the tour, we would be breaking new ground with some unfamiliar songs as well as plenty of the ones everybody knew. As things progressed, we could introduce more of the new material into the set to showcase the new album. But we had to start somewhere, and where we did start was Birmingham. It wasn't the NEC, we would be back there as part of our final UK dates right at the end of the tour, but one of the smaller, more intimate theatre venues. Even so, it was a different world from some of the fleapit clubs we played on our way up and actually held almost enough people to justify the scale of the show.

When we arrived late morning, the road crew were already busy wheeling flight cases in through the loading bay and the chief lighting engineer stood at the front of the stage, scratching his head and trying to work out how to adapt our rig to a stage half the size of the ones we'd been used to playing by the end of our previous tour.

Rafael looked up towards the overhead lighting gantries, where several people were hard at work, muttering under his breath in Spanish. He appeared to be saying something along the lines of 'there's no way you'd get me up there'. Even with harnesses, it wasn't a job I fancied either.

'Morning, Jase!' I called as we approached. I had to raise my voice to be heard over the rumble of flight cases being wheeled around somewhere backstage and the shouts from the lighting riggers who were in the middle of hoisting the last gantry into position high above the front of the stage. Somewhere out of sight, something metallic clattered loudly to the floor.

Jason moved the handheld radio he'd been speaking into away from his mouth and looked around.

'Oh, hi! You're early.' He checked his watch. 'I didn't think you guys would be here for another two hours at least. We're nowhere near ready for a soundcheck yet.'

I assured him we hadn't expected to be; we just didn't want to be late.

'Well, you'd better settle in. We've got a few start-of-tour gremlins to deal with and I'm not sure if the sound guys are going to have it much better. I'd go and get some lunch if I were you.'

The rest of the band seemed to feel much as I did, just not perhaps *quite* as nervous. Dan was, as always, a ball of pent-up energy, although the ever level-headed Helena had learned how to keep him in check. I assumed the two of them had arrived at their own ways of dealing with excess nerves and would probably disappear back to the hotel once the soundcheck was complete. They appeared to still be as loved-up as they had been when they got back from their travels.

Alex always became quiet and contemplative before gigs. Like all of us, he had developed his rituals, his own ways of coping with the ups and downs of life on the road. The only one of us who appeared completely unfazed by the occasion was Rafael. The backing singers and brass section would not be joining us until mid-afternoon so I had no idea how they were feeling. Being additional hired hands, they weren't part of the creative hub of the band, so I don't think they had as much invested in it as we did. The five of us had always stood firm in the face of everything we'd faced so far. We would do again.

'Lunch?' asked Rafael. 'We might as well. I don't think we'll get much chance to eat later on if the setup runs behind schedule and it's never good to eat just before a gig. Far better to go on stage a little bit lean and hungry.'

Daniel nodded his head and pulled down the corners of his mouth.

'Sounds sensible. We might still need to keep our strength up.' Helena punched him on the arm. He grinned at her.

To be honest, I didn't drum up much enthusiasm for eating; my stomach already felt a bit queasy. I, more than anyone else, couldn't help being painfully aware of how much there was riding on this. For the sake of unity, though, I went with them although I didn't eat much; I just couldn't force it down. Until after the gig, I would drink nothing but water either; fizzy drinks and caffeine aren't much good for the voice.

By the time we returned to the venue, all the lights had been set up and the last of the sound equipment was being patched in. Curved arrays of speakers had already been hoisted into the air on either side of the stage and various banks of coloured lights were powering up and down to test they were all working correctly. Even though the house lights were still up, the stage was being bathed in a succession of colours as Jason and his crew put the lighting console through its paces. Corey the chief sound engineer, who we'd been lucky to keep on board ever since our first major tour, appeared from behind the mixing desk at the back of the auditorium and sauntered down the aisle between the seats to join us.

'Good timing. We ran behind on the lighting but we've

just about caught up with the rest of it. Nobody's been killed by falling lights yet so we're all good.' He chuckled briefly at his own joke then cleared his throat and pulled a straight face again when he could see I wasn't laughing. 'You should be able to soundcheck in about twenty minutes.'

I thanked him and went backstage to seek out Davey my guitar tech, who I found in his little cubby hole backstage, restringing the white SG I used a lot for live work. It had a gritty, edgier sound than most of the guitars I used in the studio, which suited playing live. It also weighed in a lot lighter than some of my other guitars so it didn't slow me down on stage. I wanted to remind Davey that my favourite Gibson Les Paul would not be used for most of the live gigs. Instead, I hoped she would remain on the tour bus for me to use when I had some downtime. There were about a dozen other guitars available for me to use on stage, and despite being stored and transported in toughened flight cases, accidents sometimes happened when setting up and packing down; that was just the rough and tumble of life on the road. I wanted to keep my Les Paul with me as much as possible: a little piece of home.

We ran through three or so numbers to make sure everything was working and that we had the balance right. There's always an element of guesswork as an empty auditorium sounds completely different to a full one, but Corey and his team knew exactly what they were doing and we had long since learned to trust their judgement.

Corey gave us the all-clear and we retreated backstage while the support act set up their gear. This was always the part I hated: the waiting around before a gig, the dead space. The before and after that sandwiched the event couldn't be more different from the gig itself. Up on that stage, feeding off the energy of the crowd, I could live only in the moment. Everything else faded into insignificance for those two hours. I could just be the thing I knew I was born to be: a musician, a performer. Nothing else mattered. I was free.

For now, though, the nerves and the nagging doubts were getting to me. I tried to occupy myself as much as possible. As expected, Daniel and Helena did a disappearing act, Alex retreated to the tour bus to occupy himself on the games console, and Rafael followed him, no doubt to lie on his bunk for a nap. To be honest, Rafael could sleep anywhere. He'd often been known to place several chairs in a row in dressing rooms and sleep across those, or simply lie on the floor with a book over his face.

Left to my own devices, my mind played tricks on me. I wished I could shut it out and silence the negative voices in my head.

My phone beeped. There was a message.

Linda
Good luck for the first night of the tour. Call me when you get the chance. I miss you.
KB
4:43 pm

I put the phone back in my pocket. I just couldn't deal with the emotional baggage right at that moment, and the longer it went on without us speaking to each other the harder it got to open that door again. Where the conversation led would be too predictable, and I wasn't in the headspace to cope with Linda's mental probing. Having to explain myself wasn't at the top of my list of priorities.

Drinks were always provided backstage but I stayed away from them, or at least the alcoholic ones, until after the performance. I wanted to be at my best. Unable to settle to anything I stayed backstage, pacing.

Eventually, gig time rolled around. I watched through a gap in the backdrop as the auditorium began to fill with expectant people, the hubbub of conversation steadily increasing.

I returned to the dressing room to prepare myself while the support act played their set. Trudi was waiting for me as always, and I knew the rest of the band wouldn't be far behind. I flopped into a chair, thankful to have some familiar company.

'You alright?' she asked.

'Just nerves,' I assured her. 'There's a lot riding on this tour.'

'Well don't wear yourself out stressing; there's a long way to go, even to the end of the first leg. We've got over eight months of this to go, on and off.'

'Oh, I know, I know.' I puffed out my cheeks and placed my hands on the counter in front of me. 'It's just… I just want to get on with it now. Every second of waiting around feels like torture. Hopefully, after tonight, we can all settle into a rhythm, or as close to one as you can with this crazy circus lifestyle. I used to think I couldn't put a foot wrong. But now...'

Trudi began to scrape back my hair, ready to tie it out of the way while she did my makeup.

'You'll be fine once you get started. It's all instinct with you.'

I wished I shared her confidence. My instinct, my animal sense of what to do when it mattered most had left me.

Maybe I just wasn't strong enough on my own.

CHAPTER TWENTY

As the house lights dimmed, two thousand pairs of eyes turned toward the space we were about to occupy. Having been warmed up by the support act, the audience now eagerly awaited the main event. Conversation ceased, replaced by the occasional whistle from the auditorium as our introductory music began to play. While flashes of blue-white light emerged from around the stage, punctuating the darkness, I waited in the wings, glancing across at the rest of the band who took their places in readiness.

This is it; do or die.

As the music reached its final moments I could make out the other musicians in the half-darkness, poised at their instruments, and in the centre front of the stage, a single spotlight picked out my microphone on its stand. The audience began a slow clap which gradually accelerated as the music drew to a close.

You can do this. You have to.

Right on cue, as soon as the last note of the introduction died away, the band launched into the first number. Above all else, they depended on me to do my part, to be the figurehead of the whole operation. It wasn't just them, either; it was the whole road crew, Mitchell and Penny, the fans who had shelled out their hard-earned money for tickets. Everything rested on my shoulders, and it weighed heavily.

First bar, second bar, third bar.

I threw back my shoulders, lifted my chin and strode onto the stage to be greeted by a huge cheer from the crowd. Acknowledging them with a wave, I plucked the microphone from its stand.

Don't think, just do. You've been here hundreds of times before.

But then in the past, I'd had Sadie by my side. Now she had abandoned me, I just had to go this alone. I opened my mouth and to my incredible relief the words came, the notes came. I still had the music in me. Relieved, I allowed myself to enjoy what I was doing a bit more and settled into the performance over the next couple of songs. By the time we were half an hour in, it felt like we had never been away.

What did surprise me was that some of the audience began calling out for us to play Black Roses. It hadn't been part of the setlist; none of the songs on the solo album had. What surprised me even more was that they were also calling out for Shed This Skin. Not only had we not rehearsed it but I didn't even think it was feasible without the orchestra. We hadn't even considered including it as a possibility.

The rest of the set went quite smoothly considering it was the first night. Okay, we had some technical niggles with the sound on a couple of songs and one or two of the lighting cues weren't quite right, but there was nothing that couldn't be solved before we hit our next venue in

Manchester. The audience loved hearing the songs they knew, and the smattering of new songs they hadn't heard before went down as well as we could have realistically hoped for. We couldn't afford to introduce too much of the new album into the set until it had been released, and that was still two months away. By then we would be well into our dates in continental Europe.

I came off stage feeling the same buzz I had missed for so long, high on music, having fed off the audience's energy for the last two hours. The problem I had was the same as it had always been: how to deal with that excess energy at the end of the night. It doesn't just go away by itself. Although it's usually late by the time gigs are over, sleeping it off isn't an option; everybody is too pumped up. Sex had always been one way of getting it out of my system. Sometimes, when I'd been young, carefree and single, the occasional random stranger had ended up on the receiving end of my attention, and Sadie and I had rather enjoyed half delighting, half terrifying them, but now tongues were busy wagging there was too much to lose; I couldn't do that anymore and I didn't much feel like it anyway. On stage I could bring the performance, play my part, but off stage I just wanted to retreat into my shell. Sex held no interest for me. That wasn't the answer to any of my problems anymore. To be honest, it had played its part in causing too many of them.

Daniel had always been the band's resident party animal, but even he had mellowed over time. Besides, now he and Helena had found each other they could make their own entertainment. Left to my own devices, I found solace in winding down over a bottle of wine until I fell asleep back at my hotel. In the morning I had to clear my head, force down some breakfast, and board the tour bus before we hit the road on our way to the next city.

Every other day we found ourselves in another part of the UK but the story was always the same: we kept hearing calls for the solo stuff. By the time we reached Glasgow, it had practically become a chant. We hastily called a band meeting on the tour bus after the gig, and Clive joined us around the table.

'What do you think?' I asked, looking around for the expected signs of dissent. 'I never thought the solo stuff was going to be on the cards but the audience seems to want it. It seems a bit unfair to ask since you guys played no part in that record.'

Alex shrugged.

'We never held that against you. I reckon we could pick up Black Roses quickly enough. It's not one of your more complex songs and you take the lead in that one anyway. Show us the chords and we can learn our parts while we're on the road. If we make it to venues early enough we can rehearse it all together as a band.'

The others all nodded.

'You don't mind?' I asked. This time they shook their heads.

'Shed This Skin is a bit more of a problem,' Helena added. 'I mean, I could mimic the orchestra on the keyboards but it wouldn't have the same power. I reckon if we can use backing tracks for that, it could be turned into a big number, a real highlight of the set. There are other layers of keyboards I can fill in with and we'd all have our part to play in it. What does it matter that it hasn't actually been released as a single? Stairway to Heaven wasn't. Bohemian Rhapsody almost wasn't. Who gives a flying fuck if the record company doesn't like it? They're not here are they? Personally, I think it's genius.'

We all stared at Helena, open-mouthed. I don't think any of us had ever heard her swear more than once or twice in all the time we'd been playing together.

'What?' Realisation dawned. 'So I said fuck. So what? You don't spend too long around Dan without getting a bit more relaxed about language.' She straightened her back. 'Funnily enough, I've found myself using that word quite a lot lately.'

Daniel grinned and threw up his hands in supplication as all the eyes around the table turned towards him.

'I guess it's all about context.' He looked towards Helena and winked. She blushed.

Rafael sat back with his hands behind his head.

'I'm in. If it's what the audiences want then why not? That's what the gigs are about, right? What do you think, Clive?'

Still looking thoughtful, Clive leaned forward and placed his hands on the table.

'From an organisational point of view, it's a bit late in the day to start throwing major new numbers into the production apart from the new material we'd already planned for, but I agree. If it's going to get audiences on your side then go for it. You don't have to introduce either of the songs into the set until they're ready. If we are going to attempt an ambitious song like Shed This Skin, then I need to talk to Mitchell about getting Steve Bowes to send us a mix of the orchestral backing tracks for live use and I need to coordinate with Jason to come up with a workable lighting design. Daniel, you're going to have to work to a click track for this one.'

Daniel shrugged his shoulders and tapped his ear.

'I do for quite a few numbers anyway, and I keep my IEM in all the time. It's a lot less cumbersome than relying on the wedge monitors we used to use. Some of the looser, simpler songs we freestyle, but a lot of the more complicated stuff has sequencing to coordinate the effects and the lighting. I guess there's no escaping technology these days.'

Clive looked around the table.

'Well then, we seem to be in agreement. Can I just say, right here and now, you're all absolutely fucking barmy making major changes partway into a tour but you know what? This might actually work.'

-0-

Over the next few gigs, we spent some time in the afternoons rehearsing Black Roses, and by the time we got back down south the orchestral backing tracks were ready and waiting for us. The time we should have had to ourselves before hitting mainland Europe was largely eaten up by rehearsal and preparation for the inclusion of Shed This Skin into the set. We only had four days to whip it into shape. At least we returned home, albeit briefly, which meant I could spend some precious time with Poppy before the band flew to Italy and rejoined the road crew, who by now had driven all the way down to Milan.

It broke my heart to leave Poppy behind again. Poppy was changing so fast and although it pained me to be away from her, life on the road was no place for a restless and inquisitive child of two. Her safety and wellbeing had to be my top priority. Besides, she would have my mum, Jeff, Karina and Francesca, plus all her friends at playgroup around her and, God help me, Guy when he wasn't over in the US filming now he'd found himself another movie role. When she was older she could come to gigs and experience everything from backstage, but for now, it wasn't a safe place for her to be. At least, whenever there was enough of a break in the schedule I would be able to fly home, and Karina could bring Poppy out to join us from time to time too. Even in the early stages of tour planning, I had ensured there would be a few days off here and there, enabling me to come home. It felt especially important now Poppy was old enough to appreciate what was going on and had I failed to be there for my daughter, Guy's mother was bound to have used it as emotional capital. She always seemed ready to have a dig at me, given an excuse.

Milan had to be the biggest venue of the tour so far, and although there were still some empty seats there had been a last-minute run on tickets with the new album only weeks from release. A frisson of excitement had already begun to spread about it so I could only assume the advance reviews hadn't been too scathing. To be honest, we'd been too busy to keep abreast of everything being said in the press. Sales of my solo album had been as encouraging in Italy as anywhere else so we felt reasonably confident about including the new songs. Had we rehearsed them enough? I guessed we were about to find out.

Black Roses went down well enough; the audience seemed to appreciate its quirkiness. Shed This Skin had been scheduled for much later in the setlist since it would provide a great set-piece, totally different to anything else we did, before winding the energy back up towards our biggest hits at the end. Devil On My Shoulder had been saved for the encore.

The moment arrived. The moment of truth.

Would the audience like what they heard? Would I even be able to sing it without the emotions it stirred up becoming too much? After all, I couldn't have bared my soul and made this song any more personal if I'd tried.

I handed the guitar I'd been using for the previous song to a waiting roadie at the side of the stage and took my place at the piano, bathed in white light from overhead. I checked my in-ear monitor was still firmly in place and positioned myself in front of the microphone, hands poised above the keyboard, ready to play.

'Ladies and gentlemen, as a special treat we're going to do something completely different for you, a song which means a lot to me. It's the first time we've ever played this in front of a live audience, so please bear with us. It's called Shed This Skin.' A murmur went up from the crowd, followed by cheering from some quarters. 'Grazie. Spero che vi piaccia.'

Hopefully, I got the few phrases I'd hastily picked up from Francesca right. The audience seemed to appreciate my attempts at saying a few things in Italian anyway.

A hush descended, broken only by the audible cue coming from the click track in my earpiece.

My fingers found the keys and as always the music simply took me over. Swirls of colour danced in my mind as I played through the introductory bars, which intensified when the orchestral parts joined in. Instinctively, I leant just a little towards the microphone in front of me as if somehow communicating with each member of the audience directly. I couldn't look at them, though; my emotions would have overwhelmed me. Immersing myself in the music, I closed my eyes to sing while a kaleidoscope of colours and images danced in my head.

For the next six and a half minutes, time stood still while I lost myself in my musical wonderland.

As the last note died away, returning from my reverie I became aware that the audience was on its feet, not just those in the standing areas but the whole audience. Overcome with a mixture of emotions, including relief, I could barely breathe.

'Thank you,' I said, turning towards them before the spotlight left me and the band started the next song. It gave me a vital few seconds to compose myself before rising to my feet and taking centre stage again.

A little over half an hour later we sauntered off after our final encore, bristling with excitement and all trying to talk at the same time. Even Rafael and Alex couldn't contain themselves.

'Oh, wow! That was absolutely electric. Did you see their faces?' Helena jumped up and down on the spot. 'I don't think it mattered whether they could understand all the words or not. The music spoke for itself. We're keeping it. Considering that was our first performance, it can only keep on getting better.'

'You're all happy with that, then?' I asked.

'Yeah!' they all chorused, somehow surprised I had even asked.

Even though he hadn't needed to play until halfway through, Daniel seemed equally enthusiastic.

'I think the set just got a new centrepiece,' he said. 'It gives the whole thing shape and meaning. It's got to be the most emotional thing you've ever done.'

-0-

Back at our hotel, and still pumped up after the gig, I couldn't sleep. We'd all allowed ourselves a few drinks backstage, and then a few more in the bar at the hotel, but my mind was racing. I left my suite and knocked on the door of Helena and Daniel's room. Helena answered, hastily securing the belt of a bathrobe around her waist. She looked a little ruffled and her hair was a mess.

'Oh, Rebecca, it's you. I wasn't expecting anybody. What's up?'

'Listen, I know you've had trouble sleeping sometimes. You don't happen to have any sleeping tablets, do you?'

'Yeah, I think so. They are over-the-counter ones but they're quite strong. Are you alright?'

'I'm fine,' I assured her. 'It's just with our schedule the way it is, I can't afford to go without a decent night's sleep and right now I'm wide awake.'

She checked her wrist for a watch that wasn't there.

'What time is it?'

I told her it was about half-past two.

'Well if you take them now you might have trouble getting up in the morning. You need to take them as soon as the gig's finished really.' She disappeared into the bathroom and came back a few moments later with a packet in her hand. 'Have these anyway. If you're still tired in the morning you can sleep it off on the tour bus. If needs be, when we get to Rome, try seeing a doctor and see if you can get a prescription for something proper if you're having problems.'

I thanked her and returning to my room, took two tablets. Even so, just as Helena predicted, it was another hour or so before they kicked in properly. Even though my phone alarm went off in time to wake me in the morning, still groggy I turned it off and slept through, missing breakfast. It wasn't until the time came to board the tour bus and Helena came to get me after I failed to appear that I realised how late it was.

'Maybe they're not such a good idea alongside alcohol,' she suggested. 'At least you got some decent sleep so that makes one of us.' Helena raised one eyebrow. 'I don't think anyone will see much of either me or Dan until tonight. Thank God the Rome gig isn't till tomorrow. The schedule starts getting more packed after that.'

I don't think she had any idea at that moment how prophetic her words would turn out to be.

CHAPTER TWENTY-ONE

By the time we reached Dortmund, we were getting closer to the new album release and nearly everywhere we played the auditoriums were now almost full. At least Ariva records had bothered to put their weight behind this one in advance of it coming out. I suppose we had much to be grateful for given the financial nervousness that had accompanied the planning stages of the tour.

Unfortunately, I wasn't faring so well. The only way I could get to sleep after gigs was with the aid of sleeping tablets, topped up with alcohol. At least it worked. The alcohol part I kept quiet about since I had no desire to deal with Helena's disapproval after her warnings to me. The trouble was, it made it very difficult to get going the next day. Even though my preference was for tea, I'd taken to drinking several cups of strong coffee in the mornings to get me fired up but I still struggled. I just couldn't get myself on an even keel.

I was still toying with the breakfast on my plate when my phone rang.

'Good morning, Rebecca.'

'Oh, hi Mitchell!' I said, trying to sound perkier than I felt. 'What's happening?'

'I've got a bit of news. It just so happens that Whispered Scream will be in Berlin at the same time as you. Different venue, of course! I've had a call from their management, who didn't realise until yesterday that you were going to be in town at the same time, asking if you'd consider joining them on stage for a rendition of The Halls of Hades the night after your concert. It isn't normally on their setlist for obvious reasons, but they're making a live video of the concert and thought it would be great if you could join them for a one-off. I promise it won't affect your planned visit home.'

Shit! This is all a bit sudden. Having only ever actually sung it once, I'd have to download the song to remember what the hell I did.

'I'll have my work cut out. I only ever did it in the studio.'

'Listen, I know it's a big ask but given the extra exposure it will win you and the potential it has to reach out to a different audience, I thought you might be interested.'

You've changed your tune since the first time I told you about the recording.

'Yes, I am.'

There goes my chance to normalise.

It *was* too good an opportunity to miss, though.

'You've got some time to practice it. After all, you've still got Munich, Prague, and Vienna to go before you hit Berlin. You'll have to liaise with Trudi because I guess you're going to need something different in the wardrobe department when it comes to a metal concert. I would imagine it's not going to be your usual kind of stage outfit.'

I agreed; it probably wasn't. As soon as I'd finished on the phone with Mitchell, I went over to have a word with Trudi. She had just started helping herself to the breakfast buffet.

'Graubrot, sliced ham, salami and cheese with holes in. You are going native.'

Trudi shrugged her shoulders.

'You know what they say. When in Rome, even if we're no longer actually in Rome.' She gave me an enquiring look. 'What's going on? You look like you're brewing up for something.'

'Kind of. I might have a little job for you as soon as we get back down to Munich,' I confessed. 'Fancy a little shopping trip? I've got an extra gig to do, something a bit out of the ordinary, and I'm going to need a completely different look.'

She placed her plate down on the counter and rubbed her hands together.

'Ooh, sounds interesting! Tell me more.'

-0-

With our Berlin concert under my belt, I only had the performance with Whispered Scream to go before I could catch a plane home and hold Poppy in my arms again, if only for a few days. In the meantime, the whole tour would decamp to Sweden, ready to begin our journey south again, crisscrossing Europe as we went.

While we played at a large, indoor venue close to the river Spree which ran through the centre of Berlin, Whispered Scream had set up at the Waldbühne, an outdoor arena in the forest just outside the city. If the weather held, they would have a fantastic summer evening for it. Thankfully, the weather forecast still looked good; it could have been a miserable experience in the rain.

Most of my free time on the tour bus had been spent whipping my vocals into shape. There would only be one opportunity to rehearse on the afternoon of the concert so I needed to be sure I could nail it. I didn't want to let anybody down. At least all the setting up had been done well in advance since this was Whispered Scream's second sold-out night there.

Trudi and I arrived in plenty of time, and although I still felt a bit delicate from the previous night's concert I kept a brave face on. On our arrival, we were met by a small delegation. I thanked Werner, our driver, and was led through a concrete tunnel which opened out suddenly into the auditorium at one side of the stage, to be faced with a giant horseshoe of twenty-two thousand or so tiered seats. The low rumble of bass bounced around the arena, reverberating off the seating. Beside me, the stage itself was covered over by a high canopy, so at least if it did rain the equipment would be protected. The audience wouldn't be quite so fortunate. To the rear of the stage, the surrounding forest was clearly visible, tall trees rising up the hillside behind it.

'Whad'ya think? Not a bad place to shoot a concert, is it?' Zakk had made his way down from the stage and was currently striding towards us. 'It was originally built for the Berlin Olympics. It's good to see you,' he said, giving me a hug followed by a quizzical look with his head to one side. 'Have you lost weight? I wouldn't have thought you needed to.'

I shrugged my shoulders.

'That's life on the road for you. I'm not on a diet or anything. So,' I said, changing the subject, 'what's the plan?'

'We're just having a sort out because one of the bass heads went down. Better now than halfway through the gig, I suppose. We should be ready to rehearse in about fifteen minutes.'

'Well I've been practising my part for the last five days on the tour bus, so hopefully, my memory won't let me down. There's nothing like being thrown in the deep end, is there?'

Zakk chuckled.

'That's a musician's life for you; adapt or die. It was only by accident that we found out you were going to be around and it was one of those 'wouldn't it be great if' scenarios. You know what it's like.'

I did.

'Oh, by the way, this is Trudi,' I added, suddenly remembering she was standing beside me. She's responsible for making me look the part tonight.'

Zakk's eyes lit up as he reached out his hand to greet her.

'Please. Call me Nigel.'

The normally forward Trudi looked unusually coy. Perhaps she had a bit of a superstar crush on him.

'What was all that about?' I asked when five minutes later we found ourselves backstage looking for the dressing rooms.

Trudi certainly looked a bit flustered. She cleared her throat.

'I'm just a bit of a fan, that's all. It might sound a bit

odd considering I work with famous people all the time, but Zakk Kaos is a bit of a hero of mine.'

I gave her a penetrating look.

'Are you sure that's all it is?'

'Hmm…no.'

I'd never thought of him in that way, but each to their own. The band were just friends to me.

The rehearsal went okay after a couple of false starts. It was a different experience bouncing off Zakk's vocals in a live situation compared to working over prerecorded tracks in the studio, and one or two bits of the song had evolved since I recorded my parts. The other thing that threw me was working with conventional monitors placed along the front of the stage as opposed to hearing the band through an earpiece. This was old-school, and even though the front-of-house PA was only working at a fraction of its gigging volume, everything sounded so much louder on stage.

'Holy shit!' I shouted, even though the band had stopped playing. 'How come you guys don't go deaf?'

Andre, one of the guitarists, grinned at me and shrugged his shoulders.

'It's metal, what else are we gonna do?'

'Besides,' added Zakk, 'you get to put one foot up on the monitor for effect. You can also lean out toward the front rows without toppling. It adds to the stage presence, makes you project out into the audience more.' Zakk hesitated. 'Plus, standing on something gives you a bit more, um…height.' The last word sounded more like a question than a statement, as if he thought twice about saying it, unsure what my reaction would be. I just laughed.

Once we were happy the song was going to sound the way we wanted and I had taken on board as many tips as I could about what would come across well at this kind of gig, everybody retreated backstage. We were back to the usual purgatory, the endless waiting around before getting dressed up and taking the stage that I hated the most. I wanted to bring some energy to the performance but inside I still felt like a half-charged battery.

Restless, I went for one of my habitual wanders and in one of the backstage corridors, I passed a member of the road crew reaching out his hand to accept something from a man I hadn't seen previously. He didn't look like the typical rock fan. They became awkwardly silent for a moment as I passed them, but I knew what was going on.

Rounding the corner, I shook my head. I'd spent long enough in the business to know how prevalent it was. Although it simply wasn't part of our band's lifestyle, there were always unknown faces coming and going backstage, different ones in every city. We all knew what they were there for, and as fast as we got rid of one, another would take their place ready to meet demand. I suspected one or two of our own road crew indulged but I had no proof. What could we do? It was so ingrained in the culture of touring, in fact, the music business in general.

I had always resisted the temptation but maybe there was a reason why it was so popular. Maybe just a little bit of the magic white powder would energise me, give me the boost I needed. Perhaps I could give it a try, just this once, to see if it helped.

Don't be so stupid. It's a road you don't want to go down.

But then again…

The world of celebrity is powered by the stuff; it has been for years. What have you got to lose? If you don't like it, you don't have to do it again. After all, it's not like it's heroin.

Not for the first time in my life, I had an angel whispering in one ear and a devil speaking into the other. Right now the devil was winning.

'Fuck it!' I muttered under my breath.

I turned around and caught up with the roadie again. The stranger in the baggy, black leather jacket had already gone.

'Hi!' I waved the roadie down before he could disappear too. 'Listen, is your friend still around? I could do with a little refreshment before tonight.'

He looked a little overawed that Rebecca Taylor was actually talking to him. Perhaps thinking this might have been a setup or a prank, his eyes darted around, scanning for hitherto unseen cameras. There were none.

'I don't know what you're talking about.'

I gave him a penetrating stare.

'Yes, you do. Look, I'm not trying to get you into trouble, I just… I just thought you could help me. I didn't want to go up and buy it myself. I'm sure you understand.'

Looking nervous, he checked both ways down the corridor.

'I suppose for a small finder's fee I could get hold of some more.' He felt in his pocket. 'Or you could have this one. It's only a gram; I'm not exactly loaded.'

'That'll do. How much did you pay for it?'

'Erm…eighty. It's the good stuff, though. Clean, you know? It's not been cut with any crap.'

I pulled out a couple of notes and handed them to

him.

'Well here's two hundred Euros. Go get yourself some more, keep the change, and forget we ever had this conversation. Deal?'

He nodded, handing me the small paper wrap from his pocket then folded the notes, tucked them away and scurried off, leaving me alone in the corridor. I stared down at the tiny package in my hand.

What on earth are you doing?

More voices echoed along the corridor, bouncing off the concrete walls as a group of people came closer. Hastily, I stuffed my hand into the hip pocket of my jeans and strode off to find my dressing room again.

Nothing ventured, nothing gained. Right?

-0-

'There you are, all rock-chicked up!' Makeup brush still in hand, Trudi stepped back to admire her work. 'What do you think?'

I certainly looked the part. Trudi's many hours spent trawling through boutique shops in southern Germany had paid dividends. The ensemble of black, heeled boots and black leather trousers with lace panels at the sides had been topped off with a slashed, black and white t-shirt with sparkly accents that would catch the lights. My hair, which didn't look long enough on its own any more, had been extended and given a bit more volume to complement the look, and my makeup certainly looked a lot heavier and more striking than usual. In particular, my lips and eyes had been made up much darker than they would normally be. Nevertheless, I was still recognizably me. Trudi really had thought about this look. She had excelled herself.

'I didn't want to go full-on eighties,' Trudi explained. 'Modern metal has left that look behind, but at the same time I wanted it to say something about the rock heritage in your own music. You aren't plastic teen pop and you don't fit into the dance and urban genres either. You've always been more traditional in your reliance on songwriting, musicianship, and performance rather than gimmicks, so I thought this would work. Can you move okay?'

I strode up and down the dressing room a couple of times.

'Yeah, fine. The leather trousers might be pretty clingy but they're not so tight I can't get around. I don't think I'll be able to bend over, though.'

Trudi chuckled.

'I wouldn't recommend that in front of Whispered Scream anyway. They do have a bit of a reputation.'

'I wouldn't believe everything you hear. After all, the press is full of shit about me and only a fraction of it is ever true.'

'Hmm,' she murmured, looking thoughtful.

'What?'

'Oh, it's nothing.'

'No. Go on. Spit it out,' I insisted.

Trudi hesitated.

'Perhaps it's the bits that are true you ought to be more concerned about.'

'Meaning?'

She sighed.

'You have rather invited trouble in the past. I know

you're trying to play down your old image but some mud always sticks. The attitude that there's no smoke without fire always prevails.'

If that was true then no amount of angelic behaviour on my part was ever going to change things. The devil on my shoulder could chalk up another win.

'Right! Be that as it may,' I announced, squaring my shoulders and resisting the temptation to dwell on the subject. 'Seeing as you're a bit of a Whispered Scream fan, you might as well go and enjoy the rest of the gig now your work is done. I'll see you later.'

She nodded.

'See you later. Have a good one!'

Thus dismissed, Trudi let herself out of the dressing room and once I was sure she had gone, I locked the door and reached for the little paper package in the pocket of my jeans currently lying across a dressing room chair. How was I going to do this? Looking around me, there were some straws which had thoughtfully been provided with the complimentary drinks. I'd seen it done, of course, just never been tempted to try it before.

I carefully unwrapped the paper and tipped some of the fine, white powder out onto the mirror of my compact then divided it finely with the edge of a credit card and arranged the cocaine into two neat little lines.

Here goes nothing.

I hesitated at the point of no return. Should I take the plunge?

Fuck it!

Inserting the straw into one nostril, I hovered over the mirror, pressing on the other side of my nose and inhaled. Fuck, it stung! Seeing as I still had one line to go, I swapped to the other side, forging ahead before the watering of my eyes and the urge to sneeze or blow my nose could take over.

Screwing up my face and sniffing it back, I dabbed any remaining powder on the mirror with the tip of my finger and rubbed it into my gums like I'd seen other people do. Although it was bitter, it wasn't quite as bad as I'd expected. Whacking the stuff up my nose was definitely worse.

Feeling the first, euphoric rush of energy hit me like a wave, I closed the compact then folded up the remainder of my supply, slipped it back into my jeans pocket and checked my phone.

Fifteen minutes till I'm due on stage. Time to face the world.

Clenching and unclenching my still-tingling hands, I made my way through the maze of corridors to one side of the stage, from where I could see Trudi enjoying the show from the wings on the other side. I caught her eye and waved to her. She waved back.

From where I was, I had a perfect view of the audience being whipped into a frenzy, their faces lit up by flashes of coloured light emanating from the stage while beyond them the evening sky grew ever darker above the tree line. I hopped from foot to foot in anticipation, ready to go as Whispered Scream reached the end of their song.

'Alright!' By now, Zakk was most definitely in full-on frontman mode. He glanced across to check I was ready and waiting in the wings before making his announcement. 'Seeing as this is a very special night tonight and we're filming everything, we've got a real treat for you. We were very lucky to record a song on our latest album with a certain lovely, young lady.' An outbreak of wolf whistles began across the audience. 'Normally, we don't do this song live, but tonight we're going to make an exception. However, it just wouldn't be complete without that other, special voice, so for one night only, please welcome to the stage the only singer who could truly do it justice, a woman of many talents and a true rocker at heart, the lovely lady herself, Rebecca Taylor.'

I strode onto the stage, waving out towards the darkness, and gave Zakk a hug before taking my microphone from its stand. A huge cheer went up from the audience.

'Thank you, Zakk. It's great to be here.'

'Ladies and gentlemen, we give you The Halls…' he dropped his voice and brought the mic in close, '…of…Hades.' On the last word, his voice rose again to a gravelly roar as the guitar intro burst out of the speakers and the crowd went nuts.

Propelled by the energy of the music, the audience, the novelty of the situation, and the chemicals coursing through my blood, I gave it my all, bouncing off Zakk's vocals and trading verses while from multiple angles around the stage, the cameras followed our every move. Add to that the surge of adrenaline and dopamine and I felt like I could have taken on the world…and won.

All too quickly though, the song was over; it had gone by in a blur. With a final wave, I took to the wings again while the band continued with the last half-hour of their set. They were playing a blinder and, still bristling with energy, I stayed to watch the remainder.

When I finally returned to my dressing room at the end of the gig, Trudi was waiting for me.

'That was a whole different you out there tonight. You sang like a woman possessed. Where did that come from?'

I shrugged my shoulders.

'I dunno. Just caught up in the occasion, I suppose.'

'Well, whatever it was, it worked. I don't think I've ever heard you belt out a song quite like that before. Are you ready to get changed back again?'

'Actually, before we start winding down, I think I ought to go and speak to the band. I want to thank them for having me along.' I glanced across at my jeans and a thought struck me. 'On the other hand, they'll be having a shower and a tidy up so maybe I should change first. I'll keep the makeup as it is, though. I'm rather enjoying playing the rock chick for the night.'

Trudi opened her mouth to speak but I pre-empted her.

'If you want to go back to the hotel, I completely understand. I might be a while yet.'

Looking a bit deflated, she appeared to change her mind.

'Of course. I'll see you in the morning.'

Seeing as I could hardly take it back with me, I'd be better off using up the rest of my stash before I went home. I had no idea how the members of Whispered Scream were feeling, but I wasn't done yet.

I wanted to party.

CHAPTER TWENTY-TWO

If only I'd known how bad the comedown was going to be, I might have thought twice about doing what I did. My paranoia wasn't helped by Trudi's rather offhand manner with me when I saw her just before I left for London. I wondered what the fuck her problem was.

I'd finally got back to my hotel suite about half-past three in the morning, although at least my flight back to Heathrow wasn't until the afternoon. Nevertheless, I kept my sunglasses on for the flight home; I didn't want the exhaustion, or for that matter, the guilt, to show. I could never be sure when someone might be lying in wait with a camera to catch me at my worst, and airports were always a hotspot for opportunistic photographers. They knew there was always a fair chance of somebody famous passing through, and my arrival looking anything other than perfect would have been an absolute gift.

It seemed like everybody was staring at me on my way through customs, and rightly so; I deserved it. I'd resorted to the one thing I'd always sworn I would never do. I felt...sullied. Of all the things I'd done, and all the ways I had cheapened myself, this was the worst. The high may have been high, but the low was undoubtedly lower.

None of the members of Whispered Scream had taken advantage of me in any way, although it must have been perfectly obvious what condition I was in, and had I been propositioned I don't suppose I would have turned them down. As it turns out, no isn't a word that comes easily when cocaine brings the extrovert out to play. My dilated pupils when I looked in the mirror and the fact that I incessantly talked a load of utter crap very loudly all night must have given me away. In fact, when I thought about it, Nigel had very much taken me under his wing and made sure I was alright, even escorting me to the car that had come back to collect me.

But we killed it out there, though; absolutely nailed it, and that was what counted most. Right?

At Heathrow, Derek was at the terminal to meet me, and the way he furrowed his brow for a moment when he saw me coming through the arrivals gate did nothing to ease my self-consciousness. He said nothing about it, though. Instead, he took my case and asked me about how the tour was going and whether I was looking forward to spending a few days at home. Of course, I told him I was, and I meant it; I just didn't want to face Francesca, or anyone else at home, while I felt the way I did. I wanted them to see me as I should be, not the me I currently was. Be that as it may, I had to remain strong and pull myself together for Poppy's sake. It was her I was coming home for.

It seemed unreal pulling up outside Spensford Hall again, like suddenly being back in another life, although I wasn't sure which was mine and which was someone else's. Karina led an excited Poppy down the steps, but as soon as they got to the bottom, Poppy wrenched her hand free and was running towards me before I could even step out of the car.

'Mummy!' she yelled at the top of her lungs, launching herself at me through the half-open door and flinging her arms around my neck. 'You're back!'

I held her tightly, enjoying the familiar smell of her hair and pulling her close.

'I missed you too, darling. So much!'

-0-

Three days went by so fast. It felt like no sooner had I arrived than it was time to leave once more, but I had a job to do and another life to go to.

While I was home, I concentrated on Poppy. I probably spoiled her rotten but I suppose I was trying to assuage my own guilt at not being there for her the rest of the time. Some of my family came over but I tried to keep intrusions to a minimum. I couldn't bear to face dealing with friends, some perhaps more so than others. When Linda called I pretended to be out, and when she tried my mobile I let it go to voicemail. Francesca saw me putting my phone away again, but having been shut down once or twice before when she tried to intervene, she kept her silence. Nevertheless, Francesca made it her mission to try and fatten me up again before I disappeared. I gently resisted.

I was unnerved to see Mum looking frail again. She avoided the subject when I broached it, and Jeff was less than forthcoming as well. So much went unsaid, which only added to the myriad things gnawing away inside me like a nest of rats.

By the time I was due to leave again, I felt somehow both relieved and saddened. It seemed there was nowhere I could go to escape the dark cloud that followed me. No matter what I did or where I went, it had become my inescapable companion, but for Poppy's sake more than any other, I beat it back, at least for the time being.

It broke my heart to leave her behind again but I knew it had to happen. Even so, I wasn't prepared for the wrench of having to watch her through the back window of the car, reaching out her arms and sobbing for me as we pulled away.

'Do you want to go back?' Derek asked.

It would only prolong the agony and make things worse. We'd said all of our goodbyes.

'No,' I said, only just managing to form the word. It came out as a kind of stifled sob. I couldn't bear to look behind me any more. 'Drive. Just drive.'

CHAPTER TWENTY-THREE

Having reunited with the tour at Gothenburg, everything returned to the usual dysfunctional roller-coaster of highs and lows that constitutes life on the road. With the crowds fired up in anticipation of the new release, the gigs were frenetic.

At least on stage, I could leave my thoughts behind and focus on the music, but once off it, everything came flooding back: the guilt, the feelings of worthlessness, the pain of leaving Poppy behind, and now the renewed worries about my Mum. I knew she wasn't telling me everything. Maybe Mum and Jeff thought they were doing me a kindness by keeping the details about her health from me, but all it did was leave me to worry. It was worse not knowing the truth, no matter how harsh that might be. Rather than burden everybody else with the things going on in my head, I painted a smile on for others but kept to myself as much as possible. Nobody wants misery for company, and certainly not in the claustrophobic confines of a touring show.

With the album release due any day, we were on the way to Denmark in the tour bus when Mitchell rang.

'Morning, all! Can everyone hear me?'

'Yes,' we all chorused.

'Is Clive with you too?'

'No.' I shook my head, although I had no idea why; Mitchell couldn't see us. 'He's on the other bus.'

'Okay, no biggie. I've already sent him an email and I'll update him separately. I take it you've probably noticed the upturn in attendance.'

We had.

'Well, I've got some good news for you all. It's going to put some pressure on the timelines but at least it's good for business. Seeing as Ariva have actually put some promotional weight behind the new album this time and pre-release reviews are coming back positive, there's now more demand for tickets than there are seats. I think we need to consider adding some extra nights, where possible, for the rest of the European leg. It's going to make more work for everybody in an already busy schedule, and I'm afraid a few sightseeing opportunities might go out of the window, but you've got to make hay while the sun shines.'

We agreed. For everybody's financial security, both band and crew, we could hardly turn the opportunity down, but I could sense Mitchell hesitating on the other end of the line.

'What's the catch?' I asked.

'I'm afraid it's going to impact a couple of your planned trips home, Rebecca, but instead, I would suggest bringing Poppy out to you whenever you're in one place for more than a couple of days. It will be good for her to see you and I think it will be beneficial for you too. Rafael and Alex, I believe it will afford the opportunity for your girlfriends to come out to see you as well.' They both nodded. 'I've been in this business long enough to know how isolating touring is and the toll it can take on relationships, although I'm afraid there simply isn't enough room on the tour bus for them all to travel with you.'

He was right, of course, as usual. Conditions were a bit cramped already. We were all glad of some individual space whenever we reached hotels. Despite all getting on so well generally, small things could soon become big issues and tempers sometimes frayed when we had little escape from each other for days or weeks on end. Helena and Daniel were pretty self-contained these days so for them the tour was going swimmingly. They had no problems with home-sickness.

'Oh, and by the way, I'm sending out another truck with the reserve stage equipment in, so we can leapfrog between venues. It's the only way we'll get everything up and down in time for some of the turnarounds between gigs.'

We thanked Mitchell, and I went forward to speak to the driver and confirm where we were. He reliably informed me we were only about an hour outside Copenhagen and I rejoined the rest of the band so we could discuss the day's developments.

'If we're on the road anyway, why not make the most of it?' Rafael encouraged.

It was alright for him, he didn't need to expend as much energy on stage as Daniel, I, or even Alex did. All eyes were on me for most of the time so I had nowhere to hide. I had to be on the case, bringing my A-game, night after night. Maybe I was going to need some assistance again. While my angel and my devil were busy debating the issue in my head I heard Daniel's voice in the distance, pulling me back.

'Sorry, what's that?' I asked, snapping to.

'I said do you want a drink from the fridge?'

'Oh, just a coke, please.' Maybe it was a Freudian response. Actually, I fancied something stronger than just a cola but perhaps this wasn't the time.

He stood up to make his way down the aisle to the galley and barely made two steps before being suddenly thrown to the floor. With a squealing of tyres, then a sickening crunch of metal against metal and the shattering of glass, we were all jettisoned from our seats in a rain of personal effects as the bus lurched before coming to a sudden halt.

And then silence…almost. No more low rumble of road-noise, no more chatter of voices, just the sound of a distant car horn blaring and somebody screaming.

We disentangled ourselves among the chaos of personal possessions that had been launched forward by the impact and looked around.

'Is everybody alright?' Helena asked, checking herself over. 'Thankfully, I don't think we were going particularly fast.'

Alex sat up, clutching his hand to his head, and removed it to reveal a palm smeared with blood.

'I think I must have caught the edge of something. What the fuck happened?'

Behind us, I could hear traffic coming to a halt, then feet running. The side door opened and Jason the lighting engineer poked his head around the frame.

'Are you guys okay? We were right behind you.'

'I think we're all present and correct, apart from a few

bruises,' I assured him. 'Alex might need seeing to. Who else is involved?'

'Another couple of cars, one of which looks like it went straight in front of the bus. I'd stay right where you are until told otherwise If I were you. It's a bit of a mess out here. Emergency services are already being called. I think we're going to need another tour bus; this one's not going to be going anywhere for a while.'

'What about Jens, the driver?'

Jason popped his head back out of the door again and I could hear a hurriedly shouted exchange outside. He reappeared with a grimace.

'He's conscious but I don't know much more than that. Somebody's with him now. The cab's, um, not in the best shape so I can't vouch for his injuries.'

'And I thought today was going so well. I shouldn't have opened my big mouth,' Rafael reflected as Helena helped Dan back into a seat. He appeared to have taken a bit of a whack when he went down, but nothing worse.

'Trust me,' Jason informed Rafael, 'you're having a better day than the poor bastard in the car that crossed your path. Two of our first aiders are doing what they can until the ambulance arrives.' I stood up to go and help but Jason shook his head and held up his hand. 'Unless you're any good at CPR, I don't advise it.'

Within minutes we were surrounded by blue, flashing lights, and the police had closed off the motorway while fire crews cut the top off the car in front of us. A helicopter touched down on the tarmac and whisked the driver of the car and his distraught wife to the hospital. Jens didn't appear to be in as life-threatening a condition and was dispatched by ambulance. Alex was patched up at the scene but taken away for checks.

In the meantime, we retrieved what we could from the bus before it was towed away. It was only at the last minute that I remembered my favourite guitar, still under the bunk in its case and thankfully still undamaged by the experience. I handed it to my guitar tech to put with the other guitars for now. At least it would be safe.

It was only once we eventually reached Copenhagen in the remaining vehicles and checked into our hotel that the reality of the situation hit us like a brick wall. The crew, including the first aiders among them, didn't even have time to take stock of the situation, even though they must have been similarly in shock. The relentless gigging schedule waited for no one.

Since we had moved on to larger venues, the setup now included projection screens to the sides as well as the rear of the stage, more pyrotechnics, and a bigger PA and lighting rig than we'd been using at the start. Because of its complexity, everything took longer to put in place despite the operation now working like a well-oiled machine. By this stage in the game, everybody knew their job inside out and had been drilled to perfection. If the crew didn't start that day, there was no guarantee everything would be ready for the following evening. They had no time to dwell on the situation.

We, on the other hand, did, and perhaps that made things worse.

By late afternoon, Alex returned from the hospital with a couple of butterfly stitches in his scalp. Although we were glad that he wasn't more badly hurt, the news that the car driver was still in a critical condition did nothing to lift our spirits. Our driver Jens had broken his wrist and would be out of action for the remainder of the European dates. The mood remained sombre as we nursed our drinks in the hotel bar.

Clive came in to join us, looking stressed but trying to remain positive.

'I've spoken to Mitchell and he's fully aware of what's going on. Another tour bus is on its way out to us with a pair of drivers. They could have got one locally but Mitchell has a contract with the company who's supplying the replacement. It's not quite the same spec as the original but beggars can't be choosers. Still,' he added cheerily, 'coming from the UK, at least you'll still be able to plug in your hairdryers.'

He might have been trying to inject some humour into the situation but the joke fell rather flat. Daniel looked up from running his finger around the top of his glass of Carlsberg. He never seemed to have much time for Clive.

'We've got adapters anyway,' he said rather dryly before returning to his glass. Normally, Daniel would be the first to crack a joke but on this occasion, his humour had failed him.

'Right. Well then.' Clive backed away, tapping the knuckles of one hand against the open palm of his other. 'I'll leave you to it. Things to do.'

Although I might have been tempted to say something to Daniel about how he'd treated Clive, I didn't have the energy. Nobody did.

-0-

On the day leading up to the gig, we followed every scrap of news we could, local and international. Word had spread quickly about the incident and the internet was already full of it, plus it was all over the local TV and radio, not that my Danish was up to much. While I was looking through the British newspapers, one unrelated, front-page article caught my eye.

MINISTER IN DATE RAPE DRUG SEX SCANDAL

In a shocking development, Anthony Holbrook, Member of Parliament for Cransfield South and Junior Education Minister, has today been forced to resign over allegations that he drugged and raped three women. The accusations of sexual assault go back several years and came to light after one of his alleged victims was persuaded by a friend to go to the police.

Since then others have come forward and under mounting pressure, Holbrook has stepped down from politics to focus on fighting the accusations. In a letter to the House of Commons, he insisted the accusations were "preposterous nonsense, utterly without foundation" and "malicious rumour sponsored by the opposition in an attempt to disrupt the government's forward-thinking programme of reform".

The Crown Prosecution Service remains adamant that there is mounting evidence and that the case will go to trial. Adele Fowler, a senior spokesperson for the CPS stated at a news conference yesterday that there is "substantial and corroborated testimony, along with forensic evidence from a number of sources" and that there "may be many more victims we are not yet aware of. We would urge them to come forward".

Until the shock announcement, Anthony Holbrook was widely tipped to take over a senior position in the upcoming Cabinet reshuffle, but sources close to the government have admitted that he is "unlikely to come back from this one".

Couldn't have happened to a nicer guy. Teflon-coated wanker!

Maybe now some of the shit would finally stick where it was deserved. I would have considered adding my testimony to the evidence if it meant putting that bastard behind bars, but it would have dragged Linda and Ryan's private lives and business interests into the public eye. They didn't deserve that. I might have kept my distance lately, but they had never been anything other than good to me.

From my perspective, I was just starting to get back into public consciousness for the right reasons instead of the wrong ones. The last thing I or anyone around me needed was to become embroiled in a politically linked scandal. Besides, It looked like Holbrook was going to get his just deserts anyway, and I found it rather satisfying to note that all the other rats had soon abandoned Holbrook's sinking ship. Their priority had been self-preservation. Loyalty, it seemed, did not stretch to allying with lost causes.

For once, good.

By late afternoon, and with the soundcheck done, we were back into the usual waiting around when Clive came to seek us out and called a meeting backstage.

'Listen, um… I'm afraid I've got some bad news.' He shuffled from foot to foot, looking nervous. 'The driver of the car from yesterday's accident passed away about an hour ago. His injuries were just too extensive. His wife and family were with him. On a more positive note, Jens is doing well and will be released from hospital today to travel home. He's been cleared of any wrongdoing in the incident. Witnesses corroborated that the two cars collided initially and one veered in front of the bus. There was nothing he could have done to prevent it.'

'All the same, he must be feeling like shit,' Alex interjected.

'I'm sure. We'll get him any help he needs and he'll still be paid for the rest of the time he was due to be with us. At the end of the day, once he's fully recovered we want him back. He's a reliable driver.'

'Has anybody sent flowers?' asked Helena.

Dan gave a wry chuckle.

'I don't think he's a flowers kind of guy.'

'Besides, he's allergic,' added Alex.

'No, I meant to the family of the car driver.' Helena rolled her eyes.

'I think we can do better than just flowers,' I said. 'Why don't we use part of the proceeds from the gig to start a fund for the family? It seems only right.'

Everybody nodded.

'Good, then consider it done.' Clive had a resolved look about him. 'I'll get in touch with Mitchell and set things in motion. He likes to keep a tight grip on the finances so that's more his domain.'

Once our tour manager had left the room, I felt compelled to ask Daniel why he sometimes lacked patience with Clive. Dan looked uncomfortable.

'Don't get me wrong or anything, and he's a good organiser, I mean, we don't get many hiccups on the road and when we do they're not his fault, but he's not exactly Mr Personality, is he? Even Mitchell's got more about him than Clive does. On the road, you need a tour manager who's also good at the human side, someone who inspires everybody to give their best, galvanizes the troops, and he's not really a people person. He's got all the charisma of a wet lettuce.'

'It's true enough,' Alex added. 'I'd happily let him analyse tactics but I wouldn't want to follow him into battle. He's hardly a William Wallace or a Henry the fifth.'

I'd never really thought about it, but I supposed they were right. Some of the crew didn't exactly warm to him either. Perhaps it was just as well we already had a pretty close-knit community.

It still felt like we needed to do something else, though, something more immediate.

'Anyway,' I said, reverting to the original subject, 'I've got an idea for tonight. There's something we ought to do, but it will mean making some slight changes to our running order.'

Instead of our usual introductory music, that night when we took the stage we stood, shoulder to shoulder at the front of the stage until the crowd quietened. I took the microphone to make my announcement.

'Ladies and gentlemen, in case you weren't aware, we have some sad news. Our tour bus was involved in a collision with another car on its way to Copenhagen yesterday. The driver of the car has since died and our thoughts go out to his family. As a mark of respect, we will now take the time for a minute's silence. Tak.'

After brief applause, a hush fell over the crowd. Apart from the occasional cough, you could have heard a pin drop around the arena. I knew they would understand me, though. Half the audience probably spoke better English than we did, and certainly better than one or two of the road crew. That's Scandinavia for you.

Once the minute was up, without another word we took our places, and instead of the usual dramatic introductory music played a song which had only occasionally been part of our live set since the early days but was often used to soundcheck with. 'Sometimes I Wish', despite being a staple of our early gigs, hadn't made it onto the 'Come Inside' album, not because it wasn't a good song but just because it didn't quite seem to fit with the others. Now felt like the right time to bring it back. I sang my heart out for them, and despite their typically Nordic reserve, I could see the emotion on the faces in front of me. When without a word they all stood to applaud at the end, I knew we had done the right thing.

By the end of the gig, we were back on a high again with the audience eating out of our hands. I wanted the feeling to last. I wanted to keep it that way and not let the darkness back in, but I knew it would return; it always did.

Of course, there was one thing that might help, albeit temporarily, and I knew it wouldn't be too far away if I looked hard enough. Sure enough, I found the local source. By now, I knew the type. The faces changed from place to place but the mannerisms didn't. A brief exchange was all it took and I had in my possession enough to last me until we moved on.

Knowing I couldn't risk trying to take anything across borders in case we were searched, I would have to get more every time we entered a new country, but we were on a roll and I could afford it.

If it gets me through the day, fuck it!

Once I got back to my dressing room, though, the voice of doubt started to win through again. I found myself staring down at the little, open package of white powder on the table.

What are you doing? You know how shitty it made you feel

after the last time.

But the devil shouted louder. She already had the lion's share of my attention.

But it got you through it, didn't it? You're still here.

There was a knock at the door and someone tried the handle. Thankfully, I'd had the foresight to lock it; I didn't usually.

'Rebecca?' asked the muffled voice of Trudi on the other side. 'Are you alright?'

'I'm fine. I'll be out in a minute.'

There wasn't time to do a proper line. Maybe I just needed a little pick-me-up for now. I wetted the tip of my finger and dabbed it into the powder before rubbing it along my gums. Hastily, I wrapped up my guilty secret and placed it in my compact for later.

'Coming!' I smacked my lips and ran my tongue around my teeth before opening the door. 'Let's get packed up quickly and find a bar somewhere. I fancy a drink tonight.'

CHAPTER TWENTY-FOUR

A face looms over me, sneering, before a hand on his collar drags him away and I find myself alone in a park, staring up at blue sky. Around me, people are playing in the sun with their children. I hear birdsong and a woodpecker is tapping on a tree somewhere nearby, but I still feel a sense of unease. Something is wrong. The shrill ring of a telephone pierces the air and the distant sound of a woman's voice is calling out to me. I know that voice; I'm sure I do.

I opened my eyes to be assailed by a jumble of sounds. An increasingly urgent series of knocks were coming from the door to my suite and I could hear Helena calling out my name on the other side. The phone was still ringing.

'Alright, alright! Can't I get any fucking sleep around here?' I peeled myself off the bed since I wasn't even under the covers. For that matter, I was still dressed, or at least half-dressed. I still had my jeans, my bra, and one shoe on.

What time is it anyway?

I checked my mobile phone. It wasn't ringing. The time said 11:17 am.

Fuck! We're supposed to be out of the rooms by 11.30.

I'd missed breakfast but I didn't much feel like eating anyway. The hotel phone finally relented and gave up its incessant shouting.

'Rebecca, open up! Something's happened.'

I stumbled over to the door of the suite and opened it. Helena looked me up and down.

'Jesus, Rebecca! What time did you get to bed, or didn't you?'

'Morning, Helena! Love you too! You'd better come in.'

'We were hoping to let you know when you came down for breakfast but when you didn't show, I came up to find you.'

'Let me know what?' I asked, doing my best to snap myself awake.

'It's your guitar.'

'What?'

'Now before we start apportioning blame, it wasn't any one person's fault as far as we can tell.'

I felt a lurch in the pit of my stomach.

'Just tell me what's going on, will you?'

'Your...your Les Paul didn't go back in with the other guitars straight away because when you gave it to Davey, everything was already packed away in the truck. It got put to one side with a load of other cases, and when they were sorting everything out after the gig last night it...the case got crushed. Someone put it behind one of the lorries and...' Her voice trailed away.

I flopped down onto a chair with my hand over my mouth. She was my baby.

'How bad is it?'

Helena shook her head.

'The neck's broken. Thankfully the body's alright but with set-neck guitars, it's going to mean some major surgery. According to Davey, it's not like you can just bolt another one on, and it will probably be as expensive to fix as buying a whole new guitar. If you want to keep it, it'll have to go back to the UK for repair. It's going to need a specialist luthier apparently.'

There was no way I was going to let my guitar go. She had been a present for my seventeenth birthday from Mum, Jeff, and Rob. She wasn't just an instrument; she was a part of me, a link to a time when I had been so full of hope for the future, when even sex had just been one beautiful, great, innocent adventure, and long before business decisions; parenthood; betrayal; juggling agendas; arrogant, date-rape-drugging rapist bastards; and money-grabbing, lying, faithless arseholes took over my life. She still represented a life that hadn't had all the joy and the sense of adventure sucked out of it. How could I give up on her?

'Then tell them I want it done. It's not about the money. I don't care if that guitar has to be sent to hell and back to get it fixed, it's the principle of the thing.'

Helena nodded.

'I thought you'd probably say that. Arrangements are already being made.' She looked around her, momentarily wrinkling her nose at the state of the room and the empty bottles, but chose to swallow her words. 'Come on. I'll help you pack. Better pull yourself together; it's time to hit the road.'

And that's exactly what we did. The next two weeks were spent zigzagging our way gradually southwards until we hit Spain, where a four-night, two concert stopover in Madrid allowed for a visit from Poppy and Karina.

I would have to clean up my act, though, and that scared me the most. I didn't want Poppy to see me if I looked like how I felt. I'd got this far on chemical assistance, though, and I was starting to wonder if I could manage without it. I'd got pretty good at hiding my habits, or so I thought, but that was when I could retire to my suite alone. It wasn't going to be so easy for the next few days.

Even though I felt like shit, I showered and changed and took extra care with my makeup when I knew they were due to arrive. How I wished I could have gone to the airport to meet them, but it just wasn't possible. It would have caused too much of a ruckus and I still didn't want Poppy exposed to any unnecessary media attention. Without my presence, they could slip through the arrivals lounge unnoticed and unhindered.

Waiting nervously in the air-conditioned reception of the Hotel Palacio de Madrid while the rest of the band had taken the opportunity to do some sightseeing, I saw the car pull up outside. I didn't know whether to remain nonchalantly seated in a deeply upholstered armchair or to get up and greet them. In the end, my legs decided for me and I stood nervously to one side of the entrance, waiting for them to come in through the revolving doors.

Karina came through, holding Poppy's hand while a porter followed behind them with the bags. I knelt down and held out my arms to Poppy, but at first, she gave me a blank look before the light of recognition dawned in her eyes. She ran over to me, flinging her arms around my neck and I held her close.

'How was your journey?' I asked Karina as she came over to join us. 'Everybody's looking well.'

'Thank you, yes, everybody's fine. You look…' she hesitated to say the word, 'tired.'

'Oh, you know, that's just touring,' I said dismissively. 'It takes a lot out of you. I'm looking forward to coming home for a couple of weeks after Paris. There'll be just enough time to recuperate then it's off to the US, South America, and Japan.'

Karina gave me a sympathetic look and nodded her head.

I placed Poppy back on her feet and, still holding her hands, took a step back to look at her.

'Look how you've grown. I can't believe how tall you are.'

'I'm this big now, Mummy. Look!' she beamed, placing one hand on top of her head. My mouth dropped open and I stared at her in surprise at how far her speech had come on.

'You are, my darling. You certainly are.'

'Oh, just you wait,' Karina added. 'Now she's started, she doesn't stop. You can't get a word in edgeways.'

On the one hand, I felt immense pride on Poppy's behalf but also deep sadness I was missing so much by being away. I felt no small measure of jealousy that Karina should be the one to be there for Poppy, to spend time with her. To say I felt conflicted would be putting it mildly.

Nevertheless, we had three days to make the most of it, and after each gig, I headed straight back to the hotel where I had insisted on setting a bed up for Poppy in my room. I knew Poppy would be asleep, but at least I could be there with her and listen to the peaceful sound of her breathing before I went to sleep myself. It soothed me to know she was close by and in fact, I slept more soundly than I had done in weeks. When she clambered into bed with me in the morning and snuggled up, I wanted it to last forever.

'Cuggle, Mummy,' she said, wrapping her arms around my waist and laying her head against my chest. I thought my heart would burst.

I felt energized by her presence too and did my best to banish any thoughts of falling back on my chemical crutch. For those few days, it made me feel whole again like there was still some hope of salvation. Secretly, I vowed to stay clean for Poppy's sake. I'd let her down. I'd let myself down.

Of course, there was also the excitement of the new album release. In every city, the media was all over us with requests for interviews. Incoming reviews had continued to be encouraging and we were all justifiably proud of the record and what it represented; not just me, all of us. It had been a team effort, more so than ever before. Phoenix From the Ashes promised to redefine us in the eyes of the world. According to Mitchell, even my solo album was achieving something of a cult following and sales had continued to grow steadily.

'You've just got to ride the wave,' he told me during one of our weekly telephone catchups. 'That's the nature of this business; it's boom or bust.'

In fairness to him, he had always said it would be a roller-coaster ride. He wasn't wrong. Unfortunately, it was the emotional swings that came with everything else

I had trouble dealing with: the endless cycle of approval and rejection, adoration and derision, the fickleness of it all. How do you grow a thicker skin without hardening your heart? If I knew the answer to that, perhaps I had the key to survival.

Maybe it wasn't possible, and the whole thing just ate at you from the inside until there was nothing left but an empty shell of the person you used to be. No wonder suicide is so common amongst artists of all kinds and certainly among musicians. The more of a soul you have in the first place, the more there is to lose. Experiencing the world more deeply can be both a gift and a curse.

Saying goodbye to Poppy at the end of her stay broke my heart all over again. I had to watch her go, and as I did, I felt the darkness wrap around me like a suffocating blanket. I took a deep breath, choked back a tear, and prepared to soldier on.

I just had to make it through till after Paris.

CHAPTER TWENTY-FIVE

Situated in the Parc de la Villette, to the northeast of the city centre, Le Zénith de Paris rose like some kind of multi-domed, high-tech bubble from the landscape. It wasn't the biggest place we'd ever played, and we'd certainly performed to bigger crowds outdoors, but being the largest indoor venue in Paris it had a special significance to us as the final stop on the European leg of the tour, not least because French crowds always went nuts for us, or as Mitchell would say in his own inimitable if slightly dispassionate fashion, 'They're a key demographic'.

We had a three-night residency there, the first two of which had always been part of the plan. The third had been added due to demand for extra tickets. I knew it would be exhausting, but at least the endless travelling was almost over for a while. The audience would get us through it. They always did.

You've got this far. Not much longer now.

For the past few weeks, I'd kept my thoughts and my company to myself as much as I could. I didn't want to admit to anyone, let alone the other band members, why I was finding it so hard to function from day to day. To be honest, I could barely untangle it myself. Resisting the temptation to fall back on my fairy dust, as I had privately christened it, had been a struggle. Somehow, I managed.

But it came at a cost. I had hoped I would feel better for my abstinence. I didn't. The lows between gigs were lower than ever. Apart from soundchecks, I stayed out of the way, privately doing battle with my demons and taking pleasure in very little when I should have been celebrating our renewed success with my extended musical family. Behind closed doors, the malaise ate away at me while I, in turn, ate very little. I tried to use the hotel gyms where I could but each time I did, irritation with the whole process overtook me and I threw in the towel, both literally and figuratively. At least I could sleep, and when I did, the anxiousness and the self-loathing would go away, if only for a few hours. Alcohol still helped, and since it saved me from having to face uncomfortable questions, I usually drank alone.

The first two nights went okay. The good thing was when I stepped out onto that stage, everything else went away and the performer in me took over. Off it, though, I felt like I was hanging on by a thread, clinging to what little I had left of myself. I just had one more concert to get through and then I could go home and be with Poppy again. That hope kept me going.

Paris itself seemed to be a city with as much of a dual personality as me. On the one hand, many parts of it dripped history and atmosphere while right next door there would be something abstract and ultra-modern. The Parc de Villette, which surrounded the venue, bristled with angular structures, wide-open concourses bounded by water, and a huge, silver sphere which drew the eye wherever you stood. Beyond its confines, the rest of the city was mostly a crowded melee of gridlocked traffic, gallic tempers, and ceaseless bustle, the only respite from which could be found in one of the many cafés and bars that lined its streets.

I made a point of forcing myself to venture out of my room and join the band in seeing the sights for a couple of mornings, but even though we found ourselves in the city of romance, I didn't feel romantic. Alex and Rafael's girlfriends had come out to join them, and Daniel and Helena had each other, so I felt unusually out on a limb. They were all nice about it, of course, but I could tell my presence created an awkwardness I couldn't quite put my finger on. Maybe they were surprised to see me out and about. I hadn't exactly been sociable of late.

What did cheer me up was being approached by a group of excited fans who were in Paris for the concert and couldn't quite believe their luck at bumping into us while we were strolling in the Parc de Villette, taking some fresh air. I happily autographed their shirts and we posed for selfies on their phones. They went away happy.

Relieved to return to my suite again, I could prepare myself mentally for the final concert. I stood by the glass wall of the lounge and looked out over the city skyline, pondering the evening ahead before turning to face the room. A bottle of cognac stared at me, silently taunting me from the bar. I didn't even like the stuff very much. Like whisky, it had become a means to an end, not something I savoured in any way.

My hand hovered over it for a moment and I closed my fingers around its neck before putting it back on the shelf underneath the bar, out of sight and hopefully out of mind.

Not today, matey. Not today.

I didn't feel well, to be honest, but I had a job to do and do it I would. The show had to go on.

-0-

I didn't feel much like eating ahead of the gig; I rarely did. Nobody wants to jump around on stage with a full stomach and it doesn't help your voice either. Instead, I ran through my vocal exercises and warmed up on one of my guitars to keep my chops in shape while the rest of the band and crew ate. There was always a good supply of food backstage; our rider insisted on it, although promoters varied in their attention to detail. Alex was a bit sensitive to certain foods, and the results of their failure to read the small print in advance had almost cost us a gig once or twice. Thankfully, that was rare these days. Most promoters had learned the hard way when Mitchell politely tore them a new arsehole for not reading the small print.

In the distance, I could hear the support band giving it their all out there, the sound of their music reverberating down the corridors. Since they weren't booked to accompany us to the US, they knew it was their last night. We were going to have to raise our game another notch if we weren't going to be outshone. There's no such thing as 'just another night' when it comes to performing, whether you can remember what town you're in or not. Most of the audience had been looking forward to what may for them be a once-in-a-lifetime opportunity, and I didn't want to let them down. I never did. On this occasion, awareness wasn't going to be a problem; we all knew exactly where we were. What I also knew was that we needed to psych ourselves up before we went out there.

Trudi bustled into the dressing room and helped me into my costume for the first half of the performance before doing my makeup.

'Are you still losing weight? That's the second time I've had to alter your outfits and there's still room to spare. You need to feed up while you're back home or we'll be looking for a complete change of wardrobe before we go to America.'

'And if I gained weight, it would be even more of a problem. Some of the new artists coming through are like stick insects. I'm at the mercy of what's fashionable.'

She shook her head.

'Not that much. Since when have you ever been a slave what was in or out? You've always had curves and that's never stopped you being a sex symbol.'

I struggled to contain my irritation.

'Maybe I don't want to be a sex symbol anymore. Maybe I'd rather be a human being.'

'I'm sorry, I...'

'Oh, it's alright,' I relented, exhaling slowly. 'It's not your fault. I just want to be myself, only I'm not too sure what that is anymore. Anyway!' I exclaimed, standing up. 'I'm going to catch up with the others before we go on. I'll see you back here when it's time to change. You might as well enjoy the show for now.'

Taking the hint, she left me to my thoughts again and I checked myself over in the mirror. Thank goodness the foundation did a good job of hiding how sallow my complexion had become. The support act had finished playing, so I knew we had about twenty minutes to go while their equipment was cleared and the stage reconfigured. The proverbial clock was already ticking.

Actually, now I thought about it, there was a little area of makeup I wasn't totally happy with. Perhaps I'd been too hasty in dismissing Trudi, but it was nothing I couldn't fix myself; all it needed was a little blending in. Ignoring Trudi's makeup kit, I instinctively reached for the compact from my bag and opened it up.

Shit!

I didn't think I had any fairy dust left, but sure enough, there it was. I must have taken it across several borders so it was a good thing we hadn't been searched. What was I going to do with it? I could hardly take it home.

I ought to get rid of it.

Then again, perhaps I could do with the extra boost just to get me across the finish line, and then that would be it. Finished. New chapter. New start.

I closed the compact and slowly opened it up again, hoping perhaps that my imagination had been playing tricks on me and I would be spared the temptation but no such luck. It was still there.

Pacing backwards and forwards between the bathroom and the mirror, I tapped the closed compact against my palm while I wrestled with myself. The angel and the devil had never been more at war with each other, fighting their corners while I remained trapped between them, pulled from pillar to post.

And then they both fell silent.

I stopped and opened up my compact to stare at the

package again.

And the winner is…

In that moment I knew I had reached my decision.

CHAPTER TWENTY-SIX

Passing the support act in the backstage corridor, I congratulated them on their performance and thanked them for being with us over the last few months. I wished them well before knocking on the first of several dressing room doors. Alex answered.

'Oh, hi!' He checked the corridor. 'Is it just me you want to see?'

'No, I think we all need to put our heads together before we go on. I thought I'd round up the troops.'

He looked surprised.

'It's been a while since you were first in the queue. Normally we send someone down to your dressing room to get you. What's changed?'

He was right, and I felt guilty about that. In the past, I'd always made myself the driving force behind everything we did. Not so much in recent weeks. While I had been hiding away from everybody, I hadn't even managed to get on first name terms with the support band. They probably thought I was being aloof, the big star in my ivory tower. I gained the impression Alex and Rafael had got to know them quite well since they were often found together in hotel bars along the way.

'Look, I know I haven't been myself lately and I apologise for that; there's been a lot on my mind. It just seemed right tonight. There's something I want to say to you all.'

'Right, then!' He checked he had everything he needed. 'I guess we'd better go.'

We stopped next door to collect Helena and Daniel. She opened the door, straightening her outfit and looking a little flushed, while Daniel was still straightening his shorts. Typical of many drummers, he expended so much energy when he played, it was hard to tell if he was already dressed for the occasion or not. He never wore very much on stage beyond shorts, a T-shirt and trainers, and what he did wear was primarily for the sake of decency.

Rafael emerged from his dressing room before we had a chance to knock.

'I heard voices,' he said, 'so either I'm going crazy or we're preparing to get out there.'

'It's the latter,' I informed him, 'and while I've got you all together I wanted to talk to you.' They all looked expectantly at me. 'I've got a confession to make, well, several actually.'

Rafael stared at me for a moment.

'Come in,' he invited. 'Let's not do this out in the corridor.'

We stepped inside and Rafael closed the door, looking serious. I took a deep breath while I steeled myself. No one else said a word. I think they must have suspected something had been brewing.

'I know I've been rather distant lately, and probably not a very good friend to any of you, but I want you all to know I intend to change that. I've been dealing with a lot of personal shit and I haven't handled it very well. I've been missing my daughter and I think my mum is ill again, even though no one in my family will admit it, and...'

Now the floodgates were opening I couldn't stop myself. The unspoken words began to pour out of my mouth at the same time as tears began to roll down my face. It was probably going to spoil my makeup but that could be fixed. Right now, this was more important.

'...and a few months ago I was almost raped by that scumbag politician who just resigned.'

Helena gasped and put her arms around me.

'Oh Rebecca, we had no idea,' she soothed. 'Why didn't you say all this was going on?'

I shook my head and sniffed. I could feel my nose about to run.

'It gets worse. I've been drinking more than I should, to block it all out so I could sleep at night and...'

'Oh God, I thought so but I didn't want to say anything,' Helena said, putting her hand over her mouth. 'I should have been there for you. A few people have had their suspicions but no one wants to interfere. You're the star of the show. I don't imagine anyone thinks it's their place.'

'...and to get me through the gigs I've been...' This was the hardest confession of all. '...I've been...' I reached into my pocket and pulled out the small package, still with my dirty little secret inside it. '...I've been using this stuff.'

Alex looked visibly shocked.

'Is that what I think it is? But you've always been so...'

'Dead set against it. Yes, I know.'

'When did that start?' asked Daniel, looking horrified.

'Germany.' I couldn't look him in the eye.

'That fucking metal band.' He began to clench his fists. 'I'm not surprised they're to blame.'

I shook my head, though.

'It's not their fault. They had nothing to do with it. As far as I know, they're probably as clean living as the rest of you. No, this is all down to me just trying to get through the day and not making it. But I'm sick of living like that. I hate it and I want it to change before I end up hating myself any more than I already do.'

'So what are you going to do with that?' Rafael looked down at the package in my hand.

'It's going down the toilet, but I wanted to be honest with you guys first. You deserve to know.'

'Are you going to do it or do you want one of us to?' Helena asked.

'No.' I straightened my back and set my jaw. 'I'm doing it myself.'

There was a knock at the door. It was the stage manager. He tapped his watch.

'Vous êtes prêt?'

Helena held up one hand with her fingers spread.

'Cinq minutes,' she told him.

'Bof!' he exclaimed, waving his hand while turning away and mumbling something under his breath about entitled English rock stars. My French may not have been all that brilliant but I understood him well enough.

'Well, he's a charmer, isn't he?' Helena exclaimed, making light of the situation. 'Come on.' She took me by the hand. 'Let's do this, and then we're going to go out there and show them what English rock stars do best. We can talk more about it later, but personally, I think you're being very brave. You've stood by all of us in the past and we're not about to abandon you now.'

They all nodded their agreement.

We ceremonially flushed the rest of the cocaine away and watched it disappear down the pan before Helena dabbed my tear-streaked face dry and touched up my makeup.

'I know it's not quite up to Trudi's standards but she can patch you up properly at half time. Let's do this.'

Pinching my lips together, I nodded, glad to still have some good people around me. After everything we'd been through together, I still believed in them and they believed in me too, something that made me feel a whole lot better about the situation.

We huddled for a moment with our heads together and our arms across each other's shoulders, just like we had so many times before taking the stage.

'Thank you,' I said simply. 'I guess we'd better shift our arses before Monsieur Grumpy throws a hissy fit. Besides, the audience is waiting.'

Rafael checked his watch.

'Only a couple of minutes late. I think they'll live.'

Daniel grabbed his sticks and we all strode out together, making for the hidden area to the rear of the stage from where we would all emerge. We encountered the stage manager on the way and smiled sweetly on our way past as the sound of the expectant audience grew louder in our ears.

'Ready?' I asked, looking around me.

'Ready,' they all chorused.

'Right, then! See you on the other side.'

We gave the signal to a waiting crew member who spoke briefly into his headset mic and the house lights dimmed. A cheer erupted from the waiting crowd and our introductory music began to play, while the band separated to collect their instruments and carry out any last moment checks. Then, under the cover of relative darkness, they ascended the steps to take their places. Aware of movement on stage, the crowd roared, almost drowning out the music.

I waited, shaking first one foot then the other, while patches of blue and green light spread across the stage, punctuated by streaks of piercing white which darted around, illuminating sections of the audience. I could see them all as clear as day, thousands of eager, smiling faces, some with phones held aloft, ready to catch a photograph of the moment, and I knew why I was here. I knew why I couldn't let them down. They had waited a long time for this moment, especially since this tour was over two years late happening. These people had made everything possible, and without them I would still be an unknown single mother with a dull, repetitive day job and a shitty boss, struggling to keep a roof over our heads and feed and clothe us on minimum wage while dreaming of a better life. Instead, I was a worldwide recording artist with wonderful people around her and had the privilege of doing the thing she loved most in all the world. The road back to myself wasn't going to be easy, and I knew that, but I still had so much to look forward to. I couldn't just give up.

Beneath my hand, I felt fur running through my fingers for the first time in many months, and I looked down at the figure who had padded forward from the shadows to stand beside me.

'You're back,' I said, choking back tears again, but this time they were tears of joy. 'Thank you.'

Sadie looked up at me with benign calm and leant against my leg, purring softly as I stroked her head. The intro music stopped and the band struck the first notes of our opening number in a blaze of light as the crowd suddenly came alive again with a deafening roar.

'Are you ready?' I asked and she hunched her back legs, about to spring up the steps and onto the stage alongside me. 'Alright then. Let's go.'

CHAPTER TWENTY-SEVEN

We emerged onto the stage, bathed in bright light, while screens to the left and right of us afforded those at the back of the venue a better view. It didn't matter to me that nobody else could see Sadie. I knew she was back by my side, and that was what counted.

Prising the microphone from its stand at the centre of the stage, I looked out over the thousands of faces in front of me and opened my mouth to sing. I wasn't going to push my voice too hard too early, though. After all, we had another two hours to go and I knew the best was yet to come. I needed to pace myself.

At this stage in the tour, we knew all the songs so well we could have played them in our sleep, even the newer additions to the set, so I knew I could do so much more than just sing and play, more than perform them. They were *my* songs. I could *live* them. It didn't matter that I still had so much to sort out in my head; I could deal with the details later. For the moment, I had my friends. I had my music. I had Sadie. I just needed to give my all for tonight and let tomorrow take care of itself. This was what I was born to do. Despite everything that had happened, this was where I was meant to be.

The next hour went by in a flash, a blur of sound and light and colour, and by the time I made my brief return backstage to change, we had the momentum of the occasion behind us. To buy me some time, Alex had taken centre stage to sing one of his songs with the band. As always, Trudi was ready and waiting for me.

'You're on fire out there tonight, but what happened to your makeup?' she asked as I sat down after she had helped me into my new outfit. We had just under three minutes left before I had to be out of the door again.

'It's hot out there; we're really going for it. I just wish I felt a bit better but I guess that's to be expected by this stage of the tour.'

She nodded but I could tell words were going unsaid. She hadn't swallowed my explanation.

I paused. Perhaps it was time for some honesty. I owed her that. Trudi, more than any other, had put up with my highs and lows without complaint or judgement, and I hadn't always been as appreciative as I should, at least not lately. She must have known all along something was going on. Try as I might, I could run but I couldn't hide.

'Actually, before we went out there, the band and I had a bit of a moment together and it shouldn't end there, either. I've got some apologising to do.'

'For what?' With a hairbrush in her hand, she stopped and stared quizzically at me.

'I've not exactly been myself for a long time, and I need to change that, starting here and now.'

Trudi carried on brushing my hair back from my face and reached for a makeup brush, talking while she worked.

'It's been obvious you've been going through some stuff. The space you've been in, I didn't want to rock the boat.'

'Trudi, you've always been my sounding board about so many things. I don't want you to feel like you can't be honest with me. And I've been selfish.' She opened her mouth to protest but I stopped her. 'Yes. Yes, I have. If I hadn't been so wrapped up in myself, I'd have invited you to stick around and spend some time with Whispered Scream. I knew you were a fan and I just didn't think. I wasn't thinking of anybody but myself.'

She carried on dabbing to blend my makeup back in and shrugged her shoulders before reaching for an eyeliner.

'I won't deny I was a bit disappointed, but that's not important any more. I've been worried about you; we all have. Just promise me that whatever's troubling you, you'll get the right help. You're not alone.'

'Thank you,' I said touching her hand. It was as much as I could do not to start crying again.

Ever the consummate professional, she finished redoing my eyes and checked both sides to make sure I looked symmetrical.

'Right! That's you! You'd better shift. Your audience is waiting.' I hesitated, thinking there was something else I ought to say, but there wasn't time. 'Go on!' she insisted. 'You've got about thirty seconds.'

She was right. In the distance, I could hear the music drawing to a close.

'I'll see you later. And thank you.'

Trudi gave me a tight smile and nodded.

With a little wave, I hurried out of the door, along the

corridor, and dashed up the steps to the rear of the stage, heading for the wings. Thankfully, I hadn't missed my cue but it was close. I popped my earpiece back in and checked beside me to make sure Sadie was still there. She was.

'Are you coming?' I asked.

Sadie looked up at me then toward the stage and put one paw on the steps.

Time for our showpiece, then. And three…two…one.

The audience was still applauding the rest of the band when we stepped out of the shadows and into the light again. They grew louder as I took my place at the piano, before settling gradually into an expectant hush. The rest of the stage fell into relative darkness and I sat at my stool, picked out under the spotlights. I leant toward the microphone with my hands poised above the keys, ready to play the first chord.

'Ladies and gentlemen, mesdames et messieurs, we're going to play a song for you that is already very special to me, but after tonight it takes on a whole new meaning. It was the title track from a little album I released earlier this year. One or two of you might know it.'

A cheer of recognition went up and the click track in my ear counted me in.

Perhaps I was finally ready to shed my skin, to leave behind the things that had been weighing me down for so long, to be myself again, whatever life threw at me. Some things I could control, others I could not, so perhaps the secret was to take charge of the things that were within my power and to let go of the things that weren't. Easier said than done, of course, but now, at last, I finally understood what my own words were trying to tell me.

Everything faded away, and there was just me and the piano as my fingers found the first, slightly hesitant notes, muscle memory taking over as they remembered where they needed to go. I found myself back in the moment when the song first came to me, with the studio lights down low and my Steinway and silence for company, strings swirling in my head. Whether I was singing for myself or an arena full of fans it made no difference anymore; the sentiment was the same.

When all the world is pressing down
Down upon your shoulders
When everything is upside down
You suddenly feel older
When people come and people go
And every time they take a little souvenir

When all the things that some call sins
You used to think were so great
And every shadow feeds the dark
Where vampires lie in wait
When every stolen moment feels
Like just another missing piece of your heart

Don't you ever want to shed this skin?
Walk away and leave it all behind
Begin anew with a different view
A chance to be a different you
And start all over again

Although I couldn't see the rest of the band, I could feel them. I knew exactly where they were and what they were doing, and that buoyed me up. Somehow, when you know a group of musicians well, you can just sense them. I'd missed that connection while working with session players, good though they were.

Moving pools of purple and green light bathed the stage as the band joined in, the sound of the orchestra swelling behind us. Beams of brilliant white cut through the air, dancing across the ceiling above the crowd and all around the auditorium, lighters and phones were being held aloft, bodies swaying like seaweed in ocean currents as a tide of sound washed over them. I closed my eyes, holding on to the feeling behind the words, while colours more vivid than anything ever dreamed up by a lighting designer danced in my head.

When emptiness is closing in
From every side around you
There are some wars you cannot win
No matter how you want to
The things that once were such a game
Suddenly they don't seem funny any more

Don't you ever want to shed this skin?
Begin again without the pain
Leave behind the fall from grace
Move away to outer space
And find your way back home

With a change of key the song lifted, strings and oboes carrying the melody through the middle section while I carried on playing, lost in the music. With Sadie sitting beside me, I didn't care if the critics loved it or hated it.

Like me, it was what it was, and it moved people. Maybe I shouldn't care what anybody thought of me or my music. It didn't matter anymore what the critics or the media, Lafontaine or Ariva, or even Mitchell said or did. There was one person who first and foremost had to like me and my music for what they were, one person from whom there could never be an escape, no matter how much I tried to hide away, and that was myself.

When did I start caring what anybody thought of me? At what point did that overtake everything else? It had become something invasive, all-encompassing. It crept up on me, this insidious creature, like a snake that had coiled itself around my heart and choked the life out of me, crushing my spirit.

Enough!

But it wasn't even about other people's opinions, or even whether I cared what they thought. It had eaten away at me until I'd gone from being able to do no wrong to feeling like I could do nothing right. I needed to learn to like myself again, perhaps even to love being me. It would be a long road, but I'd made a start, hadn't I? And Sadie was back; that was a good sign.

I opened my mouth to sing, closing my eyes again while colours swirled behind my eyelids. Whether it was purely in my head or down to the stage lighting or both, it didn't matter anymore. It was all one thing.

You've given all you have to give
But that's just not enough
Something inside can't be denied
Refusing to give up
You're just a faded photograph

A memory of someone that you used to know

Don't you ever want to shed this skin?
But you'll never lose the scars it leaves behind
Hold on tight to what is true
A chance to be a better you
And start all over again
Start all over again

My hands left the keys as the last low string notes died away. The audience had risen to their feet, cheering, and I stood to acknowledge them. Tears were beginning to roll down my face again; I couldn't help it. I had just bared my soul to an auditorium full of strangers, but that is what real artists do. It's not about the money or the fame or the adulation, and it's so much more than mere entertainment. An artist will lay themselves on the line night after night, give themselves completely, and it's both exhilarating and exhausting. Even if only for fleeting moments, we touch lives and if we're really lucky, we get to change them forever in some small way. Music becomes a part of everyone who loves it enough to let a piece of it into their souls.

But all of that comes at a price, and one I had already paid my share of.

Yes, enough!

From the wings, Davey handed me my guitar in readiness for the next song and I made my way back to centre stage. I felt a bit light-headed but I brushed it off.

'Alright people, I think it's time to get you back up and dancing again. This one's off the Suitcase Full of Diamonds album and it's called 'Bliss'.'

It wasn't even among my proudest musical achievements, despite selling fairly well everywhere, but it was pretty upbeat, a good song to lift the mood and energy of the crowd after all the emotion of 'Shed This Skin', and I was certainly glad of the light relief. The songs everybody was waiting for were being saved for the finale and the encore. I just hoped I had the energy to see it through because, not surprisingly, the day had been emotionally draining. The dizziness wasn't going away and we still had over three-quarters of an hour's music to get through.

The show must go on.

I gathered myself as the drums led into the next song.

The crowd-pleasers followed thick and fast, one after the other, including the first single from the new album, which had been rising rapidly up the sales charts in many of the countries we had visited. A lot of the audience already seemed to know many of the new songs. I could see people mouthing the words and bouncing up and down as I sang.

Devil on my Shoulder had been saved for the encore, so we could go out on a high. Besides, that song required another lightning change of outfit. The audience expected my skintight, red suit with devil tail and horns and I wasn't going to disappoint. It was way too hot to wear for more than one song, though, too uncomfortable by far, and I would have sweated buckets into it in a live situation if I tried to wear it for longer. Come to think of it, I'd had so much on my mind and been so into the music that I hadn't even bothered with any of the bottles of water that always appeared, strategically placed around the stage at every gig. Maybe that was why I felt light-headed; it was just a bit of dehydration.

But there wasn't any time to think about that now, and I couldn't stop at this stage; we were just getting to the climax of the show. On the other side of the stage, an acoustic guitar on a stand was being brought on. Alex would play the first part of the song on that before switching back to his electric. My guitar tech handed me my SG and I passed the strap over my head, checking the light on the radio pack as I did so. I didn't need to do that; it would have already been checked, but making sure was just force of habit. A bead of sweat dripped off the end of my nose onto the body of the guitar.

'Okay, this is the last song of the set,' as one, the audience vented their disappointment with a groan and boos, 'but if you promise to make lots of noise, we might just be persuaded to come back on for one more.' Now they cheered. 'This one was a bit of a hit for us, right back at the start of everything, and we wouldn't be here without it so thank you. It's called 'Come Inside'.'

The cheering grew louder, accompanied by a series of wolf whistles from around the venue as Alex laid into the percussive, opening groove on the acoustic guitar, and I lowered my eyes, holding onto the microphone on its stand and crooning like a lounge jazz singer.

It's been a wonderful evening
And I don't want it to end
If you come with me
Then you will see
How we could be more than just friends

The audience sang with me. They knew every word,

which never ceased to amaze me given that English wasn't the first language of most places we'd been playing for the last couple of months. It put my smattering of French to shame. Helena spoke it better than I did. Despite the swimming in my head, I tapped into the seductress in me, melting into the words while Sadie brushed up against my leg.

You can come inside if you want to
Come inside if you dare
You can pull my hair
Touch me everywhere
We can do it how you like it baby, don't fight fair

Much to the audience's delight, we gave them the full, unexpurgated version with the final verse which had been deemed too raunchy for radio. Mind you, it hadn't stopped the full-length video going viral on the internet, boosting sales of the album version, and setting us on the path to worldwide success. Here they all were, just like everywhere else, singing it back to us at the top of their lungs. Whether they understood every word of it or not, I think they got the gist.

It's as plain as can be that my friend and me
Don't want to go to sleep tonight
So why don't we all
Have ourselves a ball
And take this evening out of sight?

You can tie me down to the mattress
Slam me against the wall

Beat down my backdoor
Show me what I'm good for
Baby we can do it all

You can come inside if you want to
Come inside if you dare
You can do what you do
Till we're all black and blue
I don't think we'll ever get enough of you

In a strange way, I could understand why some people saw me the way they did. Maybe they thought the song was some kind of licence to treat me as a sex object and not as a human being. But that was never the intention when I wrote it. It was about freedom, exhilaration, and discovery, not about the abuse and subjugation of another human spirit. Of course, there were some arseholes out there who couldn't tell the difference, people who were utterly wrapped up in their own selfishness and cruelty, and God knows I'd met enough of them. Their innate meanness, their lack of humanity, prevented them from understanding how liberating sexuality could and should be. It wasn't about what anybody actually did, but the spirit in which it was done.

But there was hope. Right now, with thousands of delighted faces in front of me, singing at the top of their lungs, maybe some people got it. Maybe they understood, and I had made myself the mouthpiece of that understanding. Instead of resenting the public image I had somehow ended up with, perhaps I should be embracing the empowerment it represented.

That was the message. That was what Linda had

always understood and what I had lost somewhere along the way. She had been right all along. Fuck Gil Premmel, Angelique Monet, Svetlana Markova, Anthony Holbrook and all their double standards. Fuck everyone who had ever judged or oppressed me or betrayed my trust. Even Mitchell Sacker and his excessive caution could go and take a running jump. From now on I intended to somehow get back to being me, unapologetic and with my head held high.

Do what you want to with my body
I need that rush to find my release, yeah
Give me your touch
It could never be too much…for me

I poured myself into the last, sustained note, no longer irritated by the song but proud of it again, like I used to be, the audience erupting as we played through the punchy outro. My hands slid down the strings of the guitar in a final glissando, accompanied by Dan who had to get the last word in on the drums before launching his sticks out into the front rows of the audience. A forest of eager hands reached out to catch them.

'Merci beaucoup, Paris. Vous êtes tous beaux.' I'd called them all beautiful and I meant it. Empty platitudes had never been my style.

Waving to the crowd we left for the wings, panting and sweating, where my guitar tech stood ready to take my guitar from me.

Trudi was also there.

'Ready?' she asked. I nodded, still recovering myself. 'Are you alright?'

'Yeah, I'm fine. Let's do this.'

Already, mingling with the shouts and whistles coming from behind me, a slow handclap and the stamping of feet had started. I had no time to discuss the fact that I still wasn't feeling very well.

Maybe that's just what it feels like when all the toxic emotions and the alcohol and all the other shit you've been poisoning yourself with start leaving your body.

The crowd already sounded impatient for the big encore they knew would be coming their way, and they must have worked out which big hit was still missing from the set. It was kind of obvious.

I towelled the perspiration off myself as we hurried along the corridor to the dressing room. This costume change involved getting down to my underwear and I wasn't about to strip off in the wings. We may have regarded ourselves as one big family on tour, but we weren't *that* close. It's funny how context alters our attitudes. A few months ago, and egged on by Svetlana, I hadn't thought twice about doing so much more than simply taking my clothes off, and in the company of complete strangers. Maybe anonymity makes it easier.

It hadn't been anonymous, though. I might not have been the biggest star in the world; there were others more successful than me on both sides of the Atlantic and particularly in America, but everybody still knew exactly who I was, a fact from which there was no escape. That had been part of the problem. I might not have known who they all were, but they all knew me.

All this came with the realisation that I could only ever be truly myself among the very friends I had done my best to alienate, the people who knew me as myself, not

Rebecca Taylor the star. How was I going to reach out to them again? How could I make it up to them? Linda most of all. I'd treated her the worst when all she had ever done was stand by me through everything. I had been so much less than a friend in return. Even my investment in Pulverton Manor had started to turn a healthy profit. It had already paid itself back a couple of months ago, much earlier than originally expected, so despite my ignoring her, she had remained true to her word and the payments kept on rolling in. With that and the profits from the tour, I would have enough money to finally buy Spensford Hall for keeps.

In the dressing room, we turned it around as fast as we could. Even though the outfit wasn't as ridiculously tight as the one I'd originally had made for our performance at the UK Music Awards, and there was no denying I had lost weight since we started the tour, it still wasn't exactly roomy. I squeezed myself in, trying to keep my balance while I wrestled my feet through the legs. Horns and a long, red tail completed the outfit.

I wish this fucking swimming in my head would stop.

Maybe I was coming down with a cold or the flu. That would be the last thing I needed.

One minute forty-five seconds later and suitably attired for my final, grand entrance, we found ourselves behind the stage again, along with the backing singers and brass section who would all be on stage with us for this final big number. The clapping and stamping from the crowd had built again to another crescendo.

'Everybody ready?' asked the stagehand. We all nodded and he gave the signal before saying something into his radio mic. Daniel was the first to ascend the steps and settle behind his kit. Since the house lights remained down but the stage was still partially lit, the audience had no trouble making out the figure retaking his place in the shadows. A huge roar went up.

My head began to spin, and keeping my balance in the thigh-length, red, high-heeled boots that went with the outfit wasn't helping matters. At least there was only the one song left to go before I could go home to Poppy and my family, see my friends and make things right.

Just get this out of the way and you're done.

I gave the nod and we all stepped up onto the stage, the roar intensifying.

'You wanted it; you got it,' I announced grabbing the microphone. 'This one is all about the joys of temptation, those little voices that tell you you really want to do something, even though you know perhaps you shouldn't. I think we can all relate to that.'

A few of the faces out there were nodding. The sound of Daniel's open hi-hat rang out, setting the beat.

One, two, three, four.

A short, punchy intro led straight into the main groove and we hit the ground running. Audiences always went wild for 'Devil on my Shoulder' and by now the Paris crowd had been whipped up into a frenzy. Freed from the need to play an instrument while singing, I could concentrate on the vocal line. While parts of its rapid-fire lyrics almost came out spoken, at other times it gave me the chance to stretch out and put the full extent of my range and power on show.

The rhythm section loved this one, too. Daniel could kick out some tight, powerful, technical fills while it gave Rafael the ideal opportunity to show off the funkier side of his bass playing. Within seconds, the audience were all up on their feet and dancing in the aisles.

This is the life, Sadie. This is what we're here for.

There's a voice that whispers into my ear
Putting temptation my way
And another that speaks of fire and damnation
Both want to have their say...

There might have been too many words to this one for everybody to remember but I could still see many of them singing along to the chorus when we came to it. At least, I thought I could; their faces were beginning to go in and out of focus.

Not now!

In five minutes time I could sit down and take as long a break as I wanted.

Just not now.

I took a step forward as I sang and began to stumble, but righted myself just in time. Behind me, I could feel Helena's eyes boring into my back, and out of the corner of my eye, I caught Rafael glancing towards me then at Alex, with a questioning look.

I've just got to finish this one song.

I intensified my efforts and we ploughed on, flames projecting onto the screen behind us. The intro returned, this time with vocals, before the final, singalong choruses.

Devil on my shoulder (I tried hard to be good)
Devil on my shoulder (the angel said I should)
There's a devil on my shoulder (then the devil had her say)
Yes a devil on my shoulder and she always seems to get her

way

I pumped my fist in the air, willing the crowd on. If they sang loud enough, maybe they wouldn't realise I was now struggling to remember the words myself, never mind get them out. A hot tingle had begun to spread from my fingers, all the way up my arms to my body and I could hardly breathe. But the band could tell; I could sense their continuing glances in my direction.

Devil on my shoulder (whispers to me)
Devil on my shoulder (won't let me be)
There's a devil on my shoulder (leading me astray)
Yes a devil on my shoulder and I wouldn't have it any other way

A row of pyrotechnics all along the front of the stage went off with the final note, flames and curling rings of smoke rising into the air and the crowd erupted.

We made it! Thank fuck for that.

I turned to welcome the band to the front of the stage as they stepped forward for our final bow together but I knew in that instant something was wrong by the metallic ringing in my head and the looks on their faces. Time suddenly slowed to a crawl. The band members were running towards me and Helena's mouth moved as if she was shouting something but I couldn't understand her. I could hardly hear a thing above the high-pitched whine that was growing louder and louder in my ears. I clasped my hands to my head, my vision blurring and my knees giving way.

And then the world around me wheeled and

blackened.

To be continued…

ABOUT THE AUTHOR

D.V. Williams was born and grew up in the southeast of England, excelling throughout his education at daydreaming. After eminently sensible careers in industry and teaching, while spending any free time writing songs and performing in bands, he finally sat down to write the stories that had been taking over in his head and never looked back.

The author is married with two sons, who are now both taller than he is, and lives in southwest Wales. They share their home with two cats, a neurotic collie, a crested gecko, and an ever-growing collection of musical instruments.

www.dominic-williams.co.uk

www.facebook.com/DVWilliamsAuthor

www.twitter.com/DomVWilliams

COMING NEXT . . .

THE FINAL PART OF REBECCA'S STORY

RETURN TO THE WILD

D.V. WILLIAMS

Finding the way back to yourself is never easy

Returning to her world tour after collapsing on stage, now drug-free, re-energised, and with her popularity on the rise again, Rebecca Taylor finally seems to be putting her life back together. She even has a guardian angel watching over her in the shape of her best friend Linda's brother, the dashing but mysterious Ryan, to whom she has always been attracted. But can she trust him with her heart when she has been betrayed before in so many ways?

Nothing is ever simple. Her daughter Poppy's father is determined to win Rebecca back at all costs, her mother's life hangs in the balance, and everybody's secrets are coming out into the open, including the truth about Linda and Ryan's empire of high-class hedonism. And then, just when it looks like Rebecca might find the lasting happiness she longs for, a face from the past arrives out of the blue, changing everything.

Rebecca's inner strength is about to be tested like never before.

Tigers Book Six

Printed in Great Britain
by Amazon

83156465R00192